THE VICTORY PERSPECTIVE

THE VICTORY PERSPECTIVE

E.J. KELLETT

Independent

Published by Gondor Kellett Independent Publishing Pty Ltd 2018

ISBN: 978-0-6482350-0-2

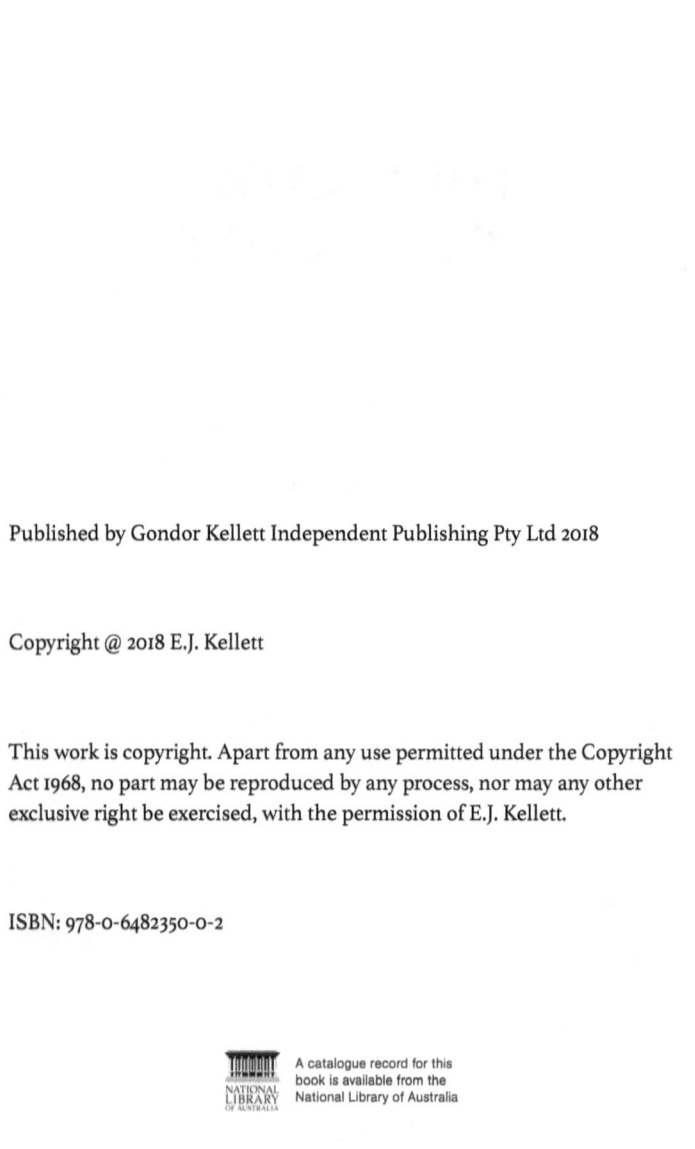

A catalogue record for this book is available from the National Library of Australia

NATIONAL LIBRARY OF AUSTRALIA

ACKNOWLEDGMENTS

Thank you to all those who supported me to write this book. Dan for being the first person to read it, reading it too many times, and giving me the time to get it to print. The Brains Trust (Maggi, Sam, Jake, Candice and Kate) for the valuable feedback and comments. Jeremy, Bobby and Zak for their cover work and Tim for the website. Also thank you to all those people who have helped with design, marketing and accounting.

Think.

There is no evidence.
There is no fact.
The world you know may not be true.
Question perspective.

ARE YOU READY?

The truth around the downfall of your race should be told. It may serve as a lesson for those who still cling to the desolate remnants of civilization or as a warning for those who may, in time, reclaim this land. Telling this story affords a sliver of hope that those of you who remain, will know the true meaning of your existence.

You were a race created and urged to flourish for one selfish and malicious purpose. So heavily manipulated to satisfy the whim of a single individual, you can hardly be blamed for your own shortcomings. You cannot be held liable for failing to see through your highly manufactured existence or for following the altered perspective of truth blindly. It was how you were made. The creation and ultimate destruction of your world made possible through one inherent and undeniable need: your need to believe.

Human belief was God's master stroke. It overcame your greatest fear; that your hard and painful lives might be pointless. In order to survive, you needed belief that you meant something, that you had a purpose. And at the end, when you left your mortal flesh, you would be taken to a place of eternal happiness.

The great human delusion you all suffered allowed God's greatest victory. By creating blind belief, God commanded ultimate control.

Your inherent desire for significance blinded you to reality. How do you know what you think is true? Is it truth at all? Your purpose must be told.

As with all stories, the best place to start is the beginning. This is the truth.

PART I

HOME

In this treacherous world, nothing is the truth nor a lie.
Everything depends of the color of the crystal through
which one sees it.
—Pedro Calderón de la Barca

THE BEGINNING

He felt like he was dying, even though he didn't know what that meant. No one should remember the moment their life began. But this memory would stay with Gabriel forever. His body slowly worked to dissolve the panic, each painful breath chipped away at the fear blocking his chest. He sat, blinded by brightness. His watering eyes moved slowly across the calm landscape. An involuntary sharp breath whistled through his teeth. Lying on the sand, was another body.

It coughed. Gabriel watched as the other came to life. "Hello," Gabriel said, his speech coming naturally.

"Hello," the other responded with a cocked, bushy eyebrow. "Who are you?"

"I am Gabriel, I think," he said, losing confidence as he spoke.

"I am Michael." The response came quickly. "I think." He finished with a smile.

"Where are we?" Gabriel asked, natural trust calmed the frayed edges of his nerves. Michael gave a heavy shrug.

"That's a fire," Michael said, nodding his head toward

the crackling flames a short way down the beach. It was a conical blaze, the sparks licked toward the blue expanse above.

"I know," replied Gabriel, pushing the question of *how* he knew out of his thoughts. By unspoken agreement, they rose to their feet, unused limbs wobbling as they found their first footfalls on the sand.

Gabriel poked around the fire, waves of heat assaulted their faces. His first lesson was quickly learned. Flames should not be touched. He jerked his hand from the heat and shook it to stop the burning sensation. To distract himself from the pain, he turned in slow circles looking at the surroundings. The wide stretch of beach sloped upward to a dense forest of brilliant greens and downward to a mass of water moving gently against the sand. Michael, too, was staring. One arm was folded across his middle. His hand cupped the opposite elbow, stubby fingers drummed against his cheek. Gabriel flitted his tongue across his dry lips, he felt a need to quench his thirst.

"What are we meant to do now?" asked Michael, not meeting Gabriel's eyes.

"I don't know. Wait for something?" Gabriel said.

THE UNFRUITFUL ENDEAVOR of waiting weathered the two companions. Aware their needs were not being met but unsure of what they required to sustain themselves, they grew weak. Their energy levels dipped, their hearts raced.

"We need to look for something," croaked Gabriel. Michael nodded, no longer attempting to speak, his dry tongue stuck to the roof of his mouth. They drew strength from each other and shuffled up the beach, legs crumpling just beyond the line of trees, the cool washed over their burning skin.

Collapsed on his back, Gabriel stared at the canopy. Green fronds obscured the sun. He felt at peace. Content with the world. If his life slipped from his body, he would be calm. Fear had left him, senses dulled to block out the pain. Through the haze, he heard a trickle. Unknowingly, he reacted to the sound, his body let out a burst of energy. Slithering through the leaves that coated the forest floor, he peered over a lip of rocks. Clear water sparkled below. Gasping, he cupped his hand, dipped it into the inviting cool, and raised it to his lips. Liquid life ran through his body, all pain forgotten. He dragged Michael to the edge of the brook, so he, too, could claw back from death.

GABRIEL LEARNED that existence was hard. His constant need for water to stave off the throbbing in his head, and foraging for food to satisfy his hunger led to continuous chores. Gabriel eyed the green plant waving gently in the breeze. Below was a moist and tender root, ready to eat. He licked his lips and readied himself to heave. The constant battle between effort and sustenance plagued him constantly. With a sharp tug, the root emerged from the dirt.

"Good, you got one," said Michael as he held out a plump-fingered hand. Reluctantly, Gabriel handed it over.

"There must be something easier," Gabriel said, hands on hips, turning his head toward the layers of shrubs that stretched into the forest. "I'm just going to take a look a bit farther in." Michael shrugged, his attention already turned to cleaning the dirt off their next meal. Once Michael had food, he could not be distracted.

Gabriel pushed his way through the delicate fronds, deeper into the forest. The mottled shards of light puncturing the trees contracted, the forest more unknown with every step. "Yes!" Gabriel cried, quickening his pace. He ran toward the glint in the green. Pushing aside a frond large enough to cover his body, he gasped. A squat plant with bulbous fruits sat behind the natural screen. He touched it, the fuzzy skin tickled his fingers. The weight of the fruit was apparent as soon as he cupped it in his hand. It seemed to glow the same color as the sky when the sun dipped past the sea. His mouth watered.

Gabriel's body jumped before he registered the noise, a large crack, a scrape through the leaves that littered the forest floor. A strange sound filled his ears, a growl. Something was coming.

His breath came fast, wild eyes drank in his surroundings. He moved without thought, crashing through the trees back to the beach. He did not want to know what he had found.

The trees lightened, he burst out of the forest. Michael's head snapped as Gabriel collapsed in the sand, trying to slow his breathing.

"What?" said Michael. Gabriel shook his head.

"Nothing, I just thought I saw something," Gabriel panted, unsure how much to say.

"Well." Michael paused. Gabriel saw a thought churning through his mind. "I found something too." Raising an eyebrow in question, Gabriel's gaze followed Michael's pointed finger. Lying on the sand, just out of the tree line, was a body. Gabriel almost mistook it for a lump in the sand. The sun glinted off the curly blond hair, just as it did off the pale ripples on the beach.

Gabriel approached with caution, his experience in the

forest fresh on his senses. It was curled on its side, knees tucked in, face peaceful. Gabriel lifted his foot and pushed on the drooping shoulder. The body gave no resistance, turning slightly with the shove. Gabriel stooped to his haunches and placed both palms on the body, shaking hard, hoping for a response. It came in a labored gasp. Eyes scrunched at the pain. Waiting for the newcomer's pain to subside, Gabriel spoke when its squinted gaze found his face.

"Hello," Gabriel said. "Who are you?"

"Alpha," the body replied.

"Does your tummy hurt?" asked Gabriel, pointing to his middle. The memory of an empty stomach pushed to the front of his mind.

Alpha nodded.

"Come with me. I'll show you where to dig."

Alpha rose and silently followed Gabriel to the nearest section of plants.

"Here," Gabriel said, beckoning to the long green stems that shot from the ground. "Pull this, hard."

Alpha did as he was told, grasping the stalks with bold hands; the small muscles on his arms engaged as he heaved.

"There," said Gabriel as the orange root lifted from the ground. "Brush the dirt off and eat it. It is crunchy and hard to chew, but it will make you feel strong."

Alpha shrugged and took a bite, dirt crunching in his teeth.

Alpha bent and heaved up two more roots. Straightening, he offered one to Gabriel. Gabriel took the offered meal and eyed Alpha, thoughts forming. "Why don't you stay here and eat as many of these as you like? You will need to eat lots of food to feel better. Then when you are done, pull up as many as you can carry in your arms, and come and find me near the fire. Down there." Gabriel pointed down the beach. Alpha nodded.

Gabriel set off down the beach, keeping a quick pace. "Michael," he hissed as he approached the fire. "Michael!"

"What?" growled Michael, his head barely lifting from his reclined position in the sand.

"He is gathering some food. I just asked him to do it," Gabriel said, thoughts racing.

"You asked him to gather food? For us?" Michael asked, receiving a curt nod in reply. "This could be good."

Gabriel's face broke into a grin that betrayed his inner thoughts. They had themselves another. He would be pliable they could mold him however they wished.

"I FOUND THEM FARTHER IN. Quite amazing, don't you think? Definitely juicier than the ones in the ground. I think they taste better. I think we should try to pick more food from the trees than from the ground. They shine like the sun," Alpha prattled as he sorted the fruits.

"Are you ever quiet?" Gabriel groaned from his nest in the sand. "Nothing but talk, talk, talk. If you spent less time talking and more time working, you could find whatever you wanted, I'm sure."

Alpha's shoulders slumped. His eyes dropped to his feet. He pressed his lips firmly together to stop any retort. The punishment was not worth it.

"I agree with Gabriel," Michael said through his current mouthful. "I want more food; every new taste makes my tongue tingle. Be good, Alpha, go and find me something else."

Alpha did not move, continuing to sort his fruit.

"Did you hear that?" Gabriel said, picking up a handful of sand. He threw it at the side of Alpha's face. Alpha shook his head, careful to keep his eyes averted. "When we tell you to do something, you do it," Gabriel shouted, pelting twigs and stones at Alpha until he ran out of range.

Head hanging in defeat, Alpha trudged toward the forest, destined to work another day for his masters. His feet instinctively stopped as he heard a rustle. His small eyes scanning the forest edge, he attempted to locate the noise. Alpha's mouth dropped open, two figures emerged from the edge of the greenery. Their eyes were wild, and their heads turned in every direction, taking in the visions of home. Alpha stood still, at once afraid and overjoyed at what this meant for him. The figures stopped.

"Hello," they said in unison. "Where are we?"

LUCIFER'S fragile nerves were immediately tested when he met the others. Gabriel and Michael's feelings toward the new arrivals were obvious from the outset, as they made their superiority clear. Long silences thickened the air. Alpha filled the gaps with his story until Lucifer gathered the courage to speak.

"So," Lucifer said, allowing the information Alpha had told him to sink in. "You all just woke up too?"

Alpha nodded.

"But what are we doing here? What are we here for? I don't understand," Lucifer muttered, casting his eyes to his new companion. He received nothing but a shrug from Raphael, whose face was still contorted with shock. His thoughts were building, words came more easily with every moment. His mind constructed a picture of his home, layering his innate knowledge with insight gathered from those who came before him.

"None of that matters," grumbled Gabriel. "All that matters is that we eat and drink, so we do not get thirsty or hungry. I don't like being asked too many questions." He finished with a sneer. "You ask Alpha how that worked out for him."

"He is right," Alpha hissed. "If you do anything to annoy them, they will punish you."

"Punish? Why? Why is he allowed to punish us..." Lucifer's questioning was cut off as Gabriel rose from his depression in the sand.

"I am in charge here. I was here first, you do as I say. Now get us more fruit. You better find something different. We are getting bored," Gabriel said, turning his back.

"Come on," said Alpha. Grabbing Lucifer and Raphael by the arms, he dragged them to the forest. "We should go."

Reluctantly, Lucifer allowed himself to be led, peering back toward Gabriel and Michael, nestled into the sand. "We will need to find some food, or they will be angry. I think there is something new over this way, it isn't too far. We have to make sure we are back before it gets dark, or we will not hear the end of it."

The edge of the forest loomed, the dark sucking them farther in with every step. Alpha bent to pluck roots from the ground as he walked.

"This is incredible," said Raphael, his mouth hanging open more with every step he took into the forest. "It feels alive, like it wants us to explore."

Lucifer smiled at Raphael, "I feel it too," he said, craning his neck to take in every layer of the forest: the crunchy leaves below his feet, the dark, soft fronds that tickled his fingertips, and the soaring trees that sprouted into a dense green canopy high above their heads. Dazzling flowers punctuated the foliage, pops of color grabbed Lucifer's attention everywhere he looked. "We need to explore," Lucifer said, a wide grin splitting his face, excitement coursing through his body, emitting a faint buzz. His eyes alight, Lucifer turned to Alpha, his forehead creased with deep lines.

"No," he said forcefully. "We can't, you don't know what will happen if we don't do as they say."

"I am not afraid of them," Lucifer replied, puffing his chest. Alpha's worried expression deepened before it relaxed with a shrug.

"Don't say I didn't warn you. I am going back." Alpha turned, slinking through the trees.

Lucifer spun back to Raphael. "What do you think, Raphael? Are you ready to explore?"

"It is what we are meant to do," Raphael said, eyes wide. "I know it."

They chose a direction and walked. Ducking through small gaps in trees, pushing aside soft green fronds, they navigated trickling streams and rested to fill their stomachs when they found new fruits.

Lucifer pushed aside a thick-stemmed branch, gasping at what he saw. A nearly sheer cliff soared above, covered with tufts of moss and grasses. Disjointed vines hung from jutting black rocks, making way for a wall of water falling from the high edge, which collected in a sparking pool. Mesmerized, Lucifer let go of the frond, which snapped back in place.

"Ouch," came a muffled voice. Lucifer spun around to see Raphael grasping his nose, eyes watering.

"Are you all right?" Lucifer said, spinning toward Raphael, half emerged from the thicket.

"I think so," he said, tenderly prodding his nose with a finger. "That hurt."

Lucifer chuckled at Raphael's expression. Raphael let a smile touch his lips and shook his head in a gesture for them to continue.

"Do you think we can get up there?" Raphael said, thinking aloud.

"I think we can," replied Lucifer. "Let's see if we can climb up using the vines."

Scrabbling for handholds, they made slow progress, the roar of rushing water was deafening. With a final heave, they reached the top and collapsed on the plateau, staring at the bright-blue sky above, breathing heavily.

"We did it," said Raphael, sitting up.

"We did," Lucifer replied, giving Raphael a firm clap on the shoulder. Fumbling to his feet, he turned slowly. Beauty overtook Lucifer's every thought, he could do nothing but stare. Below him, the forest canopy stretched into the distance, inviting, as if urging him to dive onto it and walk across the tops of the trees. He lifted his eyes and saw a jagged mountain dark against the sky, circled with cloud.

"I wonder what is up there," said Raphael absently, as if he knew what Lucifer were thinking. "This is so wonderful," he continued, raising his face and arms to the sky. Lucifer watched his nostrils flare as he took in a deep breath, twirling in a circle.

Lucifer smiled, Raphael looked happy.

Standing still, Lucifer watched Raphael skip across the plateau. He picked small plants, smelling and tasting. His energy drew Lucifer's gaze, excitement uncontainable.

"I can't describe how I feel," beamed Raphael, looking back over his shoulder. "I think something inside of me might burst." Lucifer grinned again, ambling to join Raphael near the edge of the plateau.

"I know what you mean," Lucifer said, searching Raphael's eyes.

"I just want to run around until the sun goes down. Then lie up here all night, looking at the lights in the sky." Raphael took a step and met a crumbly piece of rock. He took in a sharp breath, fear overtaking the eyes that, a moment earlier, had been alive with intrigue and joy. He reached out a hand, madly grabbing for something to hold. Lucifer lunged, just touching Raphael's fingertips before he slid over the edge. Heart beating through his skin, Lucifer ran the few steps to the edge, instincts warning him of what he might find. Raphael was in sight, clinging to a vine. He stared up at Lucifer, pleading.

"Don't move," Lucifer shouted. "I'm coming."

Unsure what to do, he looked around the plateau. He grabbed a vine hanging from the edge and tied it around his waist, leaning as far over as he could without tumbling himself. "Use your feet," he called. "Try to swing up and take my hand."

Raphael didn't move. He was frozen, clinging to the vine.

"You have to try!" Lucifer called again, desperation mounted. Raphael's fingers were white with effort, he could not hold on much longer.

"I am here. I will help you," Lucifer continued, attempting to rid his voice of panic. "I will not let anything happen to you."

Raphael took a deep breath and kicked his feet against the sheer wall of the cliff. He swung in an arc. Their fingers touched. Not enough. Raphael swung away with the momentum of the vine.

"You have to trust me!" yelled Lucifer.

Arcing back, Raphael closed his eyes and launched himself upward, losing his grip on the vine in the lunge toward his savior. Everything slowed. Lucifer did not breathe. Raphael's pale hand moved closer. Lucifer dove and grabbed the soft flesh of his forearm. A spark passed through Lucifer's body at the touch. Lucifer locked onto Raphael's wild eyes, the jolt was a mutual unknown feeling. They hung together, teetering on the edge of the cliff. With no words of encouragement left, Lucifer heaved Raphael back to the safety of the plateau.

Breathing heavily, Lucifer made his way to a crouching position. "Are you all right?" he asked Raphael, although he already felt the answer. Raphael nodded, words not yet returned. Something flickered. Lucifer snapped his head toward the movement. There was nothing there. Lucifer rose to his feet, searching. Something darted from his field of vision just before he saw it.

"What's wrong?" asked Raphael, his senses returning.

"I don't know. I thought I saw something moving," Lucifer said warily.

"We should go back." said Raphael. Lucifer nodded, still alert to the movement.

"We should tell the others," Lucifer said.

"I SAW SOMETHING OUT THERE. I'm telling you, I know there is something more!" Lucifer's frustration continued to rise as he tried to get through to his cohort back at the beach. "How can we just sit here when we know there is something to discover out there?"

"No," Gabriel said with a practiced resolve that would end any conversation. "We are happy, we have good food, we have everything we need here. I will not risk this to find what you *think* you saw. By the sounds of it, Raphael barely survived." Gabriel waved a hand at Raphael, who stood still, skin as pale as the clouds surrounding the mountains. "Your job is to get food for Michael to cook. He is getting quite good at it, and that is what we should work on, making things better for ourselves here. Not risking all we have done out there."

"But—" Lucifer started. Gabriel came close, his head craned down close to Lucifer's face. Through clenched teeth he said, "I am in charge here, I say no. I will not let your ideas ruin what I have built for myself."

Lucifer let his eyes fall to the ground. Alpha's warning about Gabriel played over in his head. With a final glare, Gabriel stomped across camp.

Lucifer sat heavily in the sand. "It is no use. I can't change his mind," he muttered.

"Perhaps that is not such a bad thing," said Raphael, sitting delicately next to Lucifer. "He is right, what happened out there scared me. I don't want to go far into the forest again. Who knows what might be in there?"

Lucifer gave a small smile. Despite his disappointment, he understood. Strong protective feelings toward Raphael rose to the surface in continuous waves.

"I suppose we have been told our place," said Lucifer. "If there is one good thing to come out of this, we can help Alpha. He does seem to be doing all the work."

"He is a little different though, don't you think?" asked Raphael.

"Different? Yes. But just because someone is different doesn't mean they should be treated this way," Lucifer continued.

"But I will say," said Raphael, "he can be a little difficult to be around. Always talking about things that don't matter. Perhaps that is why the others send him to do all the chores."

Lucifer heard a crack. He twisted, eyes darting. There was nothing there.

ALPHA KNELT at the forest edge, ripping up vegetables with all his force, muttering through clenched teeth as he threw them to a wayward pile. "I annoy them, do I? Well, I will make them see."

Gabriel's eyes flickered, opening to the bright light of another perfect day. He raised his chest, bony elbows digging into the sand. He sucked a long sharp breath. The salty scent curled up his nostrils as the breeze tickled his skin. The calming murmur of the ocean and distant chirping from the forest creased a smile on his face.

The sand was his place, comfortable and warm, molding to his body as he slept. It stretched beyond his field of vision and stopped at a thin line in the distance, where it turned into sky. The shimmering air danced above the sea. Gabriel was pulled from his fresh daze of sleep by the increasing slosh of water. The ocean was on the move. The water, calm. The clear dark blue crept up and down the sand.

Before his resting place was saturated by the inevitable reach of the sea, he rolled his unwilling body, rising to his feet to escape inundation.

Gabriel liked the water. He had stood in it once, plunging his feet up to the ankles. This small exploration was never repeated after he caught sight of a shiny sliver beneath the surface. Gabriel chose to forget the incident instead of acknowledging the well of fear that rose to his throat at the sight of something unknown. It was something he could not explain, and therefore, did not want to know.

The continuous murmur of the sea moved his thoughts to water. "Thirsty," he muttered to himself.

As he stretched his long arms above his head, a yawn escaped his lips. His wits growing with each moment of awareness, Gabriel looked around. He was alone. He took his first lazy step toward the forest edge, heading for the spring. The most accessible point of the bubbling brook was resident just inside the tree line, not too far in. Imagined pictures of fresh, cool water flowing over smooth rocks punctuated his thoughts. Glistening as dappled sunlight pierced through the canopy, the picture increased his level of thirst. He stopped. A frown furrowed his brow.

"Where are you? You should be back by now. Why should I have to get it?" he said to no one as he nestled back into the sand, expecting that someone would be along soon.

Facing the forest, his stomach growled. He could see the colorful fruits piercing through the green foliage. More delectable morsels sprang from the ground at the edge of the forest.

Gabriel's mind envisaged ripping the delicious roots from the sandy soil, dusting off the earth, and taking a juicy bite without a care for the leftover pieces of grit entering his mouth.

Hungry but unwilling to move, he rolled languidly onto his taut belly, head resting on his muscular arms. Soon enough, one of the others would be here to fetch what he needed to quench his thirst and quell his cantankerous stomach.

He drifted back into the dreamy state of semi consciousness, the sun's warm tendrils reached out to his skin. His mouth twitched up to a smile, content despite his hunger. Visions of sticky yellow flesh with a crust of char danced behind his eyes. The fruit's natural sweetness enhanced by searing on a hot stone. He sensed the sugars in the air, so real that his nose twitched.

Gabriel's eyes snapped open. Sweet, tangy roasted fruit. The unseen odor reached his nostrils. The smell was unmistakable. The proximity of food was soon confirmed as a hefty shadow blocked his sun.

Eager, he flipped up to a sitting position, narrowly avoiding the chunky thigh that still wobbled from recent movement.

Gabriel smiled, his eyes wandering up the length of Michael's substantial body, resting on the rosy-cheeked face. Food was here.

"Lunch?" Michael asked, cocking one bushy blond eyebrow, his small mouth upturned on the opposite side. The glint in his eye was always present when food was near.

"Of course, knowing you cooked it." Showing his perfect set of bright teeth, Gabriel slapped Michael on the thigh.

Michael reached out a hand, a laden leaf plastered over his meaty fingers. Relieved of the food, his frame sank into the sand.

A stew of fresh and charred fruits foraged from the forest, brought together in a sauce of crushed berries. Gabriel drank in the aroma of Michael's signature dish. The bright and enticing fruit made Gabriel's mouth water, vibrant yellows and oranges with flecks of gold that caught the sun punctured through the deep red sauce.

Gabriel shoveled food to his mouth, pinching chunks with the tips of his fingers. The tart and sweet tastes of the forest tingled his tongue. Bliss.

Gabriel's brow furrowed. His fervent chewing slackened to a slow munch as his underworked senses attempted to identify a foreign flavor. He poked around the remaining pile of food to pick out the intruder. The culprit, small, brown, and spongy, was closely examined between thumb and forefinger.

"A mushroom," Michael slurred through chomping teeth. "It comes up from the ground near the base of trees. The others found it yesterday."

Gabriel popped the morsel into his mouth. Trying new foods was the closest he got to adventure. An adventure short-lived, as the half-chewed food flew out of his mouth, thudding into the sand.

Michael roared, a solid finger pointing at Gabriel's face. "Your face!" Michael managed between wheezes. "You look like you ate your own nose!"

Emerging from the shock of the disagreeable taste in his mouth, Gabriel let a smile dance on his lips, as he punched Michael on the arm.

"That," Gabriel said, flipping his hand toward the discarded brown lump, "was not good."

"I like it." Michael rushed his words before a fresh handful filled his mouth.

"Doesn't count," said Gabriel. "You like everything."

Laughter overtook them, Michael's body heaving, trying not spit his food. Gabriel's flecked eyes twinkled in the sunlight as he went back to his meal, picking around the mushrooms.

"I love your cooking, Mikey, despite the *mushroom*," Gabriel said, hoping to distract Michael from any offense. "It is still beyond me why you bother though, you could get one of the snivelers to do it."

Michael shrugged, a wave of wobbles crossed his body "I

like doing the food. And besides, I don't trust those three, and if there is one thing that needs to be done properly around here, it's the food."

Gabriel stifled a laugh, his mind piecing together the next witty thing to say that walked the perfect line between insult and praise.

Before he could build the next piece of banter, a rustle reached his ears, and silhouettes appeared in the distance, dragging palm frond sleighs toward camp. Seeing the return of the others, a scornful noise escaped from deep in Gabriel's throat before he turned back to his food.

RAPHAEL DRAGGED the heavy bounty across the sand. The large bonfire roared. Hot coals raked to the outer edge, smooth stones heating on the bed of whitening embers. His nose twitched, Michael had been cooking. Knowing there would be no food awaiting them, he pushed the thought from his mind. There were many more chores to do before he ate the leftovers.

Raphael fixed his eyes to the fire, the dominant feature and the focus of life. The never-ending blaze was the constant force in a consistent world. It never faded, burning brightly from the first day of his memory. Drawn to the flames, he staggered close, heat radiated through his skin.

He wiped the dripping sweat from his brow, digging deep to gather the last drops of available energy. Dragging the large pile one more pace, he collapsed in the sand.

Knees drawn up, his chin on folded arms, Raphael saw the outlines of Gabriel and Michael through the shimmering air. They did not try to move.

"So hot today," Raphael said aloud, wiping his brow for a second time.

"It's always hot," came a soft voice, the whisper of an echo reaching his ear. Raphael's face broke into a broad grin. A current ran through his body, leaping out of his skin as if trying to reach for the voice behind him.

"I suppose you are right," Raphael said as he spun, the corners of his mouth twitching up at the sight of long dark hair rustling in the breeze. The delicate strands flitted across Lucifer's high forehead, brushing the long sharp nose and full pink lips. Jet black hair and alabaster skin, a striking juxtaposition of light and dark, pierced by a pair of intense bright-green eyes.

"You caught up quickly," Raphael said, groaning inwardly, regretting the stupid statement. Heart pounding in his chest, he attempted a more meaningful question. "Did you find anything after I headed back?"

Lucifer's shoulders dropped. A sigh escaped his plump lips, and a hand reached the top of his head, running through the long strands of glossy black hair. A movement Raphael knew well, an anxious impulse that escaped in times of disappointment.

"No," said Lucifer, eyes flicking down before returning Raphael's solid gaze. "I would like to go farther in, there has to be more in the forest. I can hear things in there. I just haven't seen them yet."

"You will," said Raphael, wanting badly to help fulfill Lucifer's growing need to explore. He reached out a hand, giving Lucifer's shoulder a gentle squeeze. The gesture was returned with a small smile that did not light his eyes, which remained steeped with frustration.

Raphael felt a small jump beneath his hand. Lucifer's

fine senses tweaked. He spun, and Raphael peered over his shoulder.

A squat figure made its way down the sand, shoulders heavy, head down. Sun glinted off the curly blond hair. A frond, half piled with fruits, dragged slowly.

"Alpha's caught up," said Lucifer, drooping, his disappointment multiplied with Alpha's impending arrival.

Raphael watched Alpha jerk the frond down the beach, his small strides adding to the entertainment as he vented his frustration by violently tugging the leaf.

Giving up, Alpha abandoned his contribution and trundled to the fire's edge, collapsing with a spectacular groan.

"I *cannot* do this any longer," sighed Alpha, burying his face in his arms.

Simultaneously seeking eye contact and raising their eyebrows, Raphael and Lucifer stifled their giggles, unable to contain their amusement at Alpha's continuous aversion to work.

Ribs heaving with suppressed laughter, Raphael grasped his sides. He was unable to hold it, the laughter escaped, ribs protesting with every movement. Slowly regaining the ability to breathe, he saw Alpha. Black eyes glowered with an anger that escaped the confines of his body, traveling through the air, pounding him in the stomach.

Raphael cleared his throat, avoiding Alpha's gaze. Searching for a way to remove himself from the awkward moment, he was saved by a demand from across the fire.

"Hey! About time!" called Michael. "Have you brought me anything new?"

"Not today," Lucifer yelled across the fire. "Not today," he repeated to himself.

∾

HE KNEW IT. There was something in the forest. He had felt them, seen them from the corner of his eye. The hairs prickled on the back of his neck, telling him something was near. The forest felt alive, there had to be more. Long ago, Lucifer vowed to himself to find the origins of the strange sounds he heard in the night. He would, one day, get answers.

He snapped to attention at the sound of wheezing, the sticky slapping of skin grew closer as Michael lumbered toward him, his fist shaking. Unintelligible grunts escaped his mouth. Lucifer made out the words "new" and "too long," enough to get the point. He opened his mouth to protest, he had delivered the mushroom only yesterday. Seeing Michael red in the face, spittle flying, Lucifer knew what was coming. He changed his mind. Instead of protesting, he ran.

Lucifer jumped up, zigzagging in a backward trot. Not as tall, but half the size and twice as fit; he had no trouble outrunning the lumbering figure. Agile and nimble, Lucifer darted, changing direction quickly. He forced Michael to concentrate on his footing.

Michael was fully breathless, his face adopting a red hue reminiscent of his favorite food. Laughter sprang up from deep in Lucifer's belly, the image of Michael's fat head turning into a tomato and the small appearance change that would result from such a transformation stuck in his head. Unable to stop it and seeing no harm in aggravating Michael further, he let the laughter bubble into the world.

Michael scowled and lunged toward Lucifer. Lucifer darted, barely escaping. Continuing his laughter, mocking and teasing, he picked up speed, trotting farther from Michael with every step.

Busy toying with Michael, losing track of his surroundings, Lucifer caught a double-handed wave from Raphael up the beach. His brow furrowed. What was he doing? Before the thought fully formed and his body could react, he lost his footing and crashed backward into the rippling blue sea. He dug his toes into the wet sand and raised his head above the water. With lank dark hair stuck in his eyes, he raised an arm to wave to his companions, signaling his welfare. He felt the water pull him, toes losing their grip on the sea floor. Stepping back, he scrambled for a new foothold. The world he knew disappeared as he sank over the edge of an unseen precipice.

Floating in a weightless prison, surrounded by dark, thin shafts of light pierced from above. Water crowded his ears, restricting his world to nothing but the rapid beat of his own heart. His mind told him something was wrong, this strange environment was not for him.

He felt a pressure in his chest, his throat clenched tightly, lungs screaming for air. The voice in his head urged him to kick to the surface. His senses told him this would be the end. An inbuilt understanding of basic needs forced his body to react. He clawed at the water, desperation willing him to rise. The water slipped through his fingers, he was stuck in the void.

It was useless. There was no air. He would soon leave his life behind. He would know death and ending. Acceptance soothed him. He gave in to the pull of the ocean. The last bubbles escaped his nose, his body ready for its final breath.

There was a flicker of silver, a solitary glint in the darkness. Scales flashed in the remnants of sunlight, the large-eyed creatures swam through the water, unafraid. He brushed one with his hand.

This was it, what he had been searching for. He had to survive, he had to find the answers. Kicking with the strength that only comes to one about to die, he broke the surface, water sluicing down his face. His first breath came too soon. He coughed, panting and squinting in the brightness of the sun.

Struggling toward the shore, movements anything but graceful, he found his footing a short distance from the group huddled by the edge of the water. Lucifer stood, lifting himself from the water that nearly claimed him, the ordeal evident with every movement. Senses returning, he heard the slosh of the small waves, felt the ripple around his legs and the pull of the sand at his feet. As he was about to collapse, something wriggled against his dripping leg. His hand was separate, distant, it did not belong to him. The creature from the deep wrestled in his grip. With no memory of clutching the creature, his jaw slackened. He raised his eyes to the group and was met with four identical expressions.

Willing his body to move, Lucifer waded to the shore, soon realizing the creature was not the first thing on everyone's mind. He was taken into Raphael's warm but ferocious embrace.

"Don't you ever do that again." Raphael's irritated voice was breaking, holding back tears. "I thought you were gone."

Lucifer gave him a half smile and a reassuring pat on the shoulder before dropping the creature and trudging back to camp.

3

THE FIRST DEATH

"**W**hat is it?" asked Gabriel, peering at the twitching animal spread across his upturned palms.

"I don't know," said Alpha, looking down his snub nose at the creature, leaning so close Gabriel could feel him breathing. "But it's alive."

"What do you mean *alive*?" asked Michael, voicing the collective question.

Alpha shrugged. "Well, we are alive. We move and breathe and eat. And look at this thing, it's flapping around. If there is one thing I know, this thing is as alive as you and me."

Gabriel silently willed Alpha to move, his proximity made his stomach hollow and his hair prickle. His silent plea did nothing to ease the sensation. Gabriel dropped the creature in the sand and stepped away, taking a deep breath.

Alpha noticed nothing, infatuated with the visitor from the deep. Without uttering a word, his face blank and impossible to read, Alpha strode three of his stumpy-legged paces to the edge of the fire. He stooped, inspecting the cooking rocks. He picked one from the edge that was cool enough to grasp, taking three strides back to the creature, he watched the lines in the sand move with every flap and struggle of the shining fins. Alpha placed the rock on the sand. Sinking to one knee, he roughly grasped the creature's tail. Raising his arm high, he brought the creature's head down onto the rock in a splatter of blood.

The creature's struggle ended at the instant of the blow, but Alpha continued his assault until the head transformed into a mash of flesh, an eyeball hung by a thin, fibrous strand.

Alpha sat back on his haunches. His eyes black and intense, shimmered like a piece of stone polished by time. He wiped a spatter of blood from his face with a pointed finger. Slowly, Alpha moved the blood-smeared finger to his mouth, spreading the red fluid across his lower lip.

"Or it *was* alive," Alpha said, tongue emerging, flitting across his thin lip to remove the blood. Raising his victim from the sand, he turned back toward the fire.

FOR THE FIRST TIME, Gabriel's words abandoned him. He remembered Alpha's arrival. He was different, difficult to be around. Constantly talking. Gabriel stopped his talking by giving him constant chores. He had felt Alpha's resentment rise with each day. But he never imagined his potential for aggression. He didn't think he would dare. This creature had proved otherwise.

Alpha stared at the cooking stones. What should he do with the thing? There was only one thing he knew beyond all certainty: he was meant to eat it. The kill had filled a void, an emptiness that had been sitting within him from his first memory.

Alpha blinked his eyes against the smoke, a small trickle of liquid running down each cheek was quickly wiped away.

"Alpha!" yelped a voice from behind him. He jumped in his skin, spinning on his heel, nearly toppling over into the uneven sand. "I don't like the way you are looking at my kitchen! What are you doing?"

"We should eat it," Alpha said, ignoring Michael's gruff questioning.

"Eat it?" Michael's eyes widened.

"It's dead." Alpha shrugged.

"I can see that." Michael's voice developed an edge to match his astonishment.

Alpha stood still, blocking Michael, protective of the underwater creature. With a sharp shove to the shoulder, Michael pushed past him and grabbed the cold, still tail of the animal. Giving it a quick study, he sliced it open with a shell as sharp as his voice.

"We need to cut it up, or it won't cook," Michael said, his voice muffled, head bent over the dead animal. After a few skillful cuts, the fish lay open on a cooking stone. The sweet smell of roasting flesh quickly reached Alpha's nose.

Alpha was presented a shriveled, blackened mess. The aesthetics of the meal were far from Michael's usual standard. But Alpha was not interested in the appearance or taste of the flesh. From the moment Alpha had sampled the metallic tang of blood on his tongue, he felt a wave of power surge through his body, standing his hair on end. His heart was pounding, skin tight and flushed. Electrified by his bodily response to the blood, he was only sure of one thing. He needed more.

Moving away from the fire and closing his eyes, he sank

his pointed teeth into the rubbery meat. Tough strands filled his mouth; charcoal coated his tongue. Eyes still closed, he waited. Nothing.

Alpha's heart pounded, breath coming in sharp bursts. Still nothing. He waited.

Finally, he felt it. The bolt quelled his rising panic. Life force streamed down his gullet, resting in the pit of his stomach before bursting from his body in relentless powerful waves.

Behind closed lids, his eyes rolled back, absorbing the waves that took over every muscle. His scalp prickled, each curly lock buzzing with life; the fine blond hairs on his arms stood on end. His hammering heart slowed to a dull thud as the tingles dissipated, nesting to his fingertips. He ran his wild eyes around his stunning home.

The feeling faded, the initial hit was wearing off, the lingering buzz settled into his bones.

Alpha glanced furtively back at the others, all in their places, eating small pieces of fish. No change, no leaps. No outward signs of an experience remotely akin to his own. They just sat, chewing, the same as always.

Alpha had proof, a long-held suspicion solidified. He was different from the others, he was special.

Alpha let his eyes fall on Lucifer, whose head was bent, cocked slightly to the side in deep conversation with Raphael. Their heads were so close that their hairs blew together in the breeze, red and black intertwining like sunset into night. Swallowing the remnants of flesh with a loud gulp, Alpha sprang to his feet. He was quicker, livelier. Dusting the sand from his hands, he slithered toward Lucifer.

He could use him, Lucifer was the one adamant that

"things" roamed the forest. Alpha's mind was on one thing: more. He had to recreate the feeling. Focusing on the infatuated pair, Alpha formed a plan. They would go to the forest and search for what Alpha craved most.

4

THE FOREST

L ucifer stared, his blank expression affording a thin veil to the whirlwind in his head. His brain flittered through the events of the day: his accidental discovery of life in the water, his burning lungs and bulging eyes, and the calm that washed over him, moments from death. Lucifer gathered the pieces in his head. Disparate flashes of feelings, pictures, and memories came together to form the question that hung at the murky edges of his mind. Lucifer closed his eyes, reaching out to the elusive thoughts, trying to grasp the pieces and force them together. Suddenly they disappeared, vanishing pieces replaced by wisps of white smoke.

His body refused to cooperate. Exhaustion pinned his legs to the ground. Determined to snap himself out of fatigue, Lucifer opened his eyes, shaking away the remnants of fog. Blinking in the softening light, he saw the layers of orange and purple fall into the sea from the once blue sky. The time for rest was approaching.

A familiar tingle ran through Lucifer's body. His mouth twitched up to a shy smile, the sense of Raphael's presence immediately soothing. He turned toward the fire, catching sight of Raphael a short distance away, cross-legged in the sand. His red hair caught the dying sun, each long strand appeared alight. Lucifer could see Raphael's mind was full. He sought support from the leaping flames.

Lucifer slid closer, brushing Raphael's knee with a flat palm. Jumping with a start and letting out a small yelp, Raphael grabbed his chest, breathing heavily.

"You scared me. How are you so quiet?" said Raphael, allowing humor to momentarily dance on his lips as he recovered his poise, his small mouth quickly reverting to its ponderous position.

Lucifer studied Raphael, whose lips were pressed together, shoulders tight, brows raised. Lucifer rose to his haunches, twisting himself in front of Raphael, looking deep into the troubled eyes. One eyebrow cocked in question. Lucifer's movement received the desired reaction. Raphael's shoulders loosened as he let out a long breath, the twitch of a smile returning.

"How do you always know?" Raphael said, shaking his head.

"If you could see yourself, Raph, you would know, too." Lucifer offered a kind smile. Reaching out, he touched Raphael lightly on the shoulder. "What is it?"

Raphael let out another breath, running a dainty hand through his hair, an outward signal of internal torment. "It doesn't feel right." He paused. His lashes flitted upward, eyes locked onto Lucifer's intense gaze.

Lucifer raised his eyebrow farther, a silent request for more.

"Killing and eating things," Raphael said. Lucifer felt his heart melt.

"I mean, we know nothing about them. Do you

remember when Gabriel threw that stone, and it cracked my ankle so badly I couldn't walk?" Lucifer nodded, letting Raphael find his own words. "That hurt so much I could barely breathe. What if the sea creature felt everything? I don't think any creature should feel pain like that."

Swallowing the lump in his throat, Lucifer grappled for words. He wanted to tell Raphael that his kind heart and his care for others made him special.

"You are so..." Lucifer failed to find the words. Instead he gathered Raphael into his arms, holding him close against his chest, breathing into his hair. Every drop of emotion poured into the embrace, the surge between them grew to breaking point before they wrenched apart, both holding a timid smile.

"We don't have to eat the creatures," said Lucifer, cupping his hands around Raphael's face, looking him straight in the eyes. Raphael nodded, relief flooding his face.

Lucifer's eyes dropped to Raphael's full mouth, the hairline cracks moist in his lips. He ran his thumb across Raphael's lower lip, feeling a combined shiver through their bodies. Lucifer's eyes flicked up, searching for permission.

Swishing footsteps in the sand broke the spell. Rapidly creating a greater space between their bodies, Raphael and Lucifer turned their heads. Alpha was approaching. Lucifer tried to tame his thumping heart.

"Alpha," Lucifer said with a nod. The stilted greeting was the best he could do. In return, Lucifer received a knowing grin, Alpha's eyes moved from Lucifer to Raphael.

Keen to end the awkward appraisal, Lucifer attempted to ignite conversation.

"What's going on?" he asked in his best casual manner.

"Nothing," said Alpha, his stubborn leer tightening

Lucifer's chest as if Alpha had placed a rock directly inside his body.

Alpha was enjoying this. He was going to make Lucifer work hard to pull himself from awkwardness. Increasingly flustered, Lucifer could not connect brain, throat, and tongue to form any kind of remark, let alone a witty retort.

Alpha gave up, laughing. Tension eased. Raphael and Lucifer joined with a chuckle, their bodies tight, unwilling to give in to laughter. Alpha's laugh stopped with a jolt, a frown crossing his face.

"Creatures," Alpha said without preamble.

"Creatures?" Lucifer snapped to attention.

"I want to go deeper into the forest," Alpha said. "I thought you might want to come, too, seeing as you have always spoken of finding creatures."

"Why do you want to explore? I thought you were sick of going out to gather food," said Raphael, failing to keep skepticism from his voice.

"I don't want to gather food every day just to bring it back to those two lazy lumps. I want to know what is out there." Alpha turned to Lucifer, seeking backup. "You said it yourself, Lucifer, you are sure there are more creatures."

Lucifer glanced to Raphael, the intense look silently reviving their recent conversation.

Lucifer was torn. He wanted nothing more than to grasp Alpha's offered opportunity, his long-held dream of exploration moments from reality. He saw the deep creases above Raphael's eyes intensify.

He was wary of Alpha's sudden desire to explore, the visions of Alpha crushing the head of the creature against a rock, licking its blood, and eating its flesh sent flashes through Lucifer's brain. But the secrets of their world reached out, pulling him to the forest. His heart and brain fought without resolution.

Lucifer's attempt to form a response was interrupted by Raphael's usual straight thinking.

"How are we going to explore? What about Gabriel and Michael? They will never let us go anywhere beyond where we can turn around to bring their food," Raphael said, words coming quickly. Fear covered his face. Even after all this time, he did not want to go back to the deep forest.

Lucifer looked to Alpha, shrugging in agreement. None of them had challenged the order of the group, continuing in blind acceptance of the enduring dominant forces.

"I refuse to bow to those two any longer," Alpha said through gritted teeth. "We should just go. Who cares about them? They don't care about us. Maybe they will appreciate us if we are gone for a while."

Alpha was bursting with energy, oozing confidence. Lucifer had no doubt that Alpha could and would take on anything.

Lucifer turned to seek Raphael's opinion, receiving a small shrug in answer. Alpha had a point.

Taking this as acceptance, Alpha maneuvered himself into the snug gap between Lucifer and Raphael's bodies.

"Well," grinned Alpha, clapping a hand on the shoulder of each companion, "now is as good a time as any, my friends."

Raphael swallowed, color draining from his face.

Gabriel and Michael basked in the warmth, the latest meal slowly digesting through their ever-full stomachs.

"Where are the snot bags going?" asked Michael. Gabriel lifted his head a fraction off the sand.

"Don't know, don't care," he said, barely coherent. "Gone to get some food for tomorrow? You know they always skulk around the edge of the forest."

"I guess," said Michael. "It's dark though."

"Whatever, who cares? They won't go far, they will be too scared," said Gabriel, yawning, rolling into his favorite position. He drifted to sleep.

DARKNESS. A complete blackness Lucifer had never seen. Amid the towering trees and away from the fire, he navigated by the scrunching steps ahead. Alpha led the single-file expedition, arms outstretched in the darkness. Lucifer and Raphael's only choice was to follow blindly.

Lucifer's hand stretched out behind him. Raphael clung to it, his only lifeline in a sea of black. Lucifer felt the wordless stresses pulsating through his hand. He wished he could take that fear, placing it within his own body to free Raphael from dread.

Lucifer refocused ahead. He didn't know where he was or where they were going. Alpha seemed to have a plan.

Lucifer kept his eyes steady on the back of Alpha's head, whose hair appeared white in the darkness.

"What has gotten into him?" Lucifer's question turned silently in his mind.

Alpha's sudden willingness to disobey their standing orders, his energy, his presence. Something had changed, but Lucifer could not connect the pieces.

Disorientated. Fear took hold. Lucifer spiraled down a

path of despair, close to joining Raphael in the dark pit. Escape would be impossible.

As if hearing the plea for distraction, Lucifer's mind turned back to his encounter with the underwater world. He had never seen creatures like he saw there. How different would life had been if he had stood up to his masters earlier? The possibilities of what he could have found made his head spin.

"No point. It's the past," Lucifer almost said out loud.

But how things had changed. Only yesterday, he would never have imagined walking through the forest in the black of night, following Alpha, an unlikely leader, but a leader nonetheless. Lucifer snorted. He hadn't stood up to his masters, neither had Alpha. They had just run away.

Alpha stopped. Lucifer walked right into him and fell to the ground, the cohesive line collapsing in a pile of limbs, hair, and muted yells.

"Get off me," said Alpha, his voice muffled by a variety of body parts.

Lucifer writhed, slithering out of the melee. He sat, panting. "You stopped, Alpha! It's completely dark. What did you think would happen?" Alpha said nothing. He moved swiftly, crouching with his back to Lucifer.

Lucifer groped blindly for Raphael, connection impossible with no light for guidance. Lucifer stopped. A dim glow. Long fingers crept out of the shadows. His long fingers. He turned. Alpha's body was silhouetted against a small fire.

"How did you do that?" gaped Lucifer.

"It's not that hard," said Alpha, chest puffed.

Lucifer sank to the ground, every bodily function pushed to the base of his being by awe. He had seen fire. The bonfire at camp had always been there, he never thought to create more. He did not understand how Alpha had done it. No questions formed in his mind.

"I think we sleep here," said Alpha, surveying his surroundings. "We are in a clearing."

Choosing to take Alpha's word for it, Lucifer nodded, reaching for Raphael. He helped him to his feet.

"It's been a long day," said Lucifer. "We should rest."

Alpha shrugged, lay on the spongy moss, and curled toward the fire. Lucifer helped Raphael. His expressionless face was white; the fear had claimed his senses. Lucifer lay him down, rolling him to the side on which he usually slept, pulling his sinewy body tightly into the hollow of his stomach. He cradled his head and stroked his hair. Raphael relaxed, his breathing slowed into the soft lull of sleep.

"Everything will be all right," Lucifer whispered to Raphael, but he was already gone. Lucifer continued to stroke Raphael's hair. His eyes were drawn to the other prone form in the clearing. Alpha was not asleep.

5

BLOODLUST

L ucifer gasped. Heart hammering, his breath escaped him. His eyes moved wildly around the clearing, jumping from landmark to landmark. Hyperventilating, he sat upright, fear pulsed through every fiber of his body. He spotted the fire. Memory returned to him in tandem with control over his physical body.

Alpha's small fire was still burning. It had decreased in size overnight, now it was a picturesque mixture of black, gray, and red coals. Lucifer was alone. Panic reemerged, jumping to his throat, his heart hammering once again. He fumbled to his feet, almost slipping on the spongy moss. Used to walking on sand, his first few steps were awkward. He grew accustomed to the sensation and quickly learned to dig his toes for traction.

Eyes darting, looking for evidence of life, Lucifer heard a shriek from the forest. His body reacted to the sound of distress, he ran across the spongy ground, bursting through the first layer of forest. Alpha and Raphael stood at the base of a tall tree, peering into a hole scratched between giant roots.

"There is definitely something in there," said Alpha, face flushed with excitement, black eyes gleaming. Ignoring Lucifer's entrance, his eyes did not move from the hole.

"What's going on?" Lucifer said, panting. He grasped Raphael by the shoulders and looked him over, checking for damage.

Raphael sighed. Realizing Lucifer's concern, he broke into a wide smile. "There is something moving in that hole, it just gave me a fright is all."

Lucifer let out his breath. "Don't do that. You scared me. You said the exact same thing to me yesterday if I remember rightly," Lucifer scolded, eyebrow cocked. He had not forgotten the reprimand he received the previous day when he stumbled from the ocean.

"If you two have quite finished," scowled Alpha, eyes on the tree, "we need to do something about this."

"Do what, about what?" Lucifer asked, sneaking a glance at Raphael, who returned his expression of concern.

"Well," said Alpha, speaking each word slowly through an over engineered grin, "we need to get it, obviously." His words dripped.

Raphael's eyes darted. His brain churned behind his eyes. He drew himself to full height, squared his shoulders, and locked onto Alpha's eyes.

"No," said Raphael. Trembling slightly, he stood his ground.

Alpha stared for a moment before doubling over and laughing so hard he nearly lost his footing and fell down the hole to prematurely meet his prey.

"Authority doesn't suit you, Raphael," Alpha wheezed, as the words staggered out between breaths. Shaking his head,

Alpha left them without another word, heading back toward the clearing.

Stunned, Raphael turned to Lucifer, mouth hanging open. Alpha and Raphael had never been the best of friends, but Raphael had never felt so small in Alpha's presence.

Lucifer's warm hand nestled on his shoulder, concern deep in his eyes. Overtaken with anger, Raphael shrugged Lucifer's hand away and stomped a few strides to a log. He sat with such violence that the log gave way, toppling him over, his legs in the air.

Staring at the sky, Raphael heard Lucifer chuckle. The bubbly sound soon escaped in loud whoops. The sound of Lucifer's laugh was infectious. It entered Raphael's body, warming him from the inside. He too joined in the laughter.

Lucifer reached out a hand, helping Raphael up to a safe perch on the overturned log. He sat and held Raphael's hand tightly between long fingers.

"What is this about, Raph?" he said.

Raphael sighed "I don't know," he said, eyes on the ground. "I just don't think killing things is right. I don't know why. Something about what Alpha said, I can't get it out of my head. He said the thing was as alive as you and me. And if they are like us, we shouldn't be killing them. I can't bear the thought they might feel pain."

Lucifer let out a breath.

Detecting a smile, Raphael gave Lucifer a swift sideways kick in the shin. Lucifer let out another laugh. Raphael pieced together a lecture, ready to explain everything in detail. To make him understand. Halting, he heard a heavy, fast-paced thumping reach the screen of trees.

~

ALPHA CRASHED THROUGH THE TREES. He howled. Time slowed. He was focused on the task, his need to kill taking over every sense and movement. Alpha saw Raphael and Lucifer on a log, eyes wide, frozen. Alpha's grin widened, his blood pumped, excitement palpable. He shrieked. Pent-up energy escaped his body. Anticipation welled up inside of him.

The hole. He lunged. The look of realization dawned on Lucifer's face. Alpha was too fast, determined to triumph.

Alpha's arm ached with the weight of the burning stick held high above his head. He pushed it aside, pain was unimportant.

Reestablishing his grip on the cool end of the weapon, Alpha thrust the sparking spear down the hole. Letting go, he rolled and pulled himself into a crouch, waiting.

A high-pitched scream filled with pain hummed through the air. The sound left an anticipatory buzz in Alpha's head.

The creature bounded out of the hole. Alpha lunged, fearless. Arrogant of his ability to overpower the unknown beast, he dived for the burning stick and struck with all his might, connecting skillfully with the creature's head.

It fell. Possessed by power, Alpha could not stop. He struck the unmoving creature with force, each blow strengthening. Blood spurted from its head. It splattered and covered him. Alpha's frenzy subsided as the creature's head gave way in a crack of blood and bone, small pieces of internal matter flying. Dripping down the trunks of the nearby trees.

On his haunches, flushed and elated, Alpha masked his exhaustion. He laughed, slowly at first. He couldn't contain it. The kill resonated through his body, escaping in hysterical waves.

Crouching over his victim, he reached into the crevice left by his assault, covering his hands with blood. Alpha wiped his fingers across his cheeks and down the sides of his neck. Closing his eyes, he looked up to the forest canopy in ecstasy.

HE WAS FROZEN. Shock restricted his body. Unable to signal his arms and legs, he could not stop Alpha or run from the gruesome scene. The image burned into his mind, forever imprinted.

Lucifer stared. Alpha's blond hair was highlighted with red flecks, streaks of blood dripping down his neck. He laughed. Crazed, arms raised to the sky, his legs collapsed beneath him.

Alpha's head snapped back to the dead creature, laugh ceasing. He crouched over his prey, surveying.

Alpha buried his face into an exposed piece of muscle beneath the skin, his pointed teeth ripping at the sinew. Bracing himself against the carcass, he wrestled with the tough meat. He wrenched away, a large chunk of flesh held between his lips. Grabbing the meat with both hands, he began to chomp at the dead flesh. Eyes closed, he was in another place.

Lucifer startled from his daze as Raphael bent forward and emptied the contents of his stomach on the forest floor. Before he could sympathize, Lucifer grabbed the prone Raphael by the hand and dragged him back to the clearing.

Lucifer and Raphael fell to their knees on the soft moss. Raphael continued to gag, Lucifer breathed deeply to quell the rush of vomit. Hot flushes pulsated through his body, and cold sweat prickled his forehead.

"What was that?" Lucifer rasped between breaths. Raphael shook his head, unwilling to summon the scene.

Forcing himself to a sitting position, Lucifer sat, patting Raphael on the back.

A rustle. Alpha returned. Lucifer felt Raphael stiffen and move closer, huddled against Alpha's advance. Alpha sauntered toward the fire, whistling, the sweet, piercing sound cutting through the still air.

ALPHA PASSED THE OTHERS. His exterior perfectly hid the electric waves tumbling inside his body.

Alpha was bursting with life. Everything was clear, he understood his surroundings and his place within them. With one bite of flesh, he had become invincible.

Alpha sat by the embers, poking the dying lights with a stick. Sparks hissed and wood cracked. The striking colors viewed through his new eyes sent a fresh buzz through his body.

The others left him alone, for that he was grateful. Turning his back, he held his hands in front of his face, appraising, exploring. The life force of the animal coursed through his veins, eager to escape through his fingertips.

6

ABILITIES

Spongy flowers embraced the soles of Lucifer's feet, the damp welcomed his body. His brain constantly ran since his underwater incident. The collected memories of his existence flashed behind his eyes. He reviewed events and actions, assessing, appraising.

He felt a knowledge void, there was so much he did not know. His understanding of his shortcomings came without warning. How sluggish they had been, taking everything with greed. Lucifer felt the weight of his understanding. Something had switched within him, the awareness of his ignorance struck at his bones.

Lucifer's awareness extended to Alpha. He watched Alpha on the far side of the clearing; back turned, shoulders hunched and muscles tensed. He had changed.

Lucifer tried to visualize Alpha before, he could not summon a clear picture. What he had been was gone, he was different now. Alpha seemed bigger. He filled the clearing with an aura that drew eyes to him, an over-whelming presence.

Stretching his neck, Lucifer lay his long body facedown

on the moss, cradling his head in his arms. Darkness came quickly in the forest. A wave of exhaustion washed over him, accompanied by visions of blood.

Lucifer's slide into rest was disturbed when Alpha sprang to his feet, bounding back into the forest.

Head jerking in response to the sudden movement, he grabbed his wrenched neck. Curiosity rose within him. Where was Alpha going? What was he doing? Impulsively he sprang to his feet. He froze, Raphael was foraging. He would have to wait, or Raphael would worry, not knowing where he was. His disposition to protect Raphael stopped his instinctual leap. His internal desires collided, leading to no action at all.

His brain resumed activity, torrents of feeling subsided. Curiosity willed his body to move, but before his muscles could twitch, Alpha returned, silhouetted against the trees, slabs of flesh piled high in his arms.

The slabs landed beside Alpha's fire with a heavy thump.

"We can cook it up for our dinner," said Alpha.

Raphael slunk into the clearing, arms piled high with fruits. He appraised Alpha, lip curling. Lucifer stared.

"No, I will not," said Raphael.

"Suit yourself," said Alpha with a shrug, as he threw a large slab of flesh onto the fire. Bending for a second chunk of meat, he worked on it with an object held tightly in his fist.

"What is that?" asked Lucifer, curiosity overcoming him.

"That is something I just made." Alpha opened his hand. Lying on his palm was a shiny blade of silver embedded in a wooden hilt. "A knife." He cut into the meat, showing off the utensil's wicked sharpness.

"Made it how?" said Lucifer, not bothering to hide his astonishment.

"I just made it," said Alpha, dismissing Lucifer's amazement with a flap of his hand. "I thought of it, worked out how it should look, and made it."

Raphael let out a long hiss through his teeth. "I won't watch this," he spat. "I'm going to eat my nonliving dinner over there." He stomped away, leaving the heat of the fire behind him.

"My dinner isn't living either," Alpha shouted after him, voice cracking with hidden laughter.

LUCIFER DECIDED NOT TO FOLLOW. He had been around Raphael enough to know when he needed space. Because he was angry with Alpha, he would externalize these frustrations. Lucifer did not feel like taking the blame tonight.

Lucifer had so many questions, but unable to form a coherent comment, he opted for silence, watching Alpha meticulously carve pieces of meat with his knife.

"I don't know," said Alpha.

"What?" said Lucifer, startled out of his own head.

"I don't know how I make things. I just can," said Alpha, moving the point of his knife to a small branch, testing its sharpness. "For all I know, we all can."

"Oh, right," said Lucifer. The abrupt start to the conversation caught him off guard.

Alpha gave Lucifer a solid glance. "I could tell what you were thinking, and I don't know." A brightness flashed in his eyes.

"Have you made anything else?"

Alpha stopped whittling. "No," he said abruptly. He stood, walking a little way from Lucifer, his gaze sweeping a wide arc, checking for space. He closed his eyes and brought his hands above his head, elbows straight, palms flat. A crackle formed in the air. Alpha radiated heat like a fire.

Lucifer watched, mesmerized. Before his eyes, a shape appeared, resting on the ground, slowly gaining solidity. With a snap, Alpha's invention was complete. Lucifer didn't need to ask what it was, it made perfect sense. Alpha sat down on his newly created chair and leaned back, his hands behind his head and a smug grin plastered on his face.

"Wow," said Lucifer, more words lost in the noise of Alpha's laughter.

A shuffle. Raphael had sulked enough. He came close to the fire, mouth dropping open, half-eaten fruit fell from his hand. Dragging his gaze from Alpha, Raphael's wide eyes pulled to Lucifer.

"Alpha just made it," Lucifer said.

Raphael groped for words, looking exactly as Lucifer did earlier. He gave up on speaking and continued to gape at Alpha sitting in his chair.

"Shut your mouth, Raphael, anyone would think you were not right in the head," said Alpha, finger tapping his temple.

Raphael shut his mouth with a clap of teeth, and glared, bending to swipe up his dropped fruit.

Alpha rose from his throne and repeated his creation ritual for Raphael's benefit. There was the same crackle, Alpha glowing with heat and light until the fuzzy cloud took shape. This time it was a large bowl, perfectly shaped, made of wood with swirled patterns snaking their way around the external surface.

Raphael dropped his fruit again, eyes wide, his jaw remained clenched.

"I told you," Lucifer said, holding back laughter at Raphael's expression. Alpha bent to pick up the bowl.

"Here you go. You can have this for your *fruit,*" Alpha said, sweat dripping down his face.

Alpha sauntered to the fire, wrenching the cooked slab from the coals. Shaving thin pieces off the charred meat, he extended the laden knife to Lucifer. He breathed in, inhaling the strong aroma laced with a hint of metallic blood. He took the strips with pinched fingers, hand hovering. Torn emotions halted his movements.

"Don't eat that, Luc," Raphael said, face creased.

Lucifer looked down at the meat in his hands. He stuffed the first piece into his mouth and began to chew.

RAPHAEL'S SIMMERING ANGER ERUPTED. Unease, fear, and anxiety spilled out of him in a violent deluge. He was angry at Lucifer for eating the creature's remains and at Alpha for killing it, but most of all, he was angry at himself for not stopping it. And for not understanding why these feelings spouted from his heart in a torrent so violent he could no contain it.

Raphael's usual timid nature evaporated. "Why did you do that, Luc?" Raphael shouted into Lucifer's face. Lucifer stood his ground, keeping silent. "I asked you not to."

"You didn't," said Lucifer, calm. "You told me not to. There is a difference."

A noise escaped Raphael's throat, he was too frustrated to form words. "I thought you would think about me," he managed, tears stinging his eyes, voice cracking.

Lucifer's body sank, his arm raising in an attempt to make contact. Raphael jerked out of reach.

Lucifer violently grabbed his wrist and swung him into a ferocious embrace. Raphael struggled, he could not escape. Lucifer's warmth broke down his anger. He melted into the welcoming chest, heavy sobs leaving his body.

Lucifer soothed Raphael, stroking his hair. "I'm sorry. I don't feel the same, and well, I wanted to try it."

Raphael's sobbing subsided. He looked up at Lucifer, his nose twitched with the last of the sniffing. "I'm sorry, too. I don't know what is happening."

"I know," said Lucifer. A small smile broke his concern. Raphael felt the back of Lucifer's hand brush his cheek. He returned the smile.

Lucifer stiffened. Turning, Raphael followed Lucifer's gaze to see Alpha, glaring.

Slowly detaching himself, Lucifer straightened his shoulders, giving Alpha a defiant stare, daring him.

Raphael's anger was barely below simmering point. He caved in to the craving, the need. Heightened emotions overturning his fear, he strode to Alpha, hand raised, slapping his ruddy cheek.

Unresisting, Alpha let his head turn with the slap. Raphael stood motionless, breathing hard, his eyes burning. Too late for retreat, he stood steady, awaiting Alpha's reaction.

Alpha screamed. Spittle and anger escaped his mouth, bombarding Raphael straight in the face.

Raphael stood his ground, ready for a fight. The fight did not come.

Alpha closed his eyes, taking a deep breath. Then he fixed Raphael with a fierce stare, black pupils large with something moving deep inside them.

"No, I will not fight you," said Alpha with vehemence. "Why would I bother to fight someone like you?"

Raphael huffed. "Fight me, Alpha. Show me who you really are."

"Who *I* really am?" said Alpha. "What about who *you* really are?"

"You are a killer, Alpha. You eat harmless creatures, you are disgusting. You have changed, and I don't want to be around you anymore," Raphael puffed.

"That's strange. I don't want to be around *you*. At least not the two of you. All touchy with each other, smiling and crooning and lying so close. *That* is disgusting. My eating of flesh is natural. It is what I was *meant* to do."

"You just wouldn't understand, would you, Alpha?" Raphael put on his best mocking tone. "Because no one would ever want to be with you. No one ever liked you."

Raphael saw hurt on Alpha's face. His small eyes showed momentary pain before a bright anger returned. A memory of his hard early life played behind his eyes.

Choosing retreat, Alpha bounded into the forest, leaving Raphael and a stunned Lucifer behind in the clearing.

IT WAS FULLY DARK. Lucifer lay in the glow of the dying embers, wishing for sleep. Giving up, he peered past the fire into the darkness. A dark cloud hovered, a sense of foreboding, something was amiss. For the first time in his life, he kept his troubles from Raphael. Lucifer knew he would not understand.

Lucifer had always known things. He knew fire kept you warm, but you shouldn't touch it, he knew that when you get hungry, you eat, and he knew if you were to get stuck underwater, you would die. But now, he didn't just know, he understood. His random world settled into ordered patterns.

Lucifer tried to ignore the feeling. He could not push it away. Since eating the meat, he felt different. But what disturbed him the most was not the feeling itself, but that he craved to turn to someone. That person was Alpha.

Lucifer lay down, breathing deeply, trying to relax and calm his swirling mind.

Turning his head, he saw Raphael on his back, his hands folded over his stomach and head twisted away, staring into the fire. What lay inside of Raphael was anything but peaceful.

Sensing Lucifer's eyes on him, Raphael turned, giving a small smile, confirming the torment resident within his body. Lucifer lifted his hand and brushed Raphael's flaming hair from his eyes. He had touched Raphael in this way countless times before, but now, with his senses heightened, he felt the small shiver in Raphael's skin that followed the line of his fingers. Taken by urge, Lucifer moved to kiss his pulsating skin. Raphael's lips parted, a small gasp escaped. Lucifer placed his lips to Raphael's, planting a tender kiss. Raphael jerked, adjustment taking hold, soon vigorously returning the kiss.

ALPHA WATCHED from behind the trees, seething with a force that made him shake. Breathing deeply, he pumped his fists. Oddly drawn to the display of affection, he did not understand why. What purpose did this touch have? After a momentary lapse, his anger returned, they did not matter. He was above everyone now, no one would match his brain's power and speed. His ability to create and think for himself was far beyond anything the others could imagine. His closed eyes opened, burning with hatred. The hatred washed over him, it was the only emotion he understood. Hate came to him easily, working to cover feelings he preferred not to have, those of jealousy.

7

THE RETURN

Michael stared at the water. Life had gone out of him, his previous passion for edible creations now a dull flicker. He heard graceful footfalls on the sand, he didn't turn.

"Cheer up," said Gabriel.

A slight shoulder raise was the only answer Michael thought appropriate.

"I've brought some berries from that bush over there," Gabriel said, holding a leaf stocked with fruit.

"If I eat any more of those things, I think I will just die." Michael's melodrama was adequate to rival one of Alpha's turns.

Gabriel sighed. "I know," he said heavily. "You know, Mikey, I never thought I would say this, but I miss those three. Maybe we were too harsh on them."

Michael snorted "Maybe, or maybe we just want them back to get some food that isn't a berry!" He spat. "We could always go farther ourselves."

"I have no idea where to go or what to look for," said Gabriel. "They just used to do it all, we always told them to do it, and they did. That was, until they disappeared in the middle of the night to who knows where!" A handful of berries scattered across the sand. His head dropped to his hands.

"We could try to catch one of those fish things Lucifer got," said Michael. His attention turned to water, mouth watering. His interest in food momentarily returned at the thought of experimental cookery.

"Go ahead then," Gabriel snapped. "I am going nowhere near the water. Lucifer nearly died."

Michael sighed, equally unwilling. Groaning loudly, he flopped back to the sand. His arm smashed over his eyes, incoherent sounds bubbled from his lips.

"Hush," said Gabriel, his voice interrupting Michael's wails.

"What?" said Michael, head snapping.

"Quiet," Gabriel repeated, turning toward the trees. Michael heard it, rustling from the edge of the forest. Plants, leaves, and sticks brushed and kicked. Something was coming. Scrambling to their feet, they saw two figures emerge from the forest, sacks over their shoulders. They were laughing together, strolling hand in hand down the beach.

"Alpha what?" Gabriel repeated for the third time. Lucifer and Raphael exchanged glances, neither sure how to provide Gabriel with more clarity.

"As we said," Lucifer said with a sigh, recounting again, "Alpha killed the beast, went crazy, ate the beast, *raw*. Then he gained these powers. He can make things. He showed us."

"Raw?" asked Gabriel, the word falling from his gaping mouth, his brain too busy to construct a full sentence.

Lucifer rolled his eyes, his attempt to hide his frustration banished by the stream of rotating questions.

"Raw. He didn't cook it; he just ate it. Dug his face right in and ripped chunks of flesh with his teeth," said Lucifer. The look of disgust on Gabriel's face revealed his understanding.

"Here," said Raphael, pulling a bowl out of the sack, trying to draw Gabriel's attention. "This bowl and the sacks to carry stuff in." Raphael handed the bowl to Gabriel, who took it with a dubious look, turning it over in his hands.

"Alpha made this?" Gabriel asked, looking from Lucifer to Raphael, searching their eyes, seeing only the truth there. They nodded in unison.

Gabriel's brow furrowed, unable to make sense of it. Alpha was such a little weakling. How could he have killed a beast? Let alone eat it and create things.

"Where is he now?" Michael said, eyebrows raised.

"We don't know," said Raphael. "He ran off, after we had a..." he paused, searching for the right word. Wise words were important when dealing with the upper classes. "Disagreement," he concluded.

"Ha, who would have thought it, Alpha being disagreeable?" Gabriel said, turning to Michael, searching for a laugh. Michael quickly provided the intended response, accompanied by a swift pat on the back.

"Well," said Gabriel, the air of authority returning to his voice, "now that you two are back, finally we can get on with cooking a proper dinner." Gabriel turned to Michael, whose fat face was split by his smile.

"I don't suppose you would go back into the water and

get us some more of those fish, would you, Lucifer? I think I could make it very tasty," said Michael.

The blood rushed from Lucifer's face. The feeling of immersion in water came to life. It was happening again, all in his head. Snapping himself back to the present, he saw the terrified look on Raphael's face. Giving a large outward sigh and squaring his shoulders, he spoke with confidence.

"No, no. I will not," he said and walked away to empty his sack by the fire.

LUCIFER AND RAPHAEL returned to their foraging duties, working to keep the camp running, returning to normal life.

But everything had changed. Alpha was gone. The delicate balance was upset by his disappearance. The balance of power was altered; everyone was on edge.

In addition to navigating the sudden change to the state of affairs, Lucifer had another problem. It welled up from the depths of his mind, settling in a constant heaviness in his chest.

Before, after long days hauling fruits and digging comfortable spots in the sand for his masters, Lucifer would collapse at nightfall, a deep sleep of exhaustion mercilessly dragging his consciousness to the world of dreams.

Now the fatigue in Lucifer's body was distant, locked away from the constant ticking of his mind. Mind and body operated separately. A slave to his brain, Lucifer could gain no rest. His stubborn thoughts swirled, his sleep banished by constant waves.

Lucifer's thoughts flitted, no longer moving down a stable, predictable path, but jumping from subject to subject along the thinnest strand of association.

Lying in the sand, staring into darkness, willing for sleep, Lucifer's mind settled on the most uncomfortable image that was resident in his head: flashes of Alpha's frenzy, with blood-splattered eyes gleaming and pointed teeth dripping.

Lucifer screwed his eyes shut, squeezing out the nightmarish vision and replacing it with the image that made him happiest: Raphael smiling, teeth white, flaming hair falling across his forehead. He saw his own hand swiping the stray strands from Raphael's large eyes.

Lucifer's body relaxed as the images of Alpha sunk down to the murky depths of his thoughts, lurking, ready to escape at his brain's next idle moment. But the incessant ticking of Lucifer's mind persisted. Continuous questions swirled, most of them unanswered.

Why did Raphael's touch send fire through his veins? Why did his appearance at camp send a rush of blood through his body? Why did his stomach churn when he saw a flick of fire-bright hair out of the corner of his eye? Unable to keep Alpha at bay, his face solidified in Lucifer's mind. His powers were astounding, they had appeared so quickly. What was Alpha doing out in the wilderness alone? Was he honing his powers? How was he going to use them? Lucifer thought back to Alpha's life and how he had been treated. A shudder ran through his body. Would he be out for justice? Or revenge?

Lucifer sighed, his churning stomach a constant companion, pulling him back to the world. Raphael lay nearby, buried in the sand. A slight smile touched his lips, and his face was peaceful, muscles relaxed in sleep. Lucifer examined his face. His fine, long nose turned up slightly at the end. High, pointed cheekbones, and that hair flowed over his forehead like a red river.

The focus helped. Lucifer calmed. Raphael was his escape, where he could gain solace from thoughts and feelings rushing around inside of him.

One of those emotions broke the surface, rushing from head to heart. Happiness.

GABRIEL SAT UPRIGHT, stretching his long, bony arms. He had relaxed since Lucifer and Raphael's return, glad to have his servants back. Gabriel looked to the sky, grateful that the equilibrium had returned to his little world and that Michael had a full belly again. Incessant complaints of death by starvation had ceased.

Camp life had improved for Gabriel. The absence of Alpha promoted a more harmonious environment. Lucifer and Raphael were always together, leaving Gabriel and Michael alone. Although Gabriel rarely cared what was going on with the others, living without Alpha's volatile moods was bliss.

Snapped from his private contemplation by the sound of heavy breathing and even heavier footsteps, Gabriel turned.

Panting, his red face shining, Michael lumbered, bending at the waist. Hands on his knees, he sucked in air to service his heaving chest.

Gabriel waited. It would be a while until his lungs, unacclimatized to such exertion, would allow Michael to speak. Gabriel forced his curiosity down. It must have been something big to prompt a run. Patience overtook his burning desire to attain gossip.

Surprisingly quickly, Michael stood upright, drawing a huge breath.

"Alpha. Is back," he blurted.

Gabriel's jaw dropped. Before he had time to pull his eyes from Michael, the big man's eyes rolled back in his head, and he crashed to the sand with a thump, limbs wobbling.

"Well, that's that then," Gabriel said to himself. "Back so soon." Ignoring Michael's sprawled body, Gabriel hustled in search of Alpha and proof of his supposed powers.

Gabriel found his proof not far from the forest edge. Alpha stood gleaming, objects scattered around him in the sand. Things Gabriel had never seen. His precious paradise was invaded by objects he didn't understand. But the things were not the only sight that drew Gabriel's attention. Alpha was different. The short stature and the blond hair wound in such tight curls that it looked like it would spring loose at any moment, remained the same. But something had broken the surface, a trait that had previously simmered below the skin. An attitude, a surety. Confidence.

"Well, well," said Alpha, head tilted back, peering down his nose at Gabriel. For the first time in his living memory, Gabriel felt small despite his significant height advantage.

Gritting his teeth and puffing out his chest, Gabriel rose to full height. He opened his mouth, formulating a demand in his mind. Gabriel required an explanation to Alpha's disappearance and these so-called *powers*.

Alpha's eyes flashed. Gabriel's mouth fell slack, words stuck in his throat. "What just happened?" Gabriel thought as he shrank, taking a step back.

Clearing his throat, nervous, Gabriel croaked, "You're back," regretting the facile remark.

"Very observant," Alpha sneered, still looking down his nose. Power had shifted immediately and dramatically.

"Where have you been?" Gabriel got the words through his lips, but they were forced, unsure, and anxious.

"Here and there," said Alpha, picking at a nonexistent spot on his arm, the arrogant air thick between them. Alpha was playing, teasing, making him wait for the proof of what he could do.

Gabriel surrendered to Alpha's game, he bent to appraise Alpha's inventions strewn in the sand.

MICHAEL GROANED, sure that if he opened his eyes, he would come truly to life and be fully hit by the pain. After a decent few moments of steeling himself for extreme discomfort, he cracked one eyelid, tentatively letting the sunlight restrict his pupil. Opening his eyes, he looked from side to side, patting down his body, checking it was all still there. All present and accounted for, he smiled, proud that he had the resilience to survive near death from overexertion.

Leaving his bubble, he noticed voices toward the forest. "That's right," he said aloud. "Alpha is back." He grunted as he hauled himself out of the sand to join in the crowd, eager for answers.

Michael approached the throng.

The scene was strange, off-kilter. Alpha stood tall at the head of the pack, talking, his hands waving wildly, animating every word. He pointed to an array of things scattered around him on the ground. With his chest puffed, he was proud, radiating a superior aura.

Michael growled low in his throat.

Alpha no longer thought he was better than everyone else. He knew.

Gabriel was bending at Alpha's feet, turning an object over in hands. Inspecting. Michael thumped up beside him. Craning his neck, he peered over Gabriel's head.

Gabriel's long fingers were caressing the object. It had a long blade, wide and shiny, the curve ending in a vicious point. The broad end of the vibrant metal faded into a bound wooden handle. Mesmerized, he was amazed by Alpha's ability. Michael's mouth dropped a little. He would never have thought the person to awe Gabriel would be Alpha.

"This is amazing," Gabriel said. Alpha grinned back at him, keeping his head held high, eyes traveling to Gabriel down the length of his nose. "We could cut down some of the high fruits," said Gabriel, half to himself.

"Yes," said Alpha. "That's what I made it for. But there is something else I want to do first." Gabriel's head snapped up, body rising. He said nothing, waiting for Alpha to speak.

Michael, too, maintained his silence, waiting to see what Alpha would do next. Flashing another grin, Alpha let out a laugh and moved back toward camp. Like obedient dogs at the heels of a master, the others followed without question.

ALPHA SURVEYED CAMP. He smiled. He felt powerful, and he knew the others felt it too. Finally, they were treating him with the reverence he deserved. When they saw what he could really do, they would fall to their knees in the sand. Now was the time to show his power and begin his reign as commander of their world, the great and all-powerful Alpha.

Acutely aware of the wide-eyed stares from his audience, Alpha walked into the center of camp, raised his arms high into the air, and inwardly turned his palms flat to channel the energy from the atmosphere.

Alpha had always felt this energy. But he had now eaten

the flesh of the living. He understood how to channel the energy to create and destroy. His head tilted to the sky, he closed his eyes. He felt the wind pick up, rustling through his hair. The energy throbbed through his veins as he became one with his surroundings. His brain working to maximum capacity, Alpha left his body, soul held by a thin thread, the precarious tether all that stopped his life force from floating up to the sky.

At the brink of collapse, Alpha let forth the surge of energy. He placed his hands on his knees to steady himself. Sweat stung his eyes. A gasp from behind found his ears.

Letting out a long breath through pursed lips, Alpha raised his blond head to survey his latest construction. He looked over his shoulder to the crowd and let out a laugh as he sank to the sand. He had never seen so many wide eyes and open mouths.

Lucifer stepped forward first, amazed and so surprised by Alpha's creativity. He walked forward in a trance to investigate the structure.

Sitting perfectly spaced from the large central bonfire was a shelter made of stunning stone that caught the light, vibrating a slight warmth. The door into the shelter was wooden, and it swung back and forth in the remnants of breeze, which was slowly dissipating from creation. The roof, made of perfectly placed palm leaves, sloped off to one side.

Lucifer walked close enough to touch the stone. His hand quickly moved from the surface, surprised by the residual heat. The others cowered behind him, none of them brave enough to approach.

Alpha saw Lucifer's chest rise as he pushed the door, stooping beneath the lintel, slightly too low, and stepped over the threshold.

Inside was simple. Alpha practically felt Lucifer's intake of breath as he took in his new creation. It had a soft surface for sleeping, a raised flat surface for eating, and perfectly formed vessels to hold their sitting forms. Bed, table, and chairs surrounded the new fire pit at the heart of the hut. A range of cooking equipment was scattered near the fire stones. It was dark inside, a small amount of light came in through thin, high wall openings. Lucifer was surveying the dwelling when Alpha entered behind him.

Alpha made a sound of general satisfaction, proud of his creation. He took the few steps to the fire pit, held out his hand, and started a fire in the pit with no obvious effort. Luckily, Lucifer did not see the first spark fail.

Lucifer turned to Alpha, the same expression of adoration and awe resident on his face as all the others. None of them were capable of suppressing their amazement.

"It's for living in?" asked Lucifer, looking around the little house.

"Yes," said Alpha. "More comfortable, don't you think?"

Despite the rhetorical nature of the question, Lucifer nodded. His eyes were not staying in one place for long, they drank in the feat that Alpha had accomplished in such a short time. Alpha went toward the bed and threw himself down with a skip.

He relaxed into the soft bedding and put his hands behind his head, a groan of satisfaction escaped his lips. "Come and try it, Lucifer, it's very comfortable."

Lucifer started, taken aback at Alpha's familiarity. Curiosity won out. Alpha watched the decision creep onto Lucifer's face as he moved to perch on the edge of the bed, lying down next to Alpha, careful not to touch him.

Lucifer's body melted as he let go, liquefying into the mattress.

"Oh my," he uttered.

Alpha shuffled and turned to Lucifer with a wide grin, aware of a small spark hovering between them.

"Good?" Alpha said, eyebrow raised.

Before Lucifer could reply, the door banged open. The others jostled to enter the hut.

Lucifer startled, he sprung off the bed in perfect time to look right into Raphael's face, whose expression soured in the space of seconds. Lucifer reached his hand out toward Raphael, but before he could touch him, Raphael turned on his heel and strode out the door. Lucifer took no time to follow.

Alpha remained still, his grin never subsiding.

Lucifer broke out of the house, blinded by the change in light. Eyes adjusting, he saw Raphael sink into the sand a short distance from the house, head in his hands.

Lucifer slowed his pace and sank down next to Raphael. His hands remained still, and he avoided eye contact.

Lucifer let out a breath and closed his eyes. Making a swift decision, he grabbed Raphael by the face and kissed him hard. Raphael struggled against him before giving in and kissing him back, his anger and passion flowing out of him, hitting Lucifer deep in the chest.

Lucifer pulled away, breathing hard, keeping his hands on either side of Raphael's face. Filled with inspiration, Lucifer launched into speech.

"I was just testing the bed. I didn't even touch him." And almost as an afterthought, "It's only ever you, Raph." The statement met with tears. Raphael launched himself into Lucifer's arms.

"I know, Luc, I know," he said, sniffing, his tears flowing. "It was just such a shock."

They sat, unmoving. Unspoken words gushed between them.

They pulled themselves out of their embrace to see the others standing nearby, intruders in their intimate moment.

Gabriel was agape, Michael was barely quelling laughter, and Alpha did nothing to hide a look that would reignite the dullest of fires.

8

THE TEST

Alpha watched Lucifer and Raphael. Their behavior was strange and enticing. Part of him was repelled, and part of him was intrigued. He did not understand what they felt for each other. They were the only ones, as far as he knew, who did these things. An uncomfortable and foreign feeling rose in him.

"If the other option is Michael," he thought to himself, "you would be squashed with the most minor embrace." He laughed inwardly, shuffling his feet from side to side, attempting to hide his awkward feelings. Failing, he left the scene, heading back to admire his creation. Alpha's head was brimming with ideas of what to do. He could make it so they had a life of comfort. He would never have to labor again.

Alpha built his kingdom in his mind. Planning the structures and contraptions he could develop to assist with their everyday tasks. The exhaustion of the creative process wearing off enough that he could fathom doing it all again.

His mind dwelled on the animals. He killed and ate many during the days he was alone in the forest. He no longer felt the buzz. He wasn't gaining power like he did with the early kills. His vision faded. He needed more power. Kicking the sand, he was unsure how to fulfill his need. His mind ran. One more boost was all he required. After that, he knew his brain would develop enough for him to understand the complexities of his powers, the intricacies of which were consuming him.

Perhaps if he pushed the problem aside, the answer would present itself. "A walk will help," he said to himself. Scuffing sand with each lazy step, he meandered down the beach.

He saw a figure hunched against the light. Lucifer alone, a rare sight.

Alpha scoffed to himself. Raphael and Lucifer had never been apart for long. No doubt Lucifer's redheaded appendage would be here soon.

Slowing his pace, Alpha appraised Lucifer. Sitting by the water, a large rock to one side, a pile of zucchinis on the other, he methodically ground the vegetable, plopping the resulting mush into one of Alpha's bowls. Reaching the end of the zucchini, he threw the leftover pieces into the water.

The muscles in Lucifer's arm tensed with the throw, Alpha's eyebrow raised as he watched the scraps sail in the air, the sound of the landing swallowed by distance. Alpha saw movement where the scraps hit the water, fish, dancing for their treats. Alpha came up behind Lucifer, sitting firmly behind him.

Lucifer startled. "Alpha!" he yelped, holding his hand to his heart. "You scared me." Lucifer gave a brief faint smile before turning back to his task.

"Why are you doing this?" asked Alpha.

"What?" said Lucifer, asking for clarification before he processed the question. "Oh, right. I'm just preparing vegetables for Michael. He wanted to cook them in patties with some fish. And I don't want to get the fish." A visible shiver ran down Lucifer's spine.

"I see," said Alpha. "Well, let me help you." Alpha shuffled a little closer to the rock. He held his hands over the rudimentary utensil, closing his eyes. An idea popped into his head. Perfect. Not too taxing.

Alpha concentrated on the rock, mentally melding it with his nebulous idea. The vision solidified in his head. The familiar tingle ran through his body, the intangible materialized in front of his eyes.

Lucifer had come closer, staring at the rock.

Alpha smiled. He would never tire of this reaction, the wonderment at his powers.

Alpha reached close over Lucifer's lap to grab a zucchini from the pile. He grabbed the end of the vegetable, scraping it back and forth against the contraption now embedded in the rock.

Grabbing the bowl, Alpha threw Lucifer's zucchini mush into the water, replacing it with the fine gratings delivered by his newest invention.

Lucifer took the bowl from Alpha's hand. Still silent, he ran his fingers through the freshly grated strands, sharp green eyes raising to meet Alpha's.

"You have the most ingenious ideas, Alpha," Lucifer said, voice sincere. He paused, a question lingering on his lips.

"Your abilities," said Lucifer, jumping in. "Did they come after you killed the thing in the forest?"

Eyes downcast, Alpha created the illusion of thought. "Mostly," he said, nodding his head, "but I felt the first change after we ate the fish."

Lucifer's face went red. He averted his eyes.

Alpha raised an eyebrow.

Lucifer took a deep breath, lifting his head to meet Alpha's gaze again. Alpha studied him intently, eyes alive with understanding.

"You felt it too, didn't you?" Alpha asked, with an underlying tone of demand hardening his voice.

Lucifer sighed, "Yes," he said choosing his words carefully. "I have felt something, more alive, more aware. Not so much after the fish, but after"—he paused, as if reliving the memory—"what happened in the forest."

Alpha grunted. What did this mean? "Can you make things like I can?" he asked Lucifer.

"I haven't tried," said Lucifer, honesty plastered on his face. "How do you do it?"

Alpha pursed, his lips sucking in air, stalling. He was torn between keeping the power for himself and curiosity at what may be within Lucifer. The desire to know how an animal's life force affected another burned within.

"Come on; stand up. I'll show you."

ALPHA DRILLED LUCIFER FOR HOURS, telling him to visualize and meld the real world with that of his imagination. If he could master that, he could do anything. They made no progress.

Lucifer was frustrated and ready to give up. Alpha continued to hound him, forcing him to continue. A trickle ran across Lucifer's skin. Before Alpha could urge him to chase the feeling, Lucifer's shoulders slumped.

"What were you thinking of then?" asked Alpha.

"Just a bowl, like the ones you have done," Lucifer replied.

"It started that time, then fizzled," said Alpha.

Lucifer collapsed to the ground, throwing his arms up before rubbing his eyes.

"Oh well, you said it yourself, Alpha. Maybe I don't have enough ability."

Alpha nodded and sat down next to Lucifer.

"I don't mind if I can't do it," Lucifer continued. "But I feel better you understand. It makes me feel less alone."

Alpha smiled. His chest swelled, his whole body prickled with the new sensation of appreciation.

An unfamiliar urge swept over his body. He needed to cement his newfound intimacy. Alpha leaned to Lucifer, quickly and sharply kissing him on the mouth.

Alpha received nothing in return. No spark, no tenderness. The lack of feeling apparent in the short moment before Lucifer pulled away and wiped his mouth.

"Alpha! What are you doing?" he said, voice raised. "You have got the wrong idea completely."

Alpha said nothing. He sat, eyes down. Not knowing what to do, his body swam with hurt. For the first time since his powers cemented, he didn't know what he wanted. Alpha watched Lucifer rise and walk back toward camp. Back to Raphael. Lucifer had turned his back and rejected him.

Alone, Alpha strode into the water. He would get Lucifer's reverence through force, if necessary. He will never show this weakness again.

9

THE FALL

lpha stood knee-deep in the water, enjoying the sight of the sinking sun over the far horizon. One day he would explore the sea. But for now, his priorities lay elsewhere.

Conscious he must conserve his energy, he pushed his desires aside. In the past few days, Alpha had created so much that he was close to exhaustion.

He spent much of his time alone, the weakness born of fatigue was something he preferred to keep hidden from the others. He had built up a persona, successfully manipulating the others to view him as indestructible, superior. They must not see him for what he was. Flesh and blood, just like them.

Determined to wipe his failures from memory, he turned to survey his newly created village. The bonfire formed the center of the square, lined by Alpha's buildings, a house for each of the group. A kitchen for Michael, an open-fronted gazebo for Gabriel filled with various soft cushions and hammocks. A little farther back, storage sheds where Lucifer and Raphael ordered the food. The others believed it was perfectly ordered to their needs. Alpha, understanding each of their desires, created something personal for each of them. But there was only one person this paradise was created for. Him.

GABRIEL WAS DRAWN to Alpha's knives that hung on the wall in the farthest shed, each blade designed for a particular task. For the first time, Gabriel was keen to do something other than laze in the sand. He wanted to contribute. His drive only slowed when he sank into one of Alpha's hammocks, easing back into his old life.

Gabriel ran his hand along the hanging blades. He felt their movement, the slight clang at them touching. His hand stopped on the large, curved blade, it was the first one he had seen and held when he learnt of Alpha's creations. He wrapped his large hand around the handle and ripped it from its hanging place, striding through the door into the sunlight.

Alpha was standing still at the edge of the square.

"Let's do it," Gabriel said, striding up to Alpha. He received no response.

"I-I-I mean," stammered Gabriel, nervous for reasons he didn't have the patience to understand. "Let's get some of those fruits from up the top of the trees. I want to know what they are."

Michael appeared by Gabriel's side. His ability to pick up a conversation about food from the other side of camp was uncanny.

"Yes, Alpha, yes," said Michael, so excited he looked as though he might burst. "Let's get them."

Alpha sighed, his disdain for Gabriel and Michael

barely hidden, his feelings toward the stupid and facile not worthy of control.

"All right," Alpha said. "That is what I made it for, after all. But don't think I'm going up there."

Gabriel and Michael shot each other a glance. In perfect synchronization, they looked up the height of the tree to the place where the fruit hung.

Gabriel's face drained of blood, his hands shaking slightly.

Alpha rolled his eyes. "Where is Lucifer?" he said, looking around, acting bored. "He would be best to climb. He is strong."

Michael grunted. "Where do you think he is? Off with Raphael somewhere *private*," he sneered with almost as much malice as Alpha himself.

Alpha turned on his heel and stormed toward Lucifer's house. He emerged seconds later between Raphael and Lucifer, holding each by the arm. Both blinked in the light, looking red-faced.

Lucifer listened, his head bent, concentrating on his instructions from Alpha. He looked up to the tree, worry clear on his face.

Worry soon gave way to curiosity. Gabriel watched him approach the tree, appraising the obstacle. Holding the machete in one hand, he tipped the handle back and forth, a rhythmic thinking aid. The weight of the knife caused it to swing in wide arcs at Lucifer's side.

"I don't know I can climb it," he said. "How am I going to hold on?" His question was met with silence. A collective startle ran through them when Alpha stamped a foot.

Alpha growled deep in his throat and rolled his eyes. Taking the knife, he impatiently waved, adding a loop to the handle. He grabbed Lucifer roughly by the hand and looped the knife over his wrist. "There," said Alpha, his eyes kept downcast throughout the whole encounter before stepping back to join the others.

With all limbs now free, Lucifer straddled the tree, its rough bark providing a tenuous grip. He slithered upward, grabbing and halting until he reached the hard fruit in neat bunches high in the air.

~

"OK," Lucifer shouted, words falling down the bare trunk. "Here it comes." He swung the knife hard at the intersection of fruit and tree.

He heard a thud. Steeling his courage to look down, he saw Alpha bend to the fruit. Alpha hacked off some of the fibrous outer casing and deftly smashed it open with a second large knife.

"Get some more," shouted Michael, head turned up, hands cupped around his mouth. His voice entered Lucifer's ears as if he were standing on the ground.

"More?" Lucifer shouted back down. Not receiving a reply, he cut down more fruit, hoping that he wouldn't have to get up there again. Lucifer stole a look down, seeking support to make his treacherous way down the tree. They stood in a tight circle below him, heads bent, staring at the coconut. From high above, they looked like a flower with petals of different colors. Only one petal was different.

Alpha was looking upward, not at Lucifer, but at the sky. Face blank and expressionless.

Lucifer felt the tree shake. A breeze ruffled his hair, it was just the wind. He raised his knife to swing at another hanging ball.

As soon as he reached, the tree shook. His instincts

kicked in. He abandoned his stab at the coconut, attempting to regain his grip. Hand weighed down by the heavy knife, he missed his grasp. The tree shook again. The weight of the knife dragged his body to the side. He was twisting, foot slipping, knee losing its pressure hold. Time seemed to slow. Lucifer desperately shook his hand, trying to free his wrist from the knife to regain his hold to the tree. He looked down to the ground, trying to shout out to those beneath, hoping the knife wouldn't connect with one of the bent heads below. They didn't hear. The wind had risen.

Lucifer followed the knife. He felt the sand on his face, followed by darkness.

Swimming through thick liquid, he shouldn't have been able to breathe. He lost all sense of being and direction until he felt a hand grip his shoulder, followed by many others. His whole body was being clawed in desperation, souls searching for help, pleading to be saved. He heard a piecing scream and then saw the light.

Lucifer sat bolt upright. Unsure if it the scream was his own, he looked around, breathing heavily, disorientated. He was inside. He had not yet become accustomed to sleeping under a roof, feeling strange when he could not see the stars or warm sunlight.

Calm. He needed to calm. His breathing returning to normal. The piercing pain gripped him. As if his eyes may drop out of his head.

The door swung open. Raphael backed his way in,

hands full, carrying a steaming bowl of liquid. His tongue was sticking out the side of his mouth, concentrating.

Lucifer laughed. Raphael squealed. The protected bowl smashed to the floor, liquid splashing in a pattern like blood.

Lucifer's head pounded from the laugh. He covered his eyes as sunlight poured in from the flapping door.

Raphael rushed to Lucifer's side and sat by him on the bed, bowl and water forgotten on the floor. Raphael grabbed Lucifer by the shoulders and crushed him to his chest, Lucifer's face squashed into the firm warm hollow at the base of his throat.

"Ouch!" Lucifer yelled, his voice muffled. Raphael released him from the crush, taking his face between his hands instead.

"Sorry, sorry," said Raphael, his brow furrowed and eyes wide with remorse. He ran his fingers delicately across Lucifer's face. Lucifer felt the pain as Raphael traced the cuts and abrasions. "Do you remember what happened?"

Slivers of memory were running, sand, fruit, trees, wind, water, breathlessness, hands, feet, and screams still resonating in his ears. He shook his head, pain bursting with the movement.

"I think so," he said. "I'm just not sure what was real and what was a dream."

"You were out for quite some time," said Raphael, nodding. He bit his full lower lip beneath his perfectly formed top teeth. "You fell from the tree."

Lucifer moved his head, testing his limits for pain. He couldn't gather the memories. Just behind the veil of fog was a feeling. Something was not right. Lucifer studied Raphael, still chewing his bottom lip. His eyes were focused on the floor, two small lines indented between his brows. His red eyes and hollow cheeks aged him.

"What is it, Raph? What do you need to tell me?" Lucifer asked softly.

"I'm not sure exactly," he said slowly. "I just have a feeling, something about you falling and the coconuts. It doesn't feel right."

Lucifer didn't speak, waiting patiently while Raphael built what he needed to say. He always did that, and Lucifer had known him long enough to just give him the time he needed.

Raphael shot a glance back toward the door, checking there were no shadows dancing at the lower crack. "I didn't see it," Raphael whispered, still thinking which words to pick. "But I think Alpha might have done it. I don't know how or why, I just have a feeling."

At that moment, jogged by Raphael's revelation, Lucifer's memory fragments coalesced into one solid mass of recollection. Ending with the sand rushing toward him and the glimpse of Alpha from the corner of this eye, then blackness. This epiphany must have registered clearly on his face, as Raphael moved closer and took his hands.

"What is it?" Raphael said, maintaining his whisper. "Have you remembered? Was it Alpha?"

Shocked by the questions, becoming more aware of the headache plaguing his mind, Lucifer nodded and swallowed, looking at the floor.

"But why?" asked Raphael.

Lucifer swallowed again, and with another quick glance to the door to assure its emptiness, he met Raphael's eyes.

"I think I know why," he said as he broke down in tears and described his latest encounter with Alpha.

10

VANISHING

Lucifer remained in bed. Fragile both physically and emotionally, not willing to face the others, he resigned to let Raphael care for him. His companion showed outward delight, beaming with every instruction given to his patient as he took to his role of personal nurse with almost too much enthusiasm.

Lucifer was sore and bruised, his healing abrasions drove him to incessant, surreptitious scratching. The stubborn headaches were the worst. Constant dull throbbing sometimes exchanged for sharp stabbing behind the eyes, and when struck by both at once, Raphael firmly but tenderly pushed him down to his pillow, a damp cloth covering his eyes.

Raphael foraged soft and easy-to-swallow items to meet Lucifer's basic needs, the pain in Lucifer's jaw restricted his eating. Lucifer remained still and calm during Raphael's comings and goings during the day. Each evening he enjoyed the reports of camp life before drifting to sleep, safe, lying close to Raphael, feeling his warmth and shallow breath.

Reports of daily camp life were Lucifer's only remaining link to society. Raphael swore he had received no pressure regarding Lucifer's reappearance. Gabriel and Michael posed polite enquiries each day, only to ascertain if he was dead or not.

Lying together in the evening, Raphael explained to Lucifer that Alpha had created some new things and continued to succeed in catching fish. He told how Michael showed great excitement with each fish that landed on his cooking stone. Lucifer laughed, ribs aching with the movement, visualizing Michael salivating over the white flesh, continuously inventing new creative meals.

"Alpha is acting strange," said Raphael. "He burst into a rage today because he didn't like the fish. He got right up into Michael's face, demanding to know what he had done to the meat to make it so lifeless."

"An odd thing to say," said Lucifer, brow creased.

Raphael nodded. "Michael just stared at Alpha. He said he had done nothing to the fish and that if Alpha didn't like it, he could go hungry." Raphael turned to face Lucifer on the bed. "When Michael said that, Alpha glared at him, threw the plate of fish directly at his head, and walked down to the sea, waded in, grabbed a fish, and bit right into it there and then. *Alive.*"

Lucifer's jaw dropped. He winced at the pain.

"Then he stood for a moment and screeched, stamped his feet, and threw the fish back into the water. The last time I saw him, he was sprinting toward the forest," Raphael said before shrugging in response to Lucifer's look of concern.

"In fact," said Raphael. "I have not seen him around much. He is"—Raphael stopped to consider his choice of words—"distant but intense."

"You should be careful around Alpha, Raph," said

Lucifer, concern leaving deep furrows in his brow. "I don't know what is going on with him, but he has changed. I don't trust him. Something within him moved. I feel strange when I am around him."

Raphael smiled at Lucifer, a slight nod signifying his understanding. This was something he already knew. Raphael lifted his hand, stroking a stray piece of Lucifer's hair from his face. He moved his fingers down his arm in a fluid movement, taking a clammy hand.

"I know, and you should know better than anyone. I am still angry with him for kissing you, but I have made sure not to say anything," said Raphael.

"Good," said Lucifer. "I think it will make it worse, and besides, I don't think he knew what he was doing. He was taken up somehow."

A swift change of subject was required. Raphael leapt to it.

"Do you think you could face the world tonight, Luc?"

Lucifer sighed. "Perhaps tomorrow. For now, I just want you to hold me to sleep," he said, rolling onto his side toward the wall, not waiting for a reply. Raphael rose, taking care of the last of the chores.

When the sounds of clearing had ceased, Lucifer felt the bed dip and Raphael's warm body curl around him. A cocoon of safety in what had become an uncertain existence.

Lucifer slept late, the lack of natural light removing his cue to wake. Stretching, he rolled toward the door. Raphael walked in, empty-handed.

"Come on, Luc," Raphael said in his best authoritative tone. "We are going down to breakfast."

Lucifer groaned, covering his eyes with a forearm. Before a complaint could exit his lips, Raphael unceremoniously hauled him to his feet and out the door.

The sunlight hurt his eyes, but he kept the pain to himself as he followed behind Raphael. It was bliss to enter the relative darkness of the kitchen. His eyes taking a long moment to adjust, he blinked around the room, trying to focus. Eventually, he saw two bodies at a beautifully made table, their heads turned to the door, eyes full of questions.

"Well, look who it is," said Michael with a smile. "We weren't sure old Raphael was telling us the truth. We thought perhaps you were dead after all. He wouldn't let us see you since we all dragged you back to the cabin with your eyes rolled back in your head."

"Yeah," sniggered Gabriel. "We thought maybe you were dead, and Raphael was keeping your skin as some kind of plaything."

Michael laughed, spitting his mouthful across the table. Lucifer glared and moved toward an empty seat, sitting carefully.

Raphael handed Lucifer a bowl of stew. "Where's Alpha?" he asked the room. Lucifer's body stiffened.

Michael and Gabriel shrugged over their bowls. Raphael let out a breath, shot a quick sidewise glance, and dug into his own stew.

LUCIFER MANAGED most of his meal, but the walk and effort of eating real food sapped all his energy.

"I'm tired, Raph," Lucifer said, pushing his bowl away. "Will you take me back to bed?"

Raphael's brow creased. "Are you sure? You don't want to have a bit of a walk?"

Lucifer sighed. "Maybe a little one, but let's make it on the way."

The two walked back along the beach toward the cabin, detouring to the edge of the forest to give Lucifer's eyes a break from the glare of the sun and reflection of the sand.

"I'm proud of you, Luc," said Raphael, squeezing his hand "I know it's not easy to get out after what happened, whatever it was." Lucifer gave a small smile, returning the gentle squeeze. Exhaustion claimed his body, causing him to sway.

"Come on then," said Raphael. "Let's get you home, you've done well."

Upon reaching the cabin, Raphael steered Lucifer to the bed. "Lie down," Raphael said. "You sleep now," he added, planting a soft kiss on Lucifer's forehead. "I'll bring you something to eat later." Lucifer smiled and gave a diminutive nod, already drifting.

LUCIFER WOKE WITH A START, it was nearly dark. How long had he slept? His unprecedented fatigue had claimed him. Unsure of his body since the fall, he did not know how much rest he required. He looked around the cabin. No Raphael. No food on the table, no soft rustlings of general business.

Lucifer swung his legs over the edge of the bed. His exhaustion dissipated, his trip outside restoring his energy. The fresh air gave something back to him, he felt a little more normal, a little more like himself. Feeling a sudden burst of strength, he ventured out of the cabin and made his way toward the main camp buildings. It was quiet. No sounds of Michael cooking, no sacks dragging from the forest, and no orders being shouted by Gabriel from his reclined position on the body-length chair. Raphael had told Lucifer that Gabriel pestered Alpha so much for his chair that he finally gave in and made it for him, but he made sure Gabriel was aware of his displeasure at doing so.

Lucifer turned the corner past the large kitchen building. Michael and Gabriel sat face-to-face, straddling a log, a wooden board between them. Lucifer watched from behind. They were playing a game. No doubt Alpha had made up the rules for this one, rigged so he could win.

"Here again," said Gabriel, waiting some time since noticing Lucifer to bother speaking. They were concentrating hard, something that Lucifer had not seen in them before. "So strange to see you without your appendage, Lucifer, I had forgotten that you were two different people." Gabriel snickered at his own joke, looking to Michael to make sure he was also enjoying the comedic value of his statement.

Lucifer rolled his eyes. These remarks had grown into a consistent irritant. He hated to think what kind of treatment Raphael had been getting during his confinement. His heart started to thud with concern for Raphael.

"I don't know where he is," said Lucifer quietly. Michael and Gabriel ignored him. Lucifer's cheeks burned. "I mean, do you know where he is? I haven't seen him since he took me back after breakfast."

Michael twisted in his seat, concern flitting over his face for a moment before he reaffixed his mask of indifference.

"That's why there's no cooking yet, he hasn't come back with the food I ordered." Michael twisted back to the game.

Lucifer swallowed, his mouth dry. "Do you know what he was getting?" he asked.

"Coconuts," said Michael without turning around.

Lucifer's face drained to white. He dug his heel into the sand and moved with all the speed his battered body could muster.

LUCIFER ARRIVED at the coconut trees, puffing. He bent down, his head dipped low he rested his hands on his knees. Banding all his senses, hoping he wouldn't pass out, he raised his throbbing head and looked as far as he could through the trees. He was alone. No rustling of beasts, no splashing of fish, no chirping of birds. Only silence.

Lucifer drifted, his panic simmering below the surface. He pushed his way through the first screen of trees at the edge of the forest, mind darting around plans, fears, and scenarios, unable to land for long enough on any shard of thought to form a coherent picture of the situation he faced.

"This is ridiculous, you are being ridiculous," he breathed to himself, hands on his hips, puffing heavily. He put both hands to his temples to stem the throbbing and force his thoughts to work effectively.

He heard a rustle, a forest sound. There was something moving. Finally, the forest felt alive again. Lucifer crept forward, not wanting to disturb a beast that may lurk nearby, desperation nearly causing him to endanger himself. Finding decent shelter in the thick trunk of a tree, he waited. The rustle continued off to the side, heading for the beach. No heavy footsteps, no crashes.

"It must be a small creature," Lucifer thought. The danger was probably minimal, but his rational brain overtook his panic, telling him to be careful. Lucifer peered toward the space in the growth where he thought the creature would eventually appear.

He saw the light first, a pale-yellow glow preceding its owner, touching the fronds of plants, making them glow with a beauty Lucifer had never witnessed. The light grew in intensity. Lucifer squinted. When it grew almost too much to bear, he saw a figure through a gap in the undergrowth. His jaw hung open. It was no creature, it was Alpha.

Bathed in light, Alpha floated just above the forest floor. Lucifer's eyes widened, ignoring the pain the penetrating light caused to his sensitive pupils. A peculiar sensation washed over him. It filled him, leaving his chest burning. Trembling, he could not move.

Alpha's eyes were closed. His hands drifted in fluid movements, feeling but not touching. Lucifer's thoughts dissipated into a garbling mush. The only thing he registered within his muddled emotions was growing fear.

Alpha moved fast. Floating a short distance above the ground, he avoided the pitfalls of forest terrain. Alpha drew level with Lucifer's tree. Lucifer would be visible if only Alpha turned his head. He held his breath and stood still.

The forest was attuned to incarnate Lucifer's worst fears. Alpha stopped. Lucifer was powerless to move, entranced, pulled in by Alpha's light.

Alpha's feet touched the ground, his state of levitation easily controlled. He opened his eyes and turned his head over one shoulder, staring straight at Lucifer. Bathed in light, his eyes burning with power, Alpha's mouth opened in a sneer of unfathomable cruelty, which was quickly replaced by maniacal laughter. Alpha's jaw moved up and down, pointed teeth shining against the inner blackness of his mouth. The laugh boomed through the forest, bouncing off the trees, encasing Lucifer in a roaring power. There was no escape. Lucifer's brow prickled with sweat, his heart thumped in his ears.

Alpha moved so fast, Lucifer barely saw him. Standing right in front of him, he leaned nonchalantly on the tree that Lucifer had hoped in vain would grant him some protection. Lucifer appraised Alpha. He was still Alpha, but he had an air to him, the confidence and abilities he had gained from eating the fish and the first creature multiplied.

"Up and about I see," Alpha said, looking Lucifer up and down, maintaining a sly smile.

All Lucifer could do was swallow and give a short nod. Alpha pushed off the tree, standing straight in front of Lucifer. There was a fair height difference between them, but Alpha's presence made him seem taller, more imposing. He waited for a short time, eyes burning into Lucifer's head, awaiting conversation.

"Well, you are obviously OK," he said, giving up. Lucifer was not going to speak. "That's good." he added.

"What are you doing out here, Alpha?" Lucifer demanded without preamble. The words rushed out in quick succession, giving away his nerves.

Alpha replaced the half sneer on his face, one corner of his mouth curled.

"Just exploring, like always," he said, eyes flashing with a spark, they were the residence of his power and knowledge

"I-I-I," stammered Lucifer before stopping, taking a breath, and clearing his throat to start again. "I didn't know you could do that, float, I mean."

"Neither did I," said Alpha, mindlessly digging grime from beneath a fingernail with a small twig. "Until today."

He looked up. The flash came again. "And what are you doing here, Lucifer? Seems strange for you to come out here when you have barely been out of bed for days."

It was now or never. Lucifer mustered all the conviction he could. "I'm looking for Raphael," he said, careful not to break eye contact with Alpha. "I haven't seen him since we went down to the kitchen for breakfast, and Michael said he hadn't come back with dinner."

Alpha looked as though he were thinking, his stubby fingers stroking his chin. "Have you looked by the coconut trees?"

"Yes, he isn't there," Lucifer blurted.

Shrugging, Alpha turned toward the edge of the forest. "Well, I'm sure he's somewhere, Lucifer. We aren't in such a big place."

Alpha moved toward the beach, levitating with little effort, moving quickly through the forest growth.

Lucifer let out a breath, dizzy from the encounter. He walked back to camp in hope he would find Raphael in the kitchen, depositing his forage with Michael. As Lucifer walked, his head cleared. The strange buzzing emotion he felt in Alpha's presence was subsiding, returning him to his customary state of awareness. Lucifer was going over the encounter with Alpha in his mind. He could not work out what was wrong.

11

SEARCH

Alpha was standing between Michael and Gabriel, levitating on and off as they clapped and cheered, smiles stuck to their faces.

"Hey Lucifer," called Gabriel as he walked into earshot. "Have you seen this? It's totally crazy."

"Yes," Lucifer said, sitting on a chair, running his hand over his face. "We met in the forest."

Ignoring Lucifer's remark, Gabriel hounded Alpha with questions about what else he could do. Alpha showed off his new tricks by levitating objects, beckoning and bending them to his will.

Lucifer sat quietly, unsure of what had or would happen. Tiredness washed over him, a reminder of his recent injuries and the toll they had taken on his body.

After a lengthy time of Alpha admiration, Michael turned to Lucifer.

"Where is Raphael? I need my coconuts."

"I don't know," said Lucifer so quietly the others didn't hear him. Michael raised his hand, cupping it behind his ear.

"I don't know," he repeated. "I couldn't find him." Lucifer just managed to get the last word out before he sank into involuntary unconsciousness.

~

LUCIFER ROUSED to the smell of cooking. His nostrils filled with steaming fish and the sweet tang of coconut. He was still in the chair where he had collapsed on his return from the forest. His neck was sore, slumped in this awkward position for some time. Lucifer's stomach rumbled. The food smelt so good. His appetite grew for the first time since the fall.

Lucifer gasped. Cooking! Raphael must be back.

He sprang from his chair, his tender body protesting with every movement. Ignoring the pain, he bolted into the kitchen building.

Lucifer burst through the door, expecting the find Raphael at the outer table, opening coconuts or chopping vegetables. Instead, the large form of Michael was hunched over the central fire, his meaty hand wrapped around the end of a metal poker, prodding parcels wrapped in leaves with the glowing point.

"Where is Raphael?" demanded Lucifer.

Michael didn't look up. "I don't know, Alpha got this stuff." Lucifer heard the door swing open behind him.

"You should have seen it, Lucifer. Alpha parted the water just like that, leaving fish flapping on the sand. Then he just walked down there and picked them up," said Gabriel, so excited that he barely managed to get through the door. "Then we walked over to the coconut trees and made the trees shake, the coconuts just fell down."

Lucifer swallowed, his last memory of a shaking coconut

tree sending a shiver down his spine. "Neither of you have seen Raphael all day?" asked Lucifer, his rising desperation evident in the strangled sound of his words.

Michael turned, having pulled the parcels from the fire. He shared a glance with Gabriel.

"No," said Michael. "Maybe he just went a bit farther than usual, maybe he found something new deep in the forest or something. He probably decided to stay out there the night instead of trying to come back in the dark."

Gabriel took the parcels from Michael and placed them in the middle of the large table.

"But he was going for coconuts, you said," piped Lucifer, panic creeping further into his throat. "He wouldn't go into the forest itself if he were climbing for coconuts."

Gabriel shrugged as he sat down at the table. "I don't know, Lucifer. You're the one who's with him all the time. Where do you think he is?"

"I don't know," said Lucifer, eyes downcast. "But I don't think he would stay out. I think something may have happened to him." He paused, unsure how much to say. Not traditional fans of Alpha, Gabriel and Michael were viewing him in a new light since he gained his abilities, and Lucifer could no longer read the situation. Lucifer sucked in a breath and decided to come out and say it.

"Alpha was in the forest today, I saw him." Before he could say any more, the kitchen door flew open and Alpha entered, filling the room.

"Smells good, let's eat," he said, taking his place at the table. Gabriel and Michael made busy work of digging into their parcels. Not knowing what else to do, Lucifer joined them, his shaking hand reaching out, gingerly clutching a parcel.

"If he isn't back by morning," Alpha said through

mouthfuls of coconut fish, "we will all go and look." Lucifer nodded, muttering, "Thanks." This seemed reasonable, but the lump in his throat would not subside, and fear deep in his chest exploded in waves of pain.

MICHAEL, Gabriel, and Lucifer stared up at the tree. They had followed Alpha to this place, a little way into the forest. Alpha said he would be able to see a good distance from the top of this tree and may gather a clue to Raphael's location. He levitated up the trunk, using his hands to guide him, disappearing into the canopy. This tree did not look overly tall to Lucifer, but he didn't have the same perspective as Alpha.

Michael and Gabriel were uncertain of the forest. Neither of them had ventured this far before. They both hesitated at the edge. Eventually, they followed Alpha out of fear or reverence. Lucifer was unsure which it was.

Alpha floated down the tree, planted his heel nimbly on the ground, and brushed himself down, leaves and small twigs falling from him.

"Nothing," he said to the three faces staring.

Lucifer's edginess increased with every passing moment, his constant fidgeting the only way he could keep himself from tears.

"It's getting dark," said Alpha, still staring up at the sky. "We should get back, it will be too hard to navigate with these two," he said, waving a hand at Michael and Gabriel. Neither of them made a comment. They had both been silent for some time.

"But you have light, Alpha," said Lucifer, face crumpled. "We could stay out. We need to keep looking."

Alpha sighed. "No, it's too hard to be mindful of others all the time." He moved his tongue over his bottom lip, thinking. "I know. You take Michael and Gabriel back to camp, you know the forest well enough. I will keep looking. I'll stay out and see what I can find. Like you said, I have light."

Not at all sure of this course of action, Lucifer opened his mouth to speak. Before any words emerged, he felt Alpha's power wash over him. He tried to voice his opposition to the plan, but he failed. Not sure where his voice had gone or why his ability to speak had abandoned him, he gave up and just nodded.

He got out "Thank you," before he cocked his head to Michael and Gabriel and walked, disheartened, back to the beach.

∾

It was early when Alpha returned, empty-handed. He collapsed in a chair by the fire, resting his elbow on the wooden arm, palm over his face.

Lucifer leaned forward. He had been waiting sleeplessly for Alpha's return. Alpha dragged his palm down his face, stretching out his small eyes in an almost comical fashion. No one spoke. Lucifer bent as close to Alpha as he dared, in question. Michael and Gabriel sat farther around the fire, ears pricked for news.

Alpha shook his head and sighed. "Nothing," he said, not meeting Lucifer's eyes.

"Nothing?" shouted Lucifer. "What do you mean nothing? You were gone the whole night."

"The night?" said Alpha, genuine disbelief on his face.

Lucifer's brow scrunched. He searched Alpha's eyes for answers. All he saw was emptiness. Where had he been?

"You said it yourself, this isn't such a big place. He must be around *somewhere*," said Lucifer, anger turning to a desperate, pleading whine.

For the first time since he had gained his abilities, Alpha looked tired.

"Well," said Alpha, pausing, thinking, "it might be bigger than I thought."

~

ALPHA ELABORATED on his cryptic comment following Lucifer's incessant prodding.

"I can't explain it to you," Alpha said, as if Lucifer was a person of second-rate intellect. "I will have to show you."

Desperate to find any evidence of Raphael, Lucifer went against his better judgment, ignoring the feeling present in the pit of his stomach ever since he fell from the tree. He would go with Alpha. Alone.

"All right, good." Lucifer said, having decided. "Let's go then."

"No," said Alpha, shaking his head, the large black circles beneath his eyes catching the dying light. "It is some way, and you can't travel as fast as I can. We'll go tomorrow." He paused. Lucifer nodded in resignation. "Anyway," Alpha continued, cutting off Lucifer's further questioning, "I'm tired having been up all night looking for your lover." Alpha got up, reaching the hut. The door banged behind him.

Lucifer slumped. This was better than nothing.

"You need to start thinking of other options," said Gabriel, snapping Lucifer out of his internal musing. "There are so many things that could have happened to him, like falling out of a tree. That happened to you, and you were lucky you were OK. Well, sort of OK."

"But we would have found him regardless, even if he were dead." The lump in Lucifer's throat was back, blocking his words. "We would have found his body." The last word was barely audible, the admission that something may have happened to Raphael caused him more pain than any physical trauma he had encountered.

"Well," shrugged Gabriel, "just trying to help, you should be prepared. Who knows what kind of evil beasties are out there. The forest gave me the creeps. Anything could have got him."

Lucifer ignored this comment, and without farewell, he stormed toward the outer ring of camp.

He filled his arms. Sacks, rope, knives, anything he thought might be useful, before trudging toward his empty cabin.

GABRIEL AND MICHAEL volunteered to stay behind to tend camp, and be there in the event Raphael reappeared. A convenient excuse to avoid hard trekking through the eerie forest.

Lucifer and Alpha bid them farewell, undertaking the biggest expedition of Lucifer's life. Alpha navigated through the forest with ease, following tiny paths, streams, and gullies like he belonged. This was his true home.

"How much time you have spent in the forest?" asked Lucifer, puffing behind Alpha as they fought their way through some brush. Alpha walked, giving into necessity, as Lucifer could not levitate. Although it was more cumber-

some than his preferred mode of transport, he still moved
with the grace of a beast in its natural habitat.

"Don't know," said Alpha over his shoulder. "I just explore,
finding things, testing my powers." After a short pause, he
added, "I am no longer satisfied with accepting things for what
they are. I needed to know and understand. I have an appetite.
I need to feed it." Although shocked by the unusual show of
emotion by Alpha, Lucifer understood what he meant, he felt
it too, in a way. But with his mind focused on finding Raphael,
exploration and understanding would have to wait.

Breaking for food, Alpha and Lucifer ate in silence.
Lucifer was bursting with discomfort, not knowing what to
say to Alpha.

"I haven't thanked you, Alpha. Thank you for helping to
find Raphael. I know you two had your disagreements. And
that you and I...well—" he stopped short of saying anything
more.

"Don't mention it," said Alpha, focusing on the food they
had brought with them from camp, a look flashing across
his face so quickly Lucifer didn't have time to process it.

"All right," said Alpha, rising deftly to his feet. "We're not
far now." Lucifer rose, ignoring the stiffness in his joints,
following Alpha farther into the forest.

THE FOREST CLEARED. tall trees retreated, melting into squat
ferns and damp moss. Alpha climbed a small embankment
and dropped the sack from his shoulder. Lucifer panted up
the rise to take his place beside Alpha. While he caught his
breath, he surveyed the landscape. The forest opened into a
flat plain of tall grass, intersected by two rivers forming a

fork at the point where he and Alpha were standing. The rivers traveled off into the distance, forming one tributary.

"I see what you meant when you said it's bigger than you thought," said Lucifer, still panting. "It goes forever."

"Ah," said Alpha "It goes some way, that's for sure, but that is not *exactly* what I meant."

Lucifer turned to Alpha, raising an eyebrow in question, knowing Alpha could not resist flouting his knowledge. Lucifer, intrigued, allowed curiosity to punch through his wall of grief.

Alpha took a deep breath and closed his eyes. With his feet planted on the mound, he raised his hands like a chalice to the sky. Lucifer had seen Alpha do this when creating before. His curiosity burned with what Alpha was about to do.

Alpha hummed, a deep resonance buzzed from his throat. It grew to a booming sound, the opposite of his usual whine.

Wind whipped. The sharp ends of Lucifer's hair flicked and stung his face. The air crackled. Shards of bright light collected in a swirling vortex. Tiny hairs on Lucifer's arms stood on end.

The wind died down, the plain regained its normal sense of calm. But hanging in front of Alpha's mound was a shimmering circle suspended in the air.

Lucifer stood stunned, so shocked by the disc's appearance he had not noticed that Alpha had collapsed onto the mound. Snapping to attention, Lucifer bent to grab Alpha's arm, helping him to a sitting position.

"Are you all right?" Lucifer said with genuine concern.

Alpha nodded in reply. "Just hard work."

Lucifer, satisfied Alpha would not suffer any further damage, paced across the mound. He peered at the perfect circle, hovering in the air, small sparks crackling from the rim. The circle was filled with a shimmering skin. Lucifer stood close enough to touch it but refrained from doing so. Through it, he could see a forest, it looked like home. Less vibrant but the same. Lucifer walked to the edge and popped his head past the horizon. He could barely see it from the side. A thin line sparking with energy was the only clue it was still there. Behind it, the flat plain with its intersecting rivers continued, uninterrupted. Lucifer walked a full circle, seeing just a faint shimmering from the back. Emerging from behind the anomaly, he took his place beside Alpha.

"What is it?" Lucifer asked, fascination rife in his voice.

"A portal," said Alpha, raising his hand and pointing to the trees within the portal. "See there. That is exactly the same as the trees behind us. It is home but backward, like looking into still water. You see yourself and what is behind you." Lucifer turned around. Alpha was right. Lucifer made out the same specific trees behind.

"But I can't see us standing there," said Lucifer.

"No," said Alpha. "The place is the mirror of here, but we aren't in there, we are only here. I'm calling it a different dimension."

Lucifer's head hurt. He tried to comprehend Alpha's words. "Have you been in there? Is this where you think Raphael might be?"

Alpha's eyes flashed with delight. "Yes, I have been in there," Alpha grinned. "I went in yesterday when I was looking for Raphael. I managed to open the portal somehow when I came here. I just felt an energy in the air. I knew something was different about this place."

A thousand questions ran through Lucifer's brain. "But you didn't find him," said Lucifer, hopeless, realizing how big their domain was, even without another *dimension* to consider. Raphael was lost, alone, and afraid. He could be anywhere.

"No," said Alpha. "But I have been in there. I don't know if Raphael is there, but it made me understand that looking may be pointless. He could be anywhere, and we will never find him." Alpha's thoughts mirrored his own, depressing Lucifer further. If they were both thinking it, it was likely to be true.

"What was it like in there?" Lucifer asked, his feelings of guilt bubbling to the surface as he allowed his curiosity to sideline his thoughts of Raphael.

Alpha thought for a short time, choosing his words carefully. "It is the same, the place looks the same. A little duller like you can see through the portal. But I felt strange there, as if things were moving fast, as if time passed quickly. I think it does, too, because I was there for what seemed like forever, and I was only gone one night."

"But there was nothing there?" asked Lucifer, letting the new discovery sink in, thoughts of Raphael returning to the forefront of his mind.

Alpha shook his head. "No, just a bare place that looks like this one, no creatures or anything. But what I found was almost more fascinating. There may have been no creatures as we know them or no one like us. But there *was* life. Swarming life. Tiny things jostling in the swamps. When I looked back through the portal after my return, I witnessed them changing. Adapting. They may be able to turn into anything."

Alpha stood abruptly, visibly pushing down his passion. "I'm not sure how long this portal will stay open. We should try it now," he said with great care.

"Try what?" asked Lucifer.

"See if you can go through," Alpha said, pondering the portal, speaking as if this suggestion were as normal as eating breakfast.

"Oh," said Lucifer, his heart pounding, palms sweating.

"We need to make sure it works the same for everyone," said Alpha. Mischief flashed in his eyes. Lucifer felt a lurch in his stomach. "If I am the only one who can go through, then Raphael definitely isn't there, is he?" said Alpha, intense eyes gleaming.

Lucifer swallowed, wiping his palms through his hair, attempting to rid them of the continuously sprouting prickles of sweat.

"OK," he said, mustering all his courage. "What do I do?"

"Just step through it as if you were stepping through a door," said Alpha, shrugging. "We'll see what happens." Lucifer heard the amused smile in Alpha's voice.

Inhale. Exhale. Lucifer closed his eyes and without hesitation, stepped into the portal. A jolt ran through his body, the blackness behind his closed eyes deepened. He was in a void, weightless. Moaning reached his ears, the sound of pain and despair wrenching at his chest. Lucifer clawed toward the sound. One word stood out from the pain. "Lucifer."

"Lucifer?" He heard his name through the fog. "Lucifer," the voice called out, each sound elongated. He heard a distant groan and screwed his eyes shut, not ready to face whatever had happened.

Brought abruptly back to the world by a hard crack across his cheek, his eyes sprung open to see Alpha's face, so close their noses nearly touched.

"Oh good, you're alive," Alpha said, sitting back on his haunches.

Lucifer instinctively raised a hand to his stinging cheek. "Did you slap me?"

Alpha laughed. "Only to wake you up."

"What happened?" Lucifer asked, his head beginning to throb again.

"Right," said Alpha, realization dawning that Lucifer had no memory of the incident that had rendered him flat on his back. "You can't go through. You just got bounced back here, straight away."

Lucifer's tumultuous feelings returned. He struggled to make sense of them. The glimmer of hope that Raphael may have fallen through the portal was ripped from Lucifer's heart.

"It was worth a try. I think we proved a point. Raphael could be anywhere except in there," Alpha said, waving a limp-wristed hand at the portal.

Lucifer raised himself, knees up he stared at the stony ground beneath him. "I'm going to stay out. I want to keep trying. If I stop looking, I will never see him again."

Lucifer raised his eyes to Alpha. He was blocking the sun, a dark shadow with shards of light emitting from his body. Alpha gave Lucifer a long, blank stare. He saw the familiar flash in Alpha's eyes.

Alpha shrugged. "Suit yourself. I'm going back to camp. I have more I want to do there."

Lucifer nodded. "I'm going to find him if it kills me."

Alpha laughed. "How very gallant. Good luck, I guess. Hopefully you find your way back to me eventually."

12

NEW DIMENSIONS

Alpha made good time back to camp, traveling quickly without the burden of followers. Alpha felt so far above the others, he had so much more. Superior understanding and ability made him feel separated in the early days, letting him rise above the petty interchanges of his home. His craving to be included, which boiled over in ways he preferred not to dwell upon, would never happen again. Alpha had found a new passion beyond that of his own realm. It made him hum with excitement, his body bursting in anticipation.

Alpha approached camp. Michael and Gabriel were sitting where he thought they would be, on their favorite log, wasting away the hours playing that silly game he invented. Alpha had devised the game to keep Gabriel and Michael busy and out of his way. It had worked perfectly.

But Alpha no longer had time to indulge the musings of his former bullies. He had purpose and vision, and a greater use for these two. A use that would fulfill his need for revenge and further his mission in one single act.

Alpha remained unseen, they were engrossed. It was the

perfect time to enact the first part of his experiment. Alpha closed his eyes and imagined his creation. Getting it right in his mind's eye made the process of actual creation almost instantaneous. Creating something quickly took more energy, a necessary cost in this case.

Gabriel saw him and jumped at his sudden appearance. He rose slightly, teetering on the balls of his feet.

"Anything then?" Gabriel asked, settling back to his perch. Alpha was counting on Gabriel's unwillingness to move, and Michael's inability to follow, to fulfill his plan.

"No," said Alpha, keeping his tone flat.

"Where is Lucifer?" asked Gabriel, wariness creeping into his eyes. His senses had not completely abandoned him.

"Stayed to keep looking," said Alpha in the same flat tone. Before Gabriel could ask another question, Alpha stole his chance, raising his hands in a quick, practiced flourish.

Alpha stepped back to appraise his swift creation. It was perfect.

Alpha watched the realization dawn on Gabriel and Michael as if it were in slow motion. This was everything he had hoped for. Alpha let out a booming laugh as Gabriel and Michael rose from their seats, eyes wide. They took in the perfectly formed cage, its strong metal bars stretching from deep in the ground, meeting in a neat box above their heads.

Michael and Gabriel moved over to the bars, grabbing them with both hands. "What are you doing?" they shouted over each other.

"Let us out! Alpha, this isn't funny," shouted Gabriel.

Alpha's laughter increased before it stopped with a jolt. His eyes were narrow, his voice low.

"Oh yes. Oh, yes it is," he said before he wandered back toward the fire and pulled up his favorite chair. Propping his feet up on a stool, crossing them neatly at the ankles, he lifted a hand, and with the flick of the wrist, levitated the wooden game and smashed it against the bars, splinters flying.

The captives screamed in pain, horror, and shock. Blood dripped from their splinter wounds. The game they had so loved was now used as a weapon against them. Alpha sat back in his chair, planning to bring their world crashing down. To make them suffer, just as they had done to him.

"As of now," Alpha said, grabbing a knife from beside his chair, "I am in charge here."

Lucifer stumbled, his feet blistered and bloody from days of roaming, scavenging food, and looking for clues. He found none.

Alpha was right, the world was bigger than he thought, even excluding the portal. Lucifer didn't always know where he was, but was able to navigate by the sun enough to get his general bearings. The vegetation was much more diverse than Lucifer had realized. He wished he had explored all this with Raphael, he would have loved these places.

Lucifer's heart was a heavy stone lodged deep in his chest. He had grown accustomed to despair. It was his constant companion, dragging him down. His feet were heavy, every step like he was wading through water.

Lucifer pushed past some fern fronds and entered a clearing. The cleansing tears pushed his anguish to arm's length. He knew where he was, finally experiencing definitive recognition. This is where Alpha had shown his abilities, and where he and Raphael had first acted upon their love. Lucifer wiped a singular tear from his cheek, his strength leaving him. He lay down in the moss and wept.

Lucifer's flood of emotion cleared his head. He felt capable of a decision for the first time in days. He had to go back, he couldn't look for Raphael alone. Lacking knowledge and understanding to search in a logical way, he had been meandering in the dim hope of finding something. Clasping his knees, rocking gently back and forth, he decided.

The best way to help Raphael now was to find out what happened to him. He would need to convince Gabriel and Michael to help.

Camp was eerie, the whole place encapsulated by the same cloud of pain that had been holding Lucifer's heart since Raphael disappeared. All was quiet in the outlying buildings. Due to Michael and Gabriel's preference for sedentary life, low levels of camp activity were common. But this was different, too quiet.

Lucifer moved toward the center of camp, heading for the main fire. He rounded the corner of the last building. Alpha, sitting in his favorite chair, faced the ocean, hands folded behind his head in restful contemplation.

Alpha sensed Lucifer's presence. He got up from his chair and turned to face him. His face was blank, showing no sympathy at Lucifer's empty-handed return, and no gloating that he knew this would be the case all along.

"No good then?" said Alpha as Lucifer drew closer. Lucifer just shook his head. Alpha already knew the answer.

Lucifer sat heavily in an empty chair. It was good to be

back from the forest. He had been getting increasingly irritated and depressed on his own, searching with diminishing hope.

The log was empty. The polished patches from consistent use were visible. The makeup of the central camp area subtly changed with minor readjustments to the usual placements of furniture and tools.

Lucifer let out a loud yawn and stretched his arms. He was looking forward to sleeping on a soft bed again, the thought elicited a stab of guilt, how could he be so selfish when Raphael was still missing?

"Where are the others?" asked Lucifer.

"In the kitchen," said Alpha. "Cooking," he added as an afterthought.

Lucifer bolted to attention. "What?" he said, so shocked it took a moment for him to gather his thoughts. "Gabriel is in the kitchen? *Cooking?*"

"Yep," said Alpha with a wicked grin. "He is helping Michael."

"*Helping?*" Lucifer said in total disbelief.

Alpha laughed again. "I told him to help, so he is helping."

Lucifer stared at Alpha, mouth open, incapable of processing what Alpha was telling him. He rose from his seat and walked to the kitchen. Rhythmic banging and scraping sounds escaped the hut. The noises were slow and tiresome. There was no conversation.

Lucifer pushed open the door. Michael was bent over the large pot in the center of the room. Gabriel sat at the side bench, gutting and chopping fish.

Two heads turned to the door as Lucifer entered, momentarily halting their tasks at the intrusion. Their movements were slow, mouths slack. Eyes dead.

Lucifer stepped farther into the kitchen building, staring at the scene. Gabriel and Michael were there, but not there.

"They serve me now," said Alpha from the doorway. "They will never bully me again, they will do all the hard work from now on." Then Alpha clicked his fingers, and the pair went back to their slow, laborious tasks.

Lucifer pushed past Alpha and strode into the light, quickly turning on his heel to face him. Nose to nose with Alpha, Lucifer felt his energy and saw the power deep in his eyes.

"What have you done to them?" demanded Lucifer.

"Nothing." Alpha shrugged.

"Don't try to spin that on me, Alpha. I see through you," said Lucifer, voice raising.

"Do you now?" said Alpha through gritted teeth, eyes flashing with an emotion Lucifer couldn't place.

Ignoring him, Lucifer continued to demand answers. "I know you did something to them. Why are they moving so slowly and not talking? And why are they suddenly following *you*?" Each question ended in a rise of anxiety.

"They have been bowing to me for some time. Since my abilities and all, I have quite been their hero," said Alpha.

Lucifer scoffed. "They may have suffered from infatuation, but it doesn't explain why they are nothing but empty bags of skin!"

Alpha shrugged. "Well, I decided as the new and natural leader that they hadn't been pulling their weight. Especially Gabriel, so I just made them more...pliable."

"*Pliable*," shouted Lucifer. "Pliable how?"

"You wouldn't understand," said Alpha, a dismissive hand waving. "All you need to know is they will happily do anything I ask, and I only plan to ask them to do fair things, like cleaning and collecting food. Just the things we have been doing our entire lives."

There was no arguing with Alpha. Lucifer did not know what he had done. Lucifer had to remember his own goals, the thing that was still most important to him. He could not afford to forget. He had to find Raphael, and with Michael and Gabriel now useless, Alpha was his only hope. He needed help.

This sat poorly, but he knew it was right. He had to remain with Alpha. He must use him to find Raphael.

It was strange living in camp alone with Alpha, or as good as alone, with Michael and Gabriel saying nothing except for the simplest of words. Their vigor had gone, although Lucifer admitted that neither of them had ever been the picture of energetic activity. Gabriel no longer spouted his self-styled managerial decisions, and Michael had no passion for food. All Michael did was make what Alpha told him, consuming only enough to satisfy his basic energy needs, eating with a mechanical chew. He was growing thin, skin beginning to hang, deep creases appearing across his body.

With next to no chores to do, waited on by servants, Lucifer relaxed for the first time in weeks. His guilt over Michael and Gabriel's condition came in alternating waves with grief for Raphael. But Lucifer felt he could do little about either situation. His adjusted plan to use Alpha to help had not eventuated as hoped.

Alpha disappeared for lengthy periods, arriving back at camp at odd times, sometimes cursing under his breath. One night after one of these strange outings, Alpha spoke.

"I think we need more life around here."

Lucifer was whittling a piece of wood, attempting to make the shape of one of the birds he had seen during his time in the forest. He jumped. The knife slipped, a deep crease of red oozed from his palm.

"Why and how?" asked Lucifer, pressing his hand to the cut.

"Well," said Alpha, pursing his lips. "We could expand and really build some amazing structures if we had more people to work for us." He stared at the blood seeping between Lucifer's fingers.

"You mean work for you," Lucifer said, his tone flat, attention remaining focused on the wound. Alpha shrugged.

"I have already been trying, but I can't get it right," said Alpha. Lucifer's attention snapped, his narrow gaze boring into the deep black of Alpha's eyes.

"You've been trying to make people?" sputtered Lucifer. This might be it. If he could get more people here, he could undertake a proper search for Raphael.

"I'll show you," said Alpha.

Alpha stood up, closing his eyes, thinking inwardly for a long time. Lucifer watched him intently, Alpha's face and body were twitching in ultimate concentration. He raised his hands to the sky in his usual creation gesture. But this time was different. Instead of the inanimate object simply appearing on the sand, the wind whipped so fiercely that the empty chairs around camp were knocked over. The main fire nearly blew to coals. Lucifer felt a strange pull, the world itself changing a little.

The wind died down, and Alpha fell to his knees, exhausted. A few inches in front of him stood a tiny, perfectly formed human. It blinked once, twice. Lucifer twitched, his hand moving out to touch the new flesh. The tiny human fell, dead.

"See," shouted Alpha. "I can't get it right." He banged his fist in the sand.

Sputtering, nothing more emitted from Lucifer's mouth. The tiny body, lifeless in the sand, caused a fresh wave of anguish. The body only showed moments of life.

"I have had an idea though," said Alpha. "We need to go back to the portal."

All Lucifer did was stare. What was Alpha planning? Why did he want to involve him? Lucifer needed to be practical, he would play along with Alpha to find Raphael, no matter how long it took.

ALPHA LED Lucifer through a particularly dark part of the forest. He didn't recognize it. Alpha didn't even stop when he walked passed a pile of tiny bodies. Lucifer gaped, a shiver ran up his spine.

"I guess this is where you have been trying to create your servants," Lucifer said under his breath. Alpha didn't hear, or pretended not to.

This was not the only place where Alpha had been experimenting. They came to a stop at the fork in the rivers where the portal had once been.

Alpha turned to Lucifer. "Do you remember how I said I thought time moves differently through the portal?"

Lucifer nodded, totally unaware of what he might be about to see. Nothing would surprise him anymore.

Alpha assumed his customary position, and with great effort, the portal opened. But Alpha did not stop there. He manipulated the portal, swiping with his hands, adjusting the view through the shimmering circle. When he was happy, he nodded. "Come and look."

Lucifer obediently moved toward the portal. He saw a large section of land. Alpha had changed the view through the portal. It was zoomed to a higher perspective. Even with the different view, Lucifer could tell he was looking at the same mirror.

But something had changed. Lucifer's brain took moments to catch up. There were creatures! Living creatures! Some were so big, they were as tall as the trees. Some were flying around, catching the breeze with giant wings. Some scampering across the open plain in little packs, hunting.

"What?" stammered Lucifer in wonderment.

Alpha grinned. He was so calm that Lucifer began to believe what he was witnessing was normal.

"How did you do it? You obviously succeeded here, in this dimension," Lucifer said, still staring through the portal.

"That's the thing. I didn't just create them out of nothing. I started with a speck. I found a tiny living thing, an *organism*, and watched it grow slowly. It changed. It developed. Over time, it grew into something else, a new creature. As the beasts evolved, I gave them a helping hand, I shaped them. I could make them look and act as I wanted, mostly," said Alpha, not waiting for a reply. "The time in this dimension is different to here. It passes quickly, so I can play around with the creatures, letting them evolve at their own pace, giving them a boost if they get stuck. I think that is what I need to do to make some people that are just like us. We are more complicated than these creatures. I need time to experiment. I have learned a lot through the portal. I have tried things that fail and have also had may successes, as you can see," Alpha said, his ability to hide his pride dissipating with every word. "But there is more to it."

Lucifer knew that Alpha could not help himself. His rant was leading to an epic boast.

"Time is not constant. I can manipulate it, just like I can everything else. It is just another element of the physical world I can control."

Lucifer stared. Alpha let out a small grunt.

"What I mean is," he said, the air of frustration ripe in his voice, "time may pass quick down there, but I can still control it. If I want to witness the individual life of one dinosaur, I can. If I want to watch a whole generation pass in one moment of our time, I can. I have the power to do as I please."

Baffled by Alpha's speech, Lucifer could only focus on his awe of Alpha's ability. "These creatures are amazing, Alpha," said Lucifer, forgetting his surroundings and all of his pain and suffering.

Alpha grinned, lapping up the praise. "There are some other differences in this dimension, too. The light and dark is different. I think our light and dark time is equal. This one changes over time. And they have different weather."

"Weather?" Lucifer asked, unsure what he meant.

"It gets cold and hot. Water falls from the sky when it gets cloudy. They have wind. It comes and goes as if at random, and when it is really cold, the water from the sky freezes and settles on the ground in a soft layer of fluff," said Alpha, explaining it as best he could.

"Oh," said Lucifer, the concept of weather beyond warm and sunny alien to him.

"So anyway," said Alpha, moving on, "I can make this the perfect environment to experiment. I can make more people, make people like us."

Lucifer didn't say a word, still speechless from seeing the majestic dinosaurs roam the plain through the portal. A thought struck him.

"If you do succeed in creating some people through there, how are you going to get them over here? If I couldn't get through, maybe they can't come the other way. Can the dinosaurs get through?"

Alpha looked pleased that Lucifer had thought to ask such a question. It was a sign that Alpha did not realize how smart he really was. His outward intelligence decreased due to the fact he was so shocked and amazed by the things Alpha regularly got up to, he rarely got words out of his mouth.

"The dinosaurs can't get through. I tried. The same thing happens to them as it did to you. But I am Alpha. I don't give up, I will find a way," he said, grinning.

"Just like you wouldn't give up looking for Raphael," Lucifer almost said aloud, his wits kicking into gear at the last minute. He kept this to himself. He had to tread carefully if he was to get what he wanted from Alpha's experiments.

13

NEW WORLD

Lucifer lay on the grass, the plain blue sky unending above his face. Alpha said there was rain and snow, thunder and lightning through the portal. Lucifer wondered why this side of the portal was different.

Lucifer's mind conjured majestic pictures of Alpha's dinosaurs, magnificent and terrifying, a little like Alpha himself. Alpha wanted to create a person in his own image. Lucifer considered that he had already succeeded, the dinosaurs seemed a perfect representation of many of his traits. He sat up and watched Alpha's back. He had been sitting cross-legged in front of the portal through days and nights, never sleeping, just watching.

Lucifer was drawn to Alpha, his appeal colliding with Lucifer's general feelings, creating swirls of doubt. One thing was for certain: trust had gone between them.

Lucifer didn't know what he had done to the others or what he was plotting. He felt Alpha's energy penetrating his being, he found it hard to question him. Hanging off every word he said. The continuous backdrop to their relationship, a shroud of fear. Lucifer survived by issuing a continuous reminder of why he was here, finding this more difficult as he got swept up in Alpha's creative process.

Watching Alpha watch his dinosaurs, Lucifer's mind drifted. He wondered why he was here. Where did he come from? Did he have a purpose? Alpha knew he had a purpose, but Alpha was special. Lucifer knew deep down that he shared characteristics with Alpha, no matter how deeply he wished to deny it. Only Alpha had the abilities. Lucifer had eaten fish and some of the creature in the forest. He felt something change within himself, but he lacked the intensity of Alpha's experience.

Near twilight, Alpha stood, stretching.

"I know what I have to do," he said, nodding, forefinger and thumb rhythmically caressing his smooth chin.

Lucifer rose to his haunches, eyes wide and bright, silently begging Alpha to divulge his plan. Alpha yawned, arms reaching high above his head, stretching the kinks from his immobile muscles. Lucifer followed Alpha's gaze to the hut, the lodging he had erected so he could spend every moment by the portal, unburdened by travel. The need to search for food had also been removed. That was what Lucifer was for.

"Tomorrow. Now I will sleep," said Alpha, walking to the rudimentary sleeping quarters. He crawled into his cot, his face relaxed into deep sleep.

LUCIFER AWOKE EARLY. Sleeping under the stars lifted his mood, the old connection with nature was restored by waking in the sun. Drinking in every minute of its rays rejuvenated his body, attacking the stone of grief lodged in his stomach.

"Right, shall we get to it then?" said Alpha, walking toward the portal, raising his hands to begin.

Lucifer hovered close by. "How long is it open for?" he blurted.

"What?" Alpha turned, his creation interrupted.

"The portal," Lucifer clarified. "When we were last here, when I tried to go through, you said you didn't know how long it would be open for."

"Oh," said Alpha waving a dismissive hand. "I can keep it open as long as I want." Considering that sufficient explanation, Alpha turned back to the portal, breathing sharply through his nose and raising his hands once more. "Let us begin."

Alpha began. Lucifer watched, horrified. His heart wrenched, his body shook. Tears streamed down his face as he watched Alpha bury the dinosaurs deep in the ground. He was witness to Alpha's destruction of all the beauty he created.

ALPHA CONCENTRATED HARD, enacting his first decision during his days of meditation. The dinosaurs had to go. He made them too well, too fierce, and too adaptive to their surroundings. His whole idea of starting small and letting things grow with a nudge here and there was a good one. It worked well, the plan would correlate to humans.

The dinosaurs had fulfilled their purpose. They taught Alpha why he had failed to create life in his realm. Creatures were complicated, intricacies of a species best honed slowly over many generations. Humans would be another challenge; the right mix of physical prowess and intellect would be difficult.

The decision to wipe out the creatures was the easy part. How to do it with minimum effort and maximum force claimed most of Alpha's time.

With a quick check that Lucifer was a safe distance away, Alpha raised his hands once more and closed his eyes. The distance was imperative for Alpha to remain sheltered from inane interruptions and physical intervention.

Alpha formed his fireball, pulling heat from the atmosphere, working through the portal. Choosing his landing site, he slammed the fireball to the ground. Dust and debris spurted, the crackle of fire remaining in the crater. Excitement coursed through Alpha's veins. The stupid creatures ran from a foe they could never escape. The race caused Alpha's heart to beat faster, breath coming fast. He knew he would win. The chase sent waves of exhilaration through his body.

The dust rose high, creeping in the sky, spreading, the fingers of shadow enveloping the land. Before he lost all his visibility, Alpha rained a series of smaller fireballs down onto the earth, taking advantage of the natural movement of the lower levels of solid and molten rock, energy flowing across the land mass. He moved the portal's view to watch the dinosaurs that had not died in the initial impacts, suffocate in the clouds of dust.

The dust cleared, dinosaurs were buried deep in the ground. The fireballs' profound impact forced sections of land across the sphere, surrounded and separated by displaced water.

Alpha brushed his hands together. He deserved a rest. The land through the portal would soon heal enough to support his slaves.

"How could you?" shouted Lucifer, tear-stained cheeks ashen. "You killed them. All of them."

Alpha gave his best grin, showing most of his extra sharp teeth. "I created them, I can destroy them. I am their master. They do what I say, even if it leads them to their deaths."

"But they hadn't *done* anything," Lucifer shouted back. Faced with abuse, Alpha remained calm.

"They had no idea what was going on. They were far from perceptive, their brains are the size of peanuts, well, most of them."

"It matters that they are sentient? All creatures created by you or anyone should have a chance at a life," Lucifer said, his voice horse.

Alpha roared with laughter at this latest statement. "They are my playthings, Lucifer. *I* am the one who decides who lives, and *I* am the one who decides who dies. It was their time, I have finished with them. Now it is time to create my image to form the perfect human who can come to serve me in Heaven." Lucifer stammered, trying to speak, but Alpha had not finished. "That is the whole point of this experiment. A bunch of stupid animals will not make this place into what I want. And besides, I owe nothing to anything or anyone. I am the creator, and I will destroy just as easily as I create. They are beneath us, Lucifer, they are not real in the same way we are. And anyway, where did you get this idea that everything deserves life?"

LUCIFER SHUT his mouth tight and kept it pressed into a thin line. The confidence born of anger and disgust dissipated with every statement Alpha made. He turned and moved away from Alpha, craving space from his overwhelming presence. He sat on the riverbank, Alpha's words ringing in his ears: "come to serve me in Heaven."

Lucifer did not return to main camp; he was unable to face the lifeless shells. Alpha was all he had now, other than Alpha, he was alone. Lucifer felt a great tug in his chest. If Raphael were here, they would run away together to a life happy with only each other for company. But now, Alpha and his creations were Lucifer's only hope at ever finding what happened to Raphael.

Lucifer pulled himself out of his daydreams and pushed them back down, deep inside himself. Raphael wasn't here. Wherever he was, it wasn't here. He had to get on with it.

Alpha rested for some time after slaughtering the dinosaurs. He took his place back at the portal, manipulating its views with practiced confidence.

Lucifer could tell Alpha was thinking. Alpha could liquidate his face to hide any emotion except for thinking. Lucifer didn't know if Alpha had emotions other than his quest for power and his penchant for destruction.

"I need to do more work on the land," Alpha said out loud for his own benefit. "This isn't quite right for humans. My fireballs might have knocked the whole mass off course a bit."

Lucifer understood none of what Alpha was saying. He stood blankly. Alpha gave a small smile, reveling in the opportunity to show off the true extent of his powers. He grabbed Lucifer by the arm and turned him so he was looking over Heaven's plain ahead.

"You see the sun?" Alpha said. Lucifer nodded. "Well, they are the mirror of us, and they have one, too. The sun is where we get all our heat and light from." Lucifer didn't question, drinking in the information. Disgust with Alpha was dwindling, with the excitement of pending creation filling its place.

"Well," continued Alpha. "I think I moved the land so the sun hits it differently. It's too dark. Humans need light to live."

Lucifer said nothing, moving to the space where he sat to watch Alpha work. Alpha shrugged, he didn't care if he got it or not.

Alpha worked all day, shifting, maneuvering, guiding, and manipulating piece by piece, bit by bit. By the end of the day in Heaven, Alpha stood back, assessing his masterpiece.

"Perfect," he said clapping his hands together once in a self-congratulatory gesture.

"Is that it?" Lucifer asked, still naive to all the elements of creation. "Are the humans growing down there?"

Alpha laughed. "No, much more work to be done. But for now, I rest. This is hard work. I can't keep going through the night."

LUCIFER HAD TAKEN on the support role at their makeshift camp, ensuring there was heat, light, and food. As Alpha had his own light, minimal appetite, and simple taste, these were easy tasks, leaving Lucifer plenty of time to watch the action. The activity through the portal constantly invaded his mind, taking over as the first thought of the day. Lucifer's compulsion to view the new world was pushing Raphael deeper into memory. His obsession led him to wonder about his own powers. He had them, he could feel them, but he was not like Alpha. During the long hours Alpha was absorbed in the portal, Lucifer would sit back and practice.

The small fizzes and pops were as far as he went in his quest to make an object. He wondered if he could do something else. Perhaps his powers were different? But what? His lack of imagination suffocated his learning progress. It was impossible to separate his potential from Alpha's. Every time he attempted to think about himself and his own strengths, his mind wandered back to Alpha and his plan through the portal.

Lucifer watched Alpha run his hands across the shimmering skin of the portal. "What happens now?" he asked Alpha, genuine interest shining through.

Alpha spoke without abandoning his task. "We need to get more atmosphere; my fireball burned it off." This time, Alpha anticipated Lucifer's blank stare. "When we breathe, we breathe in gas. You can't see it, I can though. To make humans thrive down there, we will need to make sure the right gas is in the air. At the moment, it is floating away because there is no barrier to whatever is out there. I need to replace the barrier with the same kind of thing we have here."

And again, Alpha worked all day, replacing the barrier around the earth, finishing with his customary clap and lying down to rest.

~

LUCIFER FELL INTO ROUTINE. Alpha rose, Lucifer busied himself with morning meal preparation.

Lucifer would always ask what was happening that day, intrigued by the process. Awaiting the day that humans would form. Alpha explained what he was doing with varying degrees of patience.

"Today, I need to separate some of the water. I need to

make freshwater for drinking and salt water for fish. They all got muddled with my fireball. Then I will add in some roots for plants to grow, there are some growing back, but it's a bit sparse. The humans will need more food. It will take them a while to learn things for themselves. I better make it easy for them initially, or they will die. They won't be smart like we are."

"We are or you are?" Lucifer kept this thought to himself.

The next day, the pattern repeated. "Today," said Alpha, "I need to remove all the dust from inside the barrier I put up to keep the air right. That way, people will see the sun, moon, and stars properly. It will also mean people will breathe without getting a lungful of rock, which is useful."

Lucifer's interest peaked again the following day. "Now for the fun part," said Alpha. "Let's get on to creatures." He planted the organisms for fish and birds. "There are the building blocks, and now we wait."

"What about land creatures, like dinosaurs?" asked Lucifer.

"Well," said Alpha. "They should all evolve out of the one thing if my theories are correct and we give it enough time."

"Oh, right," said Lucifer, not understanding the intricacies of what Alpha was doing, let alone how *he* knew what he was doing. "And what about the humans?"

"That is the clever part," Alpha said, his chest puffed in satisfaction, face split by a wide grin. "Do you remember me talking about the tiny organisms I encountered when I first went through the portal?" Lucifer nodded.

"Well, the building blocks for the creatures I have planted should eventually morph into something like humans. Then I can give it a little push and quick tweak, and we should get there. I hope so, at least. I know it seems long and involved, but this is the best way to grow creatures that look like us. We are complicated."

In spite of himself, Lucifer was impressed. Alpha's foresight and brain power was amazing. He could see how things would play out over a long period.

"So," said Alpha, "I think that deserves a rest. How many days did that take?"

"Six," Lucifer replied. "Not counting the whole destruction part," he said with intended vehemence.

Alpha scoffed, ignoring Lucifer's attempted dig. "Six days to create a world. Not bad, if I say so myself," he said as he lounged back on his cot, hands behind his head, feet crossed at the ankles.

"The people aren't created yet; all the work is still to come," Lucifer retorted.

"Well, *I* have done all the creating I plan to." Alpha's words were dripping with disdain. "Six days is what I will tell them, anyway."

"You mean you plan for them to *know*?" Lucifer said.

"Of course I do. I plan to make my presence quite known actually, might even go down there when the time is right. The whole point is, I'm going to bring them here so they better have respect for me," said Alpha, speaking as if he were stating the obvious.

"And they'll worship you, just like that?" said Lucifer, disbelieving.

"Of course they will. I'll tell them to, and I'll keep them stupid enough so they won't question me. I will implant a need in them. A need to gain a better life. That is where I come in, that is what I will give them. All we do now is wait."

14

THE TINKER

Alpha observed his fledgling world. He never left the portal. Lucifer moved back and forth from camp to the portal, checking on Gabriel and Michael, who were always there, slowly going about their business. Automatic chores were accepted with no free thought, they were both true slaves. Skin sagging heavily off their bones, they ate only the minimum amount to keep their bodies functioning.

Lucifer sat on the log near the central campfire. Gabriel shuffled past, a pile of knives balanced across his forearms, his wrists bent up, ensuring they didn't fall.

"Gabriel?" Lucifer said quietly. He didn't stop.

"Gabriel!" Lucifer shouted. Gabriel stopped walking, not turning. Lucifer rose to his feet and moved to stand in front of their former leader, to peer into his eyes. Gabriel, the tallest of the group, had half a head of height on Lucifer. Now he was slumped, almost eye to eye.

Dead eyes. There was nothing behind them but blankness. Longing to help, Lucifer closed his eyes. He had come close to creating something before, perhaps he could help Gabriel break out of his prison of flesh and blood. Lucifer cleared his mind, allowing single focus on his subject, just as Alpha had once taught him. He honed his mind to Gabriel, or the person he had once been, now trapped inside the body bent to Alpha's will, or gone altogether.

A small breeze whipped past his ears, a whisper of a voice. Lucifer scrunched his eyes tighter, mind focusing on the voice. But he heard and felt nothing.

Lucifer let out his breath and slumped. Gabriel remained the same, his blank face unmoved. He had no power, it was no use. He was not as special as Alpha; his spark was not enough.

Lucifer moved out of Gabriel's way. He continued to shuffle toward the knife shed to sharpen the knives, Lucifer assumed.

Lucifer felt powerless to help the two walking skins who had never been his "friends," but he felt a compassion toward them, a deep need to help his companions. All he could do was bide his time in the hope he could convince Alpha to undo whatever he had done to them. Another reason to stay in Alpha's good graces as long as he could.

Eyes lowered, shoulders drooping, Lucifer gathered his sack of supplies and walked back to the forest. Trudging through the first layer of trees, he heard a rustling straight ahead. His eyes darted around, looking for a creature. There was nothing. Shaking off the strange sensation, he kept moving.

Approaching the dark place that housed the tiny remains of Alpha's failed experiments, he felt a breeze, unusual in the forest.

It was there, a voice in the breeze. Lucifer stood and

listened. He concentrated wholly on the sound, the world fading to a black tunnel around him. The only thing present was himself and the voice. It came to him slowly, the sound distorted, like many voices forming into one.

Lucifer's eyes snapped open. The voices coalesced, ringing in his ears.

"Help."

SHAKEN, Lucifer regained his equilibrium. What could he do? Was this Gabriel? Coming to him from wherever Alpha had taken his inner consciousness? He didn't have the power to help anyone himself, and he couldn't talk to Alpha.

Lucifer felt torn between trying to help Gabriel and Michael, looking for Raphael, and watching Alpha's progress with humans. His ever-present guilt rose as he gave the other side of the portal such high priority, his personal fascination, his desire to witness the birth of a new race selfishly rising to the top.

Lucifer shook off the eerie feeling, he was alone in one of the darkest parts of the forest, made more unpleasant by the pile of bones on the other side of the clearing. The remnants were the only evidence of Alpha's attempt at creating life on this side of the portal. Skirting the trees, far from the pile of death, Lucifer was hit fiercely by a splitting pain and a blinding white flash as a sound bellowed within his head.

"Help." It was spoken by a million voices. Lucifer slapped his hands over his ears, trying to keep the screams out of his head. His own shrieks added to the racket within his skull as he bent to his knees, his body melting with agony. Mercy came when his eyes rolled back in his head, and he fell to the ground.

His last glimpse before final oblivion was of a tall tree with a high, protruding branch, a large chunk swinging back and forth, broken and charred.

LUCIFER WAS FLOATING. It didn't seem strange, a common sensation he had while drifting off to sleep or dreaming. He was facing the sky, peeking through overhanging tree branches, the sun glinting through the leaves at an ever-changing angle. Lucifer could feel he was not moving under his own steam. He turned his head from side to side. He lowered slowly to the ground and let out a small sigh of relief when he felt the grass touch his body. He sank in the welcoming, springy blades.

Alpha was there, looking down at him. "All right then, are you?" he said, his tone markedly flat.

"Yes, I think so," Lucifer said, sitting upright, stretching his arms and legs out in front of him, checking for damage.

"I found you passed out," said Alpha, waiting for explanation.

"I had a piercing headache and thought I could hear screams." Lucifer paused, unsure if he wanted to divulge anything more. "Or something," he completed.

Alpha was thinking, his eyes flashing with momentary intrigue or understanding. He shrugged, holding out his hand to help Lucifer up.

"You seem fine now. I was coming down to find you. I am nearly there with human life." Then he added as an afterthought, "How's camp?"

The memory of the two empty skins roaming around the camp sent a shiver down Lucifer's spine. "Ticking along," he said.

THE NEW DIMENSION was buzzing with activity. Birds and animals roamed the lands alone or in packs of varying size. The hustle made their home seem empty by comparison.

"Where do I look?" asked Lucifer. "I still only see beasts."

Alpha enhanced the view of the portal, zooming in on a pack of hairy creatures scampering around on all fours, occasionally lifting themselves to their hind legs to peer around. Big ones and small ones, playing and fighting and grooming one another's hair. Part of a pack, a family.

"That's amazing," Lucifer said. "They are so beautiful; I can't believe all this came from the tiny specs of life you planted."

Alpha nodded, a proud grin stretching across his pudgy face.

"But," said Lucifer, "they don't look human exactly."

"Ah," said Alpha. "That is the next step and why I need you." Lucifer waited, keen to hear what Alpha had in mind. "I have been nudging these species to evolve from time to time. Letting them change and grow alone and changing something in the environment or in the structure of the animal when I need to." Alpha paused for a moment to let his explanation sink in. "These primates," he said, over pronouncing the syllables of the word, "or this type of primate anyway, have grown apart. They use tools and communicate, in a way. They are special." Lucifer nodded, unsure where this was going, the curiosity brimming within him evaporating his concerns.

"The thing is," said Alpha, his hand moving to the back of his neck, twisting in his hair, a nervous gesture, "I need to go down there."

Alpha had said he'd been down there before. But still, the thought of Alpha going through made Lucifer's stomach turn.

"Why?" The word eventually fell from his gaping mouth.

"Well," said Alpha, thinking. "This is by far the most complicated part of the process. I could try it from here, but it is important that I get it right." Picking up the cues from Lucifer's unchanging expression, Alpha sighed. An irritated air coming over him, he rubbed his eyes and breathed out in attempt to calm his internal frustration. "I need to work on a sample of these primates. I need to take a few of them and make changes on a minute internal level. The changes to each one must be the same, or it won't work. I need to be there to make sure that none of them can get away and things like that. Then, this subset of primates will continue to evolve differently from the others, making a new species, which will, in turn, become human. Resemble us physically, more or less, but they will not be as smart or special."

Lucifer's brain was whirling, he understood the general idea. Alpha wanted the perfect human specimen, and he would work hard day and night until he got it right. Nothing short of perfection would be good enough.

"So," said Lucifer slowly. "Why do you need me exactly?"

"Ah," said Alpha, having forgotten the most important thing. "I need you in case I get stuck. I will tie a rope and leave the end through the portal. I didn't get stuck before, but I need to be sure."

LUCIFER HELD the end of the rope that was wrapped tightly around Alpha's waist. It disappeared into the portal. The rope looked different through the portal. More fragile, dull, and washed out to match the background of the human dimension.

Alpha had zoomed the portal's view. Lucifer, in all appearance, was only steps away from him. Through the portal, Alpha stood in the exact same spot as Lucifer. It was strange, like being in two places at once.

Alpha had corralled his sample, a small group of primates, male and female, including mothers with their babies. Alpha had explained to Lucifer how he got the animals to self-generate. There were two types of each species. They would join together to fertilize and incubate a new one, a pattern that continued until there were vast populations roaming the globe. Clever and much less work. Alpha did not quite share Lucifer's praise of this approach to procreation. He had to create the females to incubate, but they were not his favorite. He had to make them soft and nurturing to care for their children, rather than strong and driven like the males. But Alpha considered it necessary, so he lived with his decision. Lucifer disagreed, he had seen the female beasts fight for their young. In his eyes, they were just as strong, if not stronger than the males.

Lucifer watched Alpha go about his work. He held the beasts, one at a time. One hand on their head, the other grasping their ankles. Each one went the same way. The animal would struggle for a short time and cry out in pain before losing consciousness and falling to the ground.

When Alpha had finished his work, there was a line of bodies perfectly set out, all unconscious.

Clapping his hands together, signifying the task complete, Alpha turned back toward the portal. Lucifer, still holding the rope, maneuvered himself out of the way to allow Alpha's travel through the portal.

A sharp tug on the rope. Alpha was standing at the portal, waving, a concerned look on his face. Lucifer moved close to peer at Alpha.

"Stuck" and "pull" were on his lips. Was Alpha stuck? Lucifer positioned himself to yank the rope.

Wait. What if he didn't yank the rope? What if he threw it through the portal and never saw Alpha again? He would be safe from his moods and questionable actions, but lonely. Lucifer's skill alone was not enough to get answers about Raphael, who still felt so close. Like it or not, Alpha was all he had.

Lucifer lent back with the rope, pulling Alpha back through the portal. He fell backward as Alpha came through with ease.

"What happened?" said Lucifer.

"What?" said Alpha, offering a hand to help Lucifer up. "Oh, I think I bumped the portal on my way through. I couldn't get back to the right spot."

Lucifer's brow furrowed, something was not right. About to question him further, he studied Alpha's face, attempting to read his mood. He looked drained, minor changes in his appearance made him look haggard, older.

Lucifer couldn't contain himself. Forgetting about the question of Alpha's reentry, he blurted, "Did it work? How was it down there?" Alpha put up a hand, willing him to stop.

"Just"—he paused, head in his hands—"let me sit for a bit." Lucifer sat a short distance from Alpha, waiting. He had never seen him like this before. Weak, vulnerable, almost human.

Finally feeling strong enough to speak, Alpha said, "It feels so strange, going from here to there and back again. Everything rushes past you, time whizzes by, and you can't do anything to stop it. It's peaceful here, gentle and calm. Heaven is definitely the place to be."

15

DOUBLE HUMAN

"**D**amn," mumbled Alpha. The portal zoomed in close, he stared into the face of a human. It was human all right, but not one of his.

Alpha muttered. The being was upright, covered in animal skin for warmth. He had a large nose and forehead with masses of body hair. These ones had evolved alone, against Alpha's intentions. Alpha had set the path for his perfect humans, who were forming nicely some distance away. This unforeseen evolution left Alpha uneasy, he didn't know what to do.

Alpha shouted, venting his frustration into the face of the thing in front of him. The human startled, its eyes wide with fright as it turned in circles, attempting to locate the noise it had heard. It grunted and screeched, eventually running back to the cave where the rest of its clan clustered.

"Huh," said Alpha, impressed. "Well, you can hear me then." Alpha continued his pacing, deciding what to do about these extra humans muddying the face of his perfect world. He didn't want something that looked like that serving him in Heaven.

Alpha's humans had evolved into a good-looking species, mirroring his own structure in a general sense. They hadn't achieved the level of intellectual ability he needed, but he would fix that in time. He didn't want to rush things and disturb the fragile equilibrium of the world he had created.

The thought of intervention in his humans made his brain tick.

"Yes, yes," he muttered to himself, his thought process moving so fast he himself could barely keep up. "Then the bastard race will take care of itself."

Alpha heard a rusting behind him, and his shoulders sank. Lucifer must be back. Alpha had sent him back to camp to check how everything was going, but more so to be rid of him while he dealt with his current problem. He didn't want Lucifer to witness his dilemma. He could not afford to appear weak, or he would lose his control.

Lucifer had the annoying trait of caring so much about everything through the portal. He thought of all animals as equal to themselves. They should be cared for and treated in ways that provided them with long, happy lives. Alpha smirked to himself. He was so like Raphael in the beginning, too concerned with what substandard creatures *might* feel, that he would not further himself. This is why Alpha was in charge here, he knew how things needed to be. This was not the way of the world Alpha had created, he would do nothing that didn't further the completion of his goal. Ruthless and merciless behavior was the only way to achieve the perfect human. Alpha returned to his destructive thoughts, planning to ignore Lucifer's presence altogether. Muttering.

"What will take care of itself?" asked Lucifer, walking up

to the portal, dropping a sack of food on the small table Alpha had positioned to hold his essentials.

Alpha hung his head a little. He would not get away with ignoring him, he would have to engage, again. This is why Alpha wanted slaves, he would only engage when he wanted.

"Nothing to worry about," Alpha said, giving in. He would work it out soon enough. "There is another branch of humans over there." He moved the portal's view to zoom in on the cave.

Lucifer put his face close to the portal. "Wow," he said, the awe clear in his voice. "Where did they come from?"

"They sprang up of their own accord," said Alpha gruffly. "I believe from another branch of primates."

"They are amazing, how far are they from the others?" asked Lucifer.

"A fair way," said Alpha, moving his view back to his engineered humans. "I don't see a problem." Lucifer nodded. Satisfied with the order of things, he set about cooking up a meal. How Alpha wished that he didn't need to waste time doing things like eating and sleeping. But even he, the almighty Alpha, needed rest and sustenance.

Taking advantage of Lucifer's averted attention, Alpha reached both arms through the portal. Careful not to step all the way through, he picked up two sticks from the ground at the human's camp. Then in full view of the crowd staring at his partial appearance, he made them a fire, hoping they would pick up the technique to allow for easy recreation. The humans stared at Alpha's creation, some of them touching it, but none repeating the movements as they wrenched their singed hands from the flames. Alpha rolled his eyes. "I forget how stupid you are sometimes. At least you learn fast." He was right. One human was already attempting to copy Alpha's instruction.

The others were left in the cold. They would not receive a gift.

THE FIRE HAD BEEN NEEDED. They already killed and ate animals, but they seemed altogether happier to eat them cooked. Alpha thought this preference ridiculous, as it was not the most efficient way to get the most out of a kill. The only thing Alpha thought worth it was to smoke a carcass for preservation, as he had done so himself. Alpha had discovered that if proper care was taken, meat could remain edible almost eternally, which suited him well. But the cooking of meat had its advantages, the more the humans ate, the smarter they became. A mirror of Alpha's own experience with much less drastic results.

Alpha was leaving the humans to their own devices. They were spreading out, moving across the earth in search of better places, different food, and adventures.

It was time for Alpha to return his attention to Heaven. Although happy that the beach camp was running well under the care of his first servants, Alpha had a vision, and perhaps it was time to build Heaven, ready to accommodate the legion of slaves he would soon possess. Alpha knew what he wanted, a metropolis of perfect bodies to serve him and do everything he might want. It would take work to create this in the short term, but the day would soon come where his humans would take that off his hands, manually building and maintaining Heaven for eternity.

LUCIFER WAS on board with the decision to do more building in Heaven. Since Raphael had gone, he had been floating through a void, a limbo fueled by the waves of grief and helplessness. Helping Alpha to plan for Heaven renewed Lucifer's purpose, after all, he had a life ahead of him, and he should attempt to make the most of it. This was the best Lucifer could hope for with no closure on Raphael's fate. The internal struggle he felt became too much if he allowed himself to dwell. He could not reconcile Raphael's absence with the intermittent jolts of his presence, like he was just around the corner and would appear at any moment.

They worked together, clearing trees and erecting buildings, paving well-used paths through the forest, and connecting pieces of land by causeways and bridges over rivers and streams. Lucifer did none of the physical creation but supported Alpha's work by providing sustenance and strength.

Lucifer's weakness came to light throughout this process. With neither the vision nor the foresight to understand Alpha's master plan, he went along blindly, allowing himself to be led, never taking a moment to think for himself and what he may be part of.

LUCIFER FOLLOWED Alpha down a well-built path, his mind wandering, meandering from thought to thought, contradicting his physical movement, which was as straight as the path he walked.

Lucifer had been following Alpha for some time, not paying attention to his whereabouts. He realized, with a sudden jolt, that Alpha had led him back to the portal. They hadn't been here in some time. A familiar wave of intrigue and yearning washed over him.

Lucifer stood at the portal beside Alpha. The humans had spread and were growing, thriving.

As Alpha surveyed his little kingdom, Lucifer felt him stiffen.

"What is it?" asked Lucifer. Alpha remained silent. He adjusted the portal frantically from one place to the next before stopping, zooming in close to a couple, one sitting cross-legged on the ground, the other lying in his lap, hair splayed out. A man and a woman, the two types made by Alpha. They were touching, smiling with each gentle caress. Lucifer's stomach twisted, he bit his lip to stop from crying. This was life, just as it should be.

Quickly forcing control upon himself, he returned his attention to the scene. Alpha shook with anger.

"How could they?" he said through clenched teeth. "This is wrong, all wrong," he shouted through the portal. The couple sat bolt upright, hearing the rumble of Alpha's voice.

Lucifer saw it. He had seen the woman's face, but the man was hidden by a mane of thick black hair. He was a cave human. A gasp exited Lucifer's lips. "I didn't know they would love each other," he said. Alpha turned to him and yelled.

"They weren't supposed to love each other! They were supposed to kill each other! Now my perfect human beings are muddied by...that!" he said, waving his hand toward the portal. "Love causes all my problems. Why do they have to show such weakness? I only wrote it in to help with the procreation."

Lucifer tore his eyes away from Alpha as he shivered with anger, the light he emitted pulsating, a crackle leaping from his skin. Lucifer's hair stood on end.

The woman, still shaking from the unknown presence, beckoned, and a third human ran to her, jumping into her lap as she sheltered it with her arms.

Lucifer's brain swam. He needed to distract Alpha quickly, aware of what he would do in a rage. Lucifer grabbed Alpha by the arm, attempting to turn him away from the portal.

"Does it really matter, Alpha? They are all human, you said so yourself. They just come from different places." Alpha said nothing, his rage not abating.

"How about you come and have something to eat? We can talk about it." Alpha still said nothing, giving Lucifer a fierce look. Lucifer shrank. Alpha could see right through him.

Alpha snapped his head back to the portal and saw the family sitting all together, recovering from the fright of the mysterious bellow.

At the sight of the child, Alpha's teeth ground together, his fists clenched, redness rising in his face. Two words escaped his clenched teeth.

"Half breed."

❧

ALPHA'S REACTION was fast and ruthless. Lucifer had no chance at retort, he watched on, helpless. Alpha pointed his open palm toward the portal. An immediate wail followed. The child lay lifeless in its mother's arms.

Lucifer froze, looking on in horror. Alpha moved to the mother, exacting the same revenge.

"That will teach you to lie with scum like this," he said.

The man sat frozen, his primitive brain unable to comprehend the events. Alpha left him alone. "I'll deal with all of your kind," Alpha said, his anger subsiding, initial revenge exerted.

Lucifer's throat was tight, his stomach in knots. He knew deep in his heart, there was worse to come, he had to stop it. He could not let Alpha punish the humans, who felt pain and joy, and who loved, just as he did.

16

THE MASTER RACE

L ucifer had to pick his time. Alpha's volatility was never more obvious than after a kill.

Lucifer leaned back in his chair, assessing. Alpha had been staring into the portal for some time, seething and muttering, still wired, tweaking from exerting his ultimate authority.

Alpha eventually came over for food, sitting quietly. Lucifer could see his brain working.

"Serves me right," he said, looking dejected, his kill high dissipating. "I should have known that bringing women into the mix was a mistake."

This was the first time Lucifer heard Alpha admit a mistake.

"How could it have been a mistake, Alpha? Don't you need them, so the humans can reproduce themselves? Wouldn't it mean so much work for you, creating individually if they weren't there?" said Lucifer on the offensive, desperately plotting how to promote the merits of women to Alpha in the hope he wouldn't wipe them out, too.

"I do need them," Alpha sighed. "But they make my world imperfect."

"How do you mean?" Lucifer probed, hoping to get a grasp of the situation.

"Well," said Alpha, sitting back in his chair as if to give a lecture. "It is the women who are all emotional, I think it might be a side effect of what they need to bear children. They aren't strong like the men, either. They spend so much of their time caring for the young, they rarely come up with any ideas that push the race forward. Mostly, I don't see they will be as good as men in Heaven. What I want are strong souls, and they aren't strong."

Lucifer's face flushed, the vision of women's work filling his head. Alpha was wrong. But there was no arguing with Alpha.

"I made the need to copulate a driving force in these humans. It is how I will get them to have many children. But with the act of copulation, there seems to be another connection. What it is, I am unsure. But yes," continued Alpha, looking around at his freshly built-up Heaven. "Women are a necessary burden."

"But what does this have to do with women?" Lucifer gestured toward the portal. He wanted to say, "What does murdering an innocent woman and child without a flinch have to do with women?" but he didn't.

"Well, obviously, if it wasn't for the woman, none of that would have happened," said Alpha, conveying his opinion as fact, something he did frequently.

"The caveman looked happy with the situation," Lucifer mumbled, keeping his eyes downcast.

"He would be," Alpha shouted, throwing his bowl to the ground, the remnants of stew splattering. "That thing is *inferior*. He has this beautiful creature, who is better than him in every way. He probably idolized her." Alpha's anger was boiling over yet again. Lucifer trembled slightly, he hoped that Alpha wouldn't notice. "Everything is soiled now," Alpha yelled as he stomped off to stare though the portal.

ALPHA WAS TRAWLING across his world, moving the portal's view, zooming in, zooming out. Searching.

He stopped. "There," he shouted. Triumph was clear on his face, a rare, genuine smile.

Lucifer came close. He had been trying to form a plan to save the cave people, but thoughts always fizzled out. He seemed powerless against Alpha.

Alpha zoomed in on a single man. A good specimen, tall with light brown hair, his strong frame showing his hours of work in the sun through sweat-stained, bronzed olive skin.

"This is him," said Alpha. "This human has never encountered the cave people. He is still pure, I can tell."

"How can you tell?" asked Lucifer, his mind grasping, trying to see what Alpha saw.

"The cave people are far away. I can tell by the look of him he has never left this area. I don't think there are any women at all right here, so his purity can be confirmed. Now I need to find a woman."

Alpha blew into the portal, and the man slumped. Lucifer could tell he wasn't dead, he didn't have the vacant look dead things have. It made him think of Gabriel and Michael. With all the events through the portal, he had forgotten them. Guilt swept over him. He realized that his obsession with Alpha's work had pushed his search for Raphael to the side.

Alpha's search for a woman went on a long while, his body jittering, energy palpating with every moment.

"What a bunch of promiscuous scoundrels," he muttered. "None of them can keep to themselves. All they want to do is spread their legs at the first opportunity."

Alpha flung his hands in the air. "I give up, none of them are good enough," he said, disappointed. "I'll think of something," he added under his breath.

"Can you get more water, Lucifer?" asked Alpha, an innocent expression coming over his face. Lucifer's blood ran cold, he knew this look. Lucifer was attuned to Alpha's manipulative tactics.

"There is some in the barrel just in there." Lucifer pointed to one of Alpha's new buildings.

"Oh, OK," said Alpha, smiling, the smile that always took on a devious edge with sharp teeth showing. "Come and help me grab it then."

It was a better outcome than leaving Alpha alone. Lucifer walked with Alpha to the building. Alpha gestured for Lucifer to enter first, then, using his superior speed, he slammed the door, using his powers to seal it shut.

Lucifer pounded on the door. "Alpha! Alpha!" he shouted, there was no response. "Don't do it, Alpha. Have mercy! They have lives."

It was no use. Lucifer's banging subsided as his head split with pain. Screams filling his ears, he curled on the floor, rocking until the sound dimmed and faded from his head.

∾

ALPHA OPENED THE DOOR. Lucifer sat against the back wall.

"You can come out now," said Alpha. Lucifer didn't

move. "Suit yourself then." He waved a hand, walking outside.

Lucifer was angry at Alpha and wanted him to know it. He stormed out of the hut. Alpha was crouching on the ground, shaving pieces off a slab of shriveled brown meat.

"You killed a whole race of people," Lucifer yelled. "Thousands of them! Some of them even your own *perfect humans.*"

"They were no longer perfect," said Alpha evenly, not turning from his task. "They were soiled. I left some of them who hadn't been near the others. They can fend for themselves. I am concentrating on ultimate perfection."

Through the portal, Lucifer could see one solitary man sitting in a beautiful garden. The garden was lush with fruits, colorful birds chirping, just like Heaven. As close to Heaven as you would get on that side of the portal. A little bewildered, the man looked at a female form unconscious on the ground. She was beautiful with a similar look to the man, the same complexion and hair color. Features delicate versions of his own.

"Where did you get her?" asked Lucifer.

"I made her," said Alpha, "from him." Alpha pointed to the long scar on the man's side. "I took a section of his body and used all the little pieces to make her."

Lucifer stared. Alpha sighed.

"It's complicated," he said.

"Obviously," jeered Lucifer. "How did you make her brain work?"

"That was the clever part," beamed Alpha. "I took some of his consciousness—his essence—and split it into her. I tweaked it, so she would have the necessary"—Alpha paused to choose his word—"weaknesses."

Lucifer raised an eyebrow.

"Here," said Alpha, passing Lucifer a piece of dried meat. Lucifer did not take it, not yet ready for Alpha to get away with what he had done. "Come on, Lucifer! Peace offering?" Lucifer's stomach growled, giving away his hunger. He snatched the food and stomped over to the nearby chair. He sat, taking a bite out of the tough meat.

The flesh rolled around his tongue, a tingle spread over his body. The surge grew, ecstasy followed as it rippled across his skin. Then his heart jolted, light flashed before his eyes. Some of the meat still in his mouth, he looked up to Alpha, standing right over him.

"Feels good, doesn't it?" said Alpha through his grin.

"What is it?" Lucifer said, looking down to his hands. The dried meat mostly uneaten. Alpha laughed, his head thrown back, tears streaming down his cheeks.

"You are funny," he said, wiping his face. Alpha bent down and looked Lucifer square in the eye, so close he could feel breath on his face, and see the fire alight in his eyes. "I think you know."

What had he done? He heard a wail in his head, a cry for help. Hands over his ears, he ran. Crashing through the forest, he did not stop until his breath left him. Leaning against a jagged rock, his legs collapsed. He rolled onto his side, drawing his knees to his chest. Scrunching his eyes shut, he tried to block out the voices in his head. They told him what he had done. He had eaten Raphael.

Lucifer found a crevice, wedging his body into the gap. He lay, restricting every muscle. The constant surges of power bombarded him. He tried to ignore them, but they woke him from sleep, a continued reminder of the fate of his companion.

Weakening by the day, wishing for the end, Lucifer remained in the fissure. Raphael was gone. Alpha had taken the life of another for his own gain, and not just any person. The person Lucifer wanted the most. What Alpha had done weighed on his heart. Anger began to bubble through the power surges. Slowly, the rage overtook him, and he clawed himself free of the crevice, licking water off leaves and eating rough grasses for sustenance. His anger grew with his strength. Alpha would not get away with this.

"Lucifer," said Alpha with a smirk as he rose from his chair at the portal. "I am glad to see you again. You ran away before I could finish telling you what I have been up to."

"There is no need," rasped Lucifer, unused voice horse. Alpha said nothing, a smirk plastered to his face. Lucifer's anger grew, he felt a crackle from his skin, a pulse emitting from his body with every angry thought. "You wanted to talk, then talk," he said through gritted teeth.

Keeping his eyes on Alpha, he saw a momentary crease of concern cross his brow. Without warning, showing superior agility, Alpha appeared in front of him. Rearing back, he jerked forward, smashing his narrow, bony forehead into the top of Lucifer's nose with a sickening crunch. Reaching for the pain, Lucifer moved his hands to his face. Before they made it, Alpha grabbed Lucifer by the hair and smashed his face down onto his knee.

17

BANISHMENT

Dreaming. Splintered visions swimming in the darkness.

Raphael, tied at the wrists. Laughter. A knife slipping beneath skin, peeling, muscle visible beneath. Leg thrashing.

Hands tied to the arms of a chair, caked with dirt. Sharp splinters wedged beneath fingernails. Blood. Screams.

HE WAS BACK in the dark part of the forest, the morbid sentry of baby bones guarding the clearing. Buzzing filled his head, getting louder. A buzzing he recognized, another portal.

Lucifer's face throbbed, metallic blood coated his tongue. He tried to feel his face but couldn't.

He opened his eyes to Alpha. They were sitting facing each other, both cross-legged on either side of an old fire ring. Lucifer's hands were tied behind his back, pulling at his wrists and shoulders.

"I am so happy you finally see," said Alpha, looking up. Lucifer followed his gaze. He had seen this before, a carcass hanging from the tree above the fire, smoked and preserved for future use. "Does he feel as good to you as he did to me?" Alpha said, producing a knife and cleaning blood and dirt from under his nails.

Lucifer screamed at Alpha's face. He had no words, no movement, just anger. Blood-flecked spittle flew.

"Just admit it," Alpha hissed, leaning forward.

Lucifer said nothing, his breath coming rapidly, eyes fixed on Alpha.

Alpha rolled his eyes. "I know you know." Alpha paused. "You are no fun," he said, cocking his head to the side. "Just tell me how it feels to have eaten the dried meat of your lover? A leg, I think. I'm not sure. I dried about half of him, I would say. Not as good as fresh, but you can't have every-thing," Alpha said, holding the knife handle between thumb and forefinger, swinging it back and forth.

Lucifer turned his head and vomited on the ground. Alpha was right. He had known as soon as he swallowed the meat, there was no denying it. He had eaten Raphael. Lucifer took in the clearing. Heaven enhanced, he under-stood. All this time, Raphael was dead. Lucifer's stomach lurched again as the realization settled into the void in his soul.

Alpha cackled to himself throughout Lucifer's stomach upheaval. When Lucifer had finished coughing, he spoke. "Why?" Lucifer croaked, the only word that would form in his swimming head.

"Well," said Alpha, standing up, moving to a chair that had appeared from somewhere. He kicked out his feet and crossed them at the ankles. Leaning back, he placed his hands behind his head, settling in for a story. "There are a few answers to a few questions"—he paused—"and seeing as I don't know which question you are asking, I may as well answer them all."

"I NEEDED MORE, always did. But it wasn't until I ate the fish, I became aware of what I really needed. I was mistaken at first, of course. I saw the way you and Raphael were together. The way you behaved together, the way you touched. I thought love was what I wanted. Then you refused me, and I had never been so angry in all my life." He paused. He was speaking calmly, repeating facts with no emotion. "But then, I realized that physical togetherness with you, or anyone in fact, was not it. Now that I look back, it seems so unimportant. No, one person was not enough, I know now what I am destined for. It is not the love of one, but the love of an entire race. When I became powerful, more powerful than I ever let you know, I learned that taking a life was the most fulfilling and wonderful experience. The wielding of ultimate power gave me perspective and helped me to grow. I understood that you and he are minute in contrast to my potential. Killing Raphael was my turning point. I sucked in his life force, leveraging his soul to give me the power I craved. He had never respected me, he was the only one who never bowed to me. I know none of you ever trusted me, but you came to need me and appreciate my powers," Alpha continued.

"Now you, Lucifer." Alpha rose, still holding the knife limply in one hand, turning Lucifer to the side and crouching before him. "You were to be my protégé. You were the only other person who felt a change with the meat. Even if it wasn't as big as mine, you still felt it." Alpha sat back on his haunches, remaining close. "But you just kept fighting me, you wouldn't accept the greater good of what I am trying to do. You cannot see the big picture, you are too soft. You were so entranced with the world I created, so in awe of me and what I was doing. I had hope that you would come back to me. I tested you when I was down on Earth. You pulled me back, but I realize now that gave me false hope." Anger was creeping into Alpha's voice. "The humans down there are just my creations. They will live their short lives only so I can pluck their life force through the portal and put it into a body here. You see, that is how I will do it. Their bodies can't go through, but when they die, I will take their essence and bring them here to serve me. The bodies I create will live if I plant a soul in them."

That was enough. Lucifer's anger welled. Remaining silent, face unyielding, he spat in Alpha's face.

"Well, that is some reaction, I guess," Alpha said, wiping the spittle with his hand. "Your concern for the two buffoons back at camp was just irritating," Alpha continued as he paced, agitated, the only way he seemed capable of showing emotion. "I broke them easily. They got what they deserved. I mean, had you forgotten how they used to treat us before I became all-powerful and stepped in to save us?"

"The question now, Lucifer, is what to do with you," said Alpha, tapping the sharp point of the knife against his lower lip. "Obviously, you need to go. You have been against me for a long time, but I could handle you then, and you amused me. But now, I am so busy with my project that I can't indulge you anymore. I don't have forever to get my slaves up here, it takes too long with you butting in all the time."

"I thought about eating you, too. No doubt I would get extraordinary power, but I can feel Raphael's force within me, and it just wouldn't do to have the two of you in such proximity. I don't think that would be punishment at all," he said, looking less like Alpha and more like a crazed beast, hyped for the kill.

"I could also just kill you and resist the urge to soak up your power. But I think that I won't." He cocked his head to one side, giving an extravagant droopy frown. "I think that is what you want now. Now you know the truth about your lover and that you ate some of his flesh."

"No, that won't do either," he said, crouching once more beside Lucifer, raising the top of the knife to Lucifer's skin, tracing a line from eye to mouth.

"No," Alpha growled in Lucifer's ear, grabbing him by one tethered arm, dragging him to his feet. He spun Lucifer around so he was staring straight into the portal he had sensed since the moment he had regained consciousness.

A DARK MIRROR OF HEAVEN. Lush trees dead, a constant wind hissing formless words.

"The final answer to your question," Alpha said, pacing circles. "I didn't feed you Raphael just for fun, well, not entirely." He chuckled. "He gave me the ability to travel through the portal, one of the powers his sacrifice bestowed on me, *and,*" said Alpha, emphasizing his words dramatically, "I will bear the side effect, that you, too, have become stronger. You have obviously gained some powers that would be a concern for me here. But it doesn't matter. You will be in there."

Alpha moved close behind Lucifer, pressing his body hard against his back. Lucifer's bound hands pressed into Alpha's flesh. Alpha stood on tiptoes, hissing in Lucifer's ear.

"You are my nemesis, my adversary. You could have

joined me and chose otherwise. You were the only one who could have ever formed a decent opponent. But I have beaten you." As Alpha's words grew in vehemence, a wind picked up around them. Sparks flew from the portal, rods of electricity hitting trees nearby. Lucifer's breath was coming fast.

"I banish you to the Hell that you deserve. You will be alone, forever. I will tell my people of your wickedness and that you will come and take them to damnation if they ever see your face. You will never escape, you will never see another's face again."

Alpha drew a crooked finger down Lucifer's neck. Then, resting his hands on his shoulders, shoved.

Lucifer staggered. Barren rocks were slippery with the unrelenting rain, each droplet cold and sharp on his skin.

PART II

EARTH

The majority of men prefer delusion to truth, it soothes. It is
easy to grasp.
—Nietzsche, *The Antichrist*

18

EDEN

Alpha assessed his masterpiece. How brilliant his world was, how well he had done to chase perfection amid all the trouble he encountered, never giving up. The landscape he created gave humans everything they needed to thrive, to be strong. Consumed by the cycle of death and rebirth at his own hand, Alpha found solace in his quest for perfection.

Through this turmoil, his humans would gain all the characteristics required for entrance into Heaven.

Alpha smiled as he played Lucifer's banishment over and over in his mind. The look on his face just before Alpha closed the portal, sealing it against any possible means of escape. The picture in his mind showed the slow fall of raindrops and lightning so sluggish he could make out its path from the ground, time was slow in relation to Heaven. Lucifer's suffering would be truly eternal.

Alpha returned to the Earth portal, calculating, experimenting. He stopped time on Earth. His creations were frozen, perfectly preserved, allowing him time to play as he pleased. Alpha zoomed in the portal on his sleeping creations. Furrowing his brow in concentration, he restarted time on Earth.

Alpha had made his perfect humans a perfect garden: lush forest, plentiful food, and perfect weather where it only rained enough to maintain the spectacular greenery he meticulously planted.

Alpha had created the perfect couple. Adam and Eve were meant to be, cut from the same flesh, in the mirror of how Alpha saw himself. Taking advantage of frozen time, Alpha had tinkered with their brains to rectify the one major shortfall of his manufactured race, language. Alpha chose speech that mirrored his own. It was time for him to take a much more active role. He wanted to see them in the flesh, to touch them, and guide them.

Alpha beamed as his humans twitched with the jolt of time. He had been careful to fog the memories of the man's previous life, the woman was a blank slate, the perfect way to start his Kingdom on Earth. To fortify his place among the people of Earth, he would spend some time ensuring he was venerated. All he needed was to plant himself deep within their souls. He had wired the humans with the need for significance, a need that revolved solely around him. He taught them to believe.

Alpha knew the risks. He could not slow time while he was present on Earth. He would age, but Alpha's greatest belief was his own invincibility. And he was free. Free of judgment set upon him by Lucifer and Raphael, free of abuse by Michael and Gabriel. He oversaw his own destiny, one he was certain would lead to greatness.

Alpha was electric, his hair standing on end, excitement coursing out of his body, crackling into the surrounding air. He took a deep breath and stepped through the portal, leaving Heaven empty of true soul for the first time.

ALPHA BENT OVER ADAM. He was even more striking in person, with lean muscles running down his body, flawless olive skin, and a light sprinkling of dark hair covering his chest. Alpha ran his palm across Adam's breast, watching his eyes flick open to meet Alpha's gaze square, without fear.

"Who are you?" asked Adam, batting his long, dark lashes, brown eyes with flecks of gold adjusting to the light.

"I am your God." His tone was friendly, authority simmering below the surface. "I created you, you are here to serve me. Serve me well, and you will be with me for eternity."

"Better to start with the truth," God thought. "The skill of maintaining power in any situation is the ability to manipulate the truth."

"I will serve you always," said Adam.

God grinned. Great looks, great language, and just enough spark to ask questions, but not too much that he wouldn't take God's answer.

Adam stared up at God as if awaiting a command.

"How perfectly I did," God said in a low voice, stroking Adam's hair and face. "Perfect brawn and perfect brains."

God continued to survey his handiwork, touching Adam here and there, nodding and muttering. After God's intimate examination, he stood to assess his surroundings, mouth slightly open, taking in the beauty of the garden. Adam's eyes widened when he saw Eve's form on the ground, sleeping. He bent over her, inspecting the female form.

"Beautiful," said Adam, not taking his eyes off the woman.

"I made her for you. I made all of this for you," God said with a flourish. "You are master of this garden, Adam, you only bow to me. And she,"—he paused, locking eyes with Adam—"bows to you."

～

GOD LEFT Eve sleeping as he walked with Adam through the garden. He needed Adam to listen and obey and not be distracted by the woman. They walked side by side through the lush greenery of Eden. God had designed the garden with a specific level of accessibility, with seemingly natural pathways that always turned back on themselves. Adam and Eve would not be wandering out of Eden by accident, there was no exit a mere human could locate. God took no chances. Nothing would get in or out of Eden. He would not let his perfect specimens get soiled again.

God placed his hand on Adam's shoulder as they walked, steadying himself from a bout of dizziness, an effect of his adjustment to a new time paradigm. He covered this weakness expertly, continuing his movement by running his palm down Adam's arm, taking his hand, aiding him to touch a large fuzzy fruit hanging from a nearby bush.

A jolt ran through his body when he touched Adam, his soft skin tickling his fingertips, the sweet smell of sweat touching his nostrils. God felt the prickle of a tear for the first time in his life. Like when a mother looks at her young, yearning for constant contact, the love and concern rolled into one knot in his chest.

God felt complete. He had a purpose, Adam would love, honor, and obey him, which was all he ever wanted. He was hot with anticipation of bringing Adam to Heaven. God closed his eyes, willing himself to wait. There was much schooling to complete before he was ready.

God's lessons began. He taught Adam how to make

baskets from reeds, to collect fruits, and how best to store foods. Adam was pliable, God's brain size calculations resulting in the perfect intellect. But no matter Adam's excellence, God had to test him, test his obedience and love. God must work until he got it right. Obedience was the cornerstone of what God needed. Any soul would be a perfect match for Heaven, so long as God could count on obedience.

ADAM WAS WORKING, sitting cross-legged on a small mound, a pile of reeds placed neatly beside him. Shoulders hunched, tongue protruding, his large fingers made the work slow.

Adam's light disappeared. He felt the wash of God's presence. God was amazing, he knew so much and treated Adam like a son. Wordlessly, God extended a hand, which Adam took without question. He let himself be led through the brush to the very center of the garden.

Standing before them in a small clearing was a tree. Its twisted black trunk splintered into delicate branches covered with shining gold leaves. Each branch held a glowing fruit at its tip. Adam gasped. He had never seen a tree like it before. It seemed to hold life within its branches.

"This," said God, "is a special tree." He turned on his heel, facing Adam, ready to impart another piece of precious wisdom. Adam gaped up at the tree, speechless, moving silently toward one branch end, reaching up to take a fruit.

God moved with lightning speed and slapped Adam across the face with the back of his hand. Adam's eyes were wide, hand held to his reddening cheek. He remained silent.

"Never touch that!" God yelled. Adam's sudden fear of his creator must have impacted God, as he let out a breath through his teeth, facing his palms to the ground in a calming gesture. "That fruit," he explained, "is how you prove your love. How you show me you are grateful for all you have."

Adam stared. He didn't understand, the thought he could ever question God so far from his mind, he could not even comprehend it. God was his constant, God had taught him everything.

"If you eat it, you suffer." God added, reacting to Adam's blank expression. Adam stepped back, not wanting to be too near the dangerous tree.

God smiled. "Excellent," he breathed, his mouth remaining turned up at the corners.

"I don't want you to suffer," God added, looking Adam straight in the face. "Remember, this is your test. If you pass, you can live with me for eternity. If you fail, you will die at my hand, and I will start again." Adam, too naive and indoctrinated to understand the underlying meaning, smiled and nodded. He walked back toward the spot where Eve lay, eager to survey his woman, he forgot the tree. God continued to watch him, satisfied he had given Adam an illusion of choice. To obey or disobey, the perception of free will.

19

HELL

Lucifer had to survive. Act fast or die.

The opposite of the land of plenty in which he had spent his life, Hell was desolate and inhospitable.

Wet to the bone from relentless rain, its constant stinging drops striking his skin, his whole body ached with cold.

"Shelter," he said aloud.

Lucifer took a deep breath, the time to choose between life and death was now. He turned in a circle, trying to cement his bearings.

He knew where he was. It was a mirror, just like looking through the portal to Earth. Earth had the same trees and streams as Heaven, their color and fragility being the major difference. Here, trees were gray and lifeless, burnt at the tips from lightning strikes that made sparks and claps on the horizon. Through the dead branches, Lucifer could see what he knew as a calm stream, clear water ruffling gently over rocks, providing a sweet fresh drink to quench his thirst. Here, it was a wide torrent rushing with an anger he dare not approach.

Lucifer fought the rising panic in his chest. He needed to do something. But what? He stood still, concentrating, reaching within himself for an answer. If only Raphael were here to lend his practicality.

Lucifer's brain raced through the events that led to his banishment. Raphael was here, Lucifer had consumed him, his life force now within.

Concentrating to block out the icy rain, the roar of the raging torrent and the electricity in the air, he visualized his goal. A shelter made of wood, four walls, and a roof. Just as Alpha had once taught him.

"No," he thought, "something is not right." As if poked to life, his brain recounted a memory. Lucifer saw, behind his closed eyes, humans erecting their shelters. Roofs were always round or pitched for the rain. As he adjusted his visualization, the structure materialized in his mind's eye. He raised his hands, channeling all of himself toward his chosen spot on the ground. His body vibrated. He opened his mouth wide, something escaped him as he crashed to the ground, exhausted.

From one knee he raised his head, opening his eyes despite the sting of the rain. It was there, a small wooden shelter just as he had imagined. He dragged himself through the mud, collapsing under the barely holding timber roof.

Sprawled on his back, cradled by the mud, he wept. For Raphael, who had died so Alpha could gain the power to maim and murder thousands of creations. He wept for the humans, who were destined for death and rebirth for Alpha's never-ending cycle of pain. Chained in eternal slavery. The only thing that would save him now was the power bestowed on him by Raphael's body.

The sky peeked through a small crack at the corner of the roof, billowing clouds brimmed with thunder and lightning, echoing the feeling deep in his belly that events on Earth were destined for a great storm brought down by Alpha.

THE RAIN EASED, lessening to a more manageable drizzle. Lucifer sat cross-legged in the middle of his tiny hut. He slept in the mud, too tired to contemplate a floor.

His anger brewed and swelled, his body simmered, spilling over. He struggled to calm himself, so many feelings swirling. Lucifer knew Alpha was dangerous, that he would build up humans to serve him in Heaven. He knew he would toy with them before the day of their ultimate destruction. If there was something Lucifer understood since the explosion in his brain, it was that Alpha would stop at nothing to satisfy his desires. This had become more than slaves in Heaven, it had become a game played with the innocent lives of his creations.

Lucifer envisaged Raphael, smiling, hand outstretched, beckoning him to come. The jolt struck him like a bolt of lightning, and he channeled his anger. To avenge his love and save humankind, he would master his powers, escape Hell, and confront Alpha.

20

WOMANLY INTERVENTION

God watched Adam and Eve from the edge of the garden. Adam followed Eve around like a desperate puppy. God remained unconcerned; infatuation would soon fade.

God had sat with Adam, schooling him on the act of procreation. He explained that it was his duty to make many children to continue the growth of God's chosen people.

"But," added God, "you must wait."

"Wait?" asked Adam, not daring to question his creator openly.

"Yes," said God. "You have much to learn. When I have taught you all I know, you may go forth to raise many children in my name." God's message was met with a blank stare. He sighed, forcing further explanation out through frustration. "You must make many children and raise them well, to worship me and love me, just as you do."

"Oh," said Adam, his brow still furrowed, brain process incomplete. God flipped his hand.

Adam's children would be the lifeblood of Heaven. The

more he could make, the more perfect specimens God would have. He needed more servants.

But God found it difficult to let Adam go. The perfect man who adored him. The command he held over one human being gave him great strength. He was needed and wanted. God was learning to master control, he would use this over the entire race in time to come. The thought of manipulating feelings and understandings of these basic humans on a worldwide level satisfied God almost as much as the thought of a Heaven buzzing with activity. It was all his.

"I will serve you, God." Adam said, raising his eyes. "In any way that you desire."

"Excellent," thought God, smiling. This is what he needed. He would now guide Adam through everyday life, slowly crafting his internal morality to suit his purposes.

EVE PINCHED the base of the flower between her long thumb and forefinger. She rose up on tiptoes, placing her upturned nose into the hollow formed by drooping white petals. She closed her eyes, balancing. She inhaled deeply through her nose. The smell was bliss, the pungent perfume surrounding her, each new smell conjuring a different picture in her mind. She lowered the flower, not bothering to brush the yellow spores from the tip of her nose, too eager to drink in the rest of Eden.

She moved to the next bush, this flower had a bright yellow center enclosed with layers of tiny pink petals.

Eve sniffed, a smile dancing on her lips as she cocked her head, appraising the flower. "Not so much aroma but very pretty," she said as she plucked it from the bush, twirling it between her thumb and forefinger, mesmerized by the pattern the leaves made when moving at speed.

Eve lifted one foot from the soft grass, intending to continue her investigation, when she heard a grunt, followed by a crisp slap on the rump. She squealed, whirling around on her heel to see Adam, standing close. Staring at the hollow in his neck, she took a step back, regaining comfort in her personal space. Eve put on her best scowl. He was a fool, always groping and chasing her. She was trying to explore, to take in new plants and flowers, just wishing he would leave her alone.

At least it wasn't God sneaking up on her, his presence always put her on edge. Adam was just stupid, a vessel for God, and his obvious favorite.

"Would you stop that?" she said. Adam laughed and gave her the look that said, "I am in charge here. I do what I want." Then his eyes dropped, roaming over her body, his look changing to "I like what I see, and I will touch it all I want." Adam didn't need to say a word. Eve knew his thoughts, they were plain on his face.

Eve sighed. It was God's fault. God had told Adam that Eden was his; he was the master, and all in it served him. Adam looked upon everything as his property, Eve included. God seemed to agree with Adam's opinion on his place in Eden, as he did nothing to stop him from behaving this way. Endeavoring to ignore him, Eve moved to turn away and continue her walk through Eden. But Adam snatched her by the forearm and pulled her back to face him.

"Who said you could go?" he asked in a sickly voice, barely masking his demand.

"No one did," said Eve. "I want to look at more plants. I can do that, as far as I am aware." She put as much defiance into her voice as she dared. She had learned quickly that she had to treat both Adam and God carefully, choosing her moments to push her agenda. If she overstepped too much or at the wrong time, punishment would follow.

Adam gave her a wry smile. "I guess you are," he said, his tone patronizing. "But you should do something with this," he added, edging so close to her their bodies were almost touching. Bending down to be right at her eye level, he plucked the flower from her fingers, tucking it behind her ear, finishing the gesture by stroking her shiny hair to the curled end just above her breast. A cold shiver ran down her spine when he reached her skin, causing an instant recoil. Moving at lightning speed, Adam clapped his hands on either side of her face, staring her right in the eye with a barely restrained force. His eyes, the same light brown as her own, raked her skin, causing a fluttering in her stomach, an uneasiness she didn't understand.

"There," he said, moving his head back a little, touching the flower with the tip of his finger. "Much better." He sidled around Eve, hands clasped behind his back, looking around with exaggerated movements.

Eve let out the breath she hadn't realized she was holding, letting her eyes drop to the ground. Composed, she looked up to see God standing some distance away, watching her. "How long have you been there?" she said under her breath as God raised a hand and beckoned her. She sighed, beginning the movement toward him, but after two steps, he held up a hand. She stopped. He pointed. Eve looked back over her shoulder, following the line of God's gesture, seeing Adam still close to her, facing the other way. "Of course," Eve thought. "It's always about Adam."

"God wants you, Adam," Eve said, voice raised.

Adam whirled around, and in one fluid movement, he

waved at God and grasped Eve by the wrist, dragging her with him in the opposite direction, running from God.

"Now, shall we continue this walk?" said Adam, letting go of her wrist and placing a hand possessively on her lower back.

Still stumbling from the sudden change in direction, Eve looked back over her shoulder to an unimpressed God. She could feel his deep, empty eyes boring into the back of her head.

"INTOLERABLE WOMAN," said God under his breath, watching them walk away from him. He was angry. Adam was his, the amount of attention Eve commanded was becoming a problem. God's jealously was so strong that it boiled over his skin, making him quiver. He clenched his fists tightly, holding them close to his body. Pain registered in his outer thighs. God looked down to see that his fists were banging rhythmically against his legs. Not liking the loss of control over his own body, he sought to exert power over his extremities. God clasped his hands tight together in an iron grip and thumped slowly, purposefully, slamming against his chest until he felt his brain reach out to his fingers once more.

"OK, OK, OK," God said to himself, regaining control. He had to watch her, she had the potential to ruin everything with her inquisitive mind. He made a note to himself to doctor the minds of humans to make them less inquisitive. Adam was perfect. The spark in Eve was troubling.

God moved as fast as he could, following Adam and Eve, slowing to a leisurely saunter once they were in view. He had a persona to uphold. He knew everything. He was in charge. He *was* everything, they could not see him in any other light.

"Do you ever wonder what is over there?" Eve said, the question directed to Adam, her attention focused on the high hedge at the edge of the garden.

"Where?" said Adam, appearing beside her.

"There." Her long finger was outstretched, guiding his attention.

Adam just shrugged. "If God hasn't shown it to me, then there is nothing. He tells me everything about Eden."

Letting her own shoulders rise in a defiant shrug, she cocked her head to one side. "I'll just ask him then."

Adam looked horrified. "Ask God? Ask God what is beyond Eden? Ask God why he hasn't told us something? I wouldn't if I were you." The last few words escaped in a condescending, pompous tone.

"Why not?" said Eve. "God said himself that he made everything for us, that he wants us to be happy and want for nothing."

"Well, that's not *entirely* true," said Adam, casting his eyes down to the ground before raising them to lock on to Eve's beautiful face with burning desire. Eve's eyebrow jerked up, the rest of her body still. "He said he made everything for *me*, including you."

Eve laughed. Adam's fists clenched, his mouth pressing into a line. "What is so funny?" he demanded through tight lips.

"Get over yourself, Adam. You are not that special." Eve got the words out through hoots of laughter.

Eve's laughter halted when saw Adam raise a hand,

ready to strike. The blow's momentum ceased as she felt an icy hand clasp her shoulder.

"Ask me what?" said God.

Emboldened by her win over Adam, Eve dived in. "What is over that hedge? Are we really the only two humans? Why have you put us here? Will the fruit on that tree kill us? Why did you put it there if it was dangerous?" The waterfall of questions spilled out of her.

God's mouth opened. He blinked. A moment later, he squared his shoulders, raised himself to full height, and boomed straight into her face.

"There is nothing. You are alone. You are mine. You must never go out of Eden, or you will die. You must never question me again, or you will die." His voice raised with every word, spittle flicking on Eve's face. She stood her ground, infuriating God further.

"That fruit will kill you because"—he paused, eyes darting before resting on the glimmer of a smile at the corner of Eve's mouth—"because it just will," he finished. The glimmer was still there, one turned-up corner on closed lips, a twitch of defiance.

Eve felt a hard crack across her cheek, her head turning with the blow. She turned back to God and looked him straight in the eye with nothing but a single tear escaping her brown eyes. She said nothing. She did nothing.

"Never question me again," God added, then turned on his heel and strode down the path.

"Time to go," said God to himself. "Then they will see how much they miss me."

21

THE PLAN

Lucifer scrabbled up the sheer rock face, his fingernails worn to bloody nubs dotted with small pieces of debris. Pausing for a moment, he lifted his face upward to check his progress. Nearly there. Taking an extra moment to catch his breath, he carefully removed one hand from the wall to wipe the sweat, blood, and mud onto the cloth tied around his waist. Using the knowledge that he didn't have far to go, he forced his body to move, swinging up to the next crack in the rock that was big enough for a foothold.

He yelled as his foot became firmly wedged in the fissure, leaving him dangerously off-balance, other foot flying and his hands attempting to make up for the lack of grip. He grasped for a piece of rock jutting from the precipice, a new wave of pain striking his hand and burning up his arm.

Stealing a quick glance, he soon wished he hadn't. He could just see the sharp edge of the rock pushing under the skin on the back of his hand. The rocks were black, shiny, and sharp. Difficult to grab, they penetrated delicate skin at the slightest of bumps. Gritting his teeth, ensuring his footholds were now steady, he jerked his hand as pain shot through him like a burning knife.

His field of vision decreased, he saw nothing but a pinpoint of rock swimming in a sea of blackness. He held his focus on the prick of light, determined not to slip into unconsciousness. Positioned so far up the cliff, if he fell, all his work and planning would be for nothing.

LUCIFER HAD SLEPT and found basic sustenance in Hell. The only thing to eat was a red rubbery weed that crept across the rocks. It was tough and chewy, but it gave him energy, and there was plenty of running water. His basic needs met, he sat cross-legged in the middle of his small shelter, staring at the bare wooden wall. His only thought was to plan. To stop Alpha from lording over millions of creatures with the long-term plan of placing them into permanent slavery.

Lucifer, determined not to give in to the enormity of this task, took one step at a time. The only way to manage alone.

Lucifer's first decision was to take advantage of what he had, the few elements in his favor, in what he knew would be an epic struggle of life and death.

He knew the layout of Hell. It looked different, felt different, and was harsh and difficult, but the basic formations were the same as the place he had spent his whole life. He sat pondering his plight for hours on end, only sleeping when exhaustion took over, only eating when his reserves were running so low he had no choice but to chew on the weed. As he attempted to formulate a strategy, outside thoughts of Alpha, humans, and the ever-present visions of Raphael constantly tested his concentration. Lucifer had to block him out, he had to concentrate on his power. To understand and increase his powers were his only means of escape.

Lucifer did not know how much time had passed, but he ate enough weed and maintained enough short bursts of sleep that eventually the scheme materialized in his mind as one complete plan. His brain pieced sections together without his awareness, allowing it to come to the surface when fully formed and obvious.

And now he pulled the bulk of his body over the cliff face and collapsed into the jagged rocks above. His scrawny arms extending away from his body and legs spread wide, he lay there, exhausted, drifting into the deepest sleep since his arrival in Hell, out in the open. He had done it, conquered the first of many hurdles.

LUCIFER AWOKE AT DAWN, a thin dew covering his body. He shivered, teeth striking one another in uncontrollable convulsions. The only thing to do was keep moving. The more he pushed, the quicker he would get to the next stage of his plan.

Lucifer stood atop the cliff. He had a good view of Hell, and he cemented his bearings easily. Lucifer's temporal disorientation continued. The nights were long, leaving him no idea of how much time had passed since his banishment from Heaven. This lack of knowledge urged him to focus on his quest, fulfilling each step as quickly as he could.

The day before was not the first time Lucifer had scaled this cliff, he had been here in Heaven. His previous experience provided him with thick vines to swing on and moss-covered trees growing out of the rock. Back in the time when he lost no fingernails and his hands were pain-free, capable of a dexterity that would never return. Remembering the time he had been here with Raphael, his heavy heart sank deep into his body. Raphael's smile, his joy had been infectious. Even though the experience ended with the near-fatal fall, Lucifer smiled at the memory.

Pushing all thought of his previous life from his mind, he surveyed the plateau where he had collapsed.

There it was, he could see it. A broad grin broke across his face, an event so rare that his cheeks ached and the skin on his forehead cracked with long-dormant lines. The two rivers, coming together at the lush delta on the flat plain of Heaven, with the small mound at the exact place they met. Lucifer knew this was it, he could feel it. There was no fertile delta, and the raging rivers had worn deep grooves into the rock. But the mound was there, bare and black.

Lucifer scrabbled down the opposite face of the plateau. Still steep, but far from sheer, he skidded on his hardened feet and was soon walking the large, rocky plain.

The portal mound was ahead. Without the covering of moss Lucifer knew from Heaven, he saw it was perfectly round, a flawless boulder sticking up from the ground like the shoulder of a sleeping man. Lucifer felt an electricity pass through him as he envisioned the boulder growing moss and ferns sprouting from the ground. Shaking his head, he couldn't afford to get distracted now. He was so close; he had to get back to Heaven.

Atop the boulder, Lucifer threw his crudely fashioned pack, shut his eyes, and lifted his hands to the sky that bristled with storm. He had no patience to wait, he made it this far and would not give up now.

His body shook. His eyes scrunched so tightly shut, and his teeth clenched with such force, he felt his face may implode. He let go, tentatively cracking one eye. Nothing. He let his breath whistle through his teeth as his shoulders sagged.

Lucifer adopted the stance again, closing his eyes. He felt a stronger rush of energy and sprang his eyes open, hoping to see an open portal. All he saw was a tiny stab of light dancing in the air, which fizzled like a dying fire ember.

Lucifer brought his hands to his face, covering his eyes and mouth. He let his arms drop to his hips, fingers digging into the protruding bone.

"Well, I'll just have to try harder," he said, steeling himself.

He collapsed onto the boulder, his brain working as fast as his tired body would allow.

"That's it," he said to Hell. "I came in the hope Alpha wouldn't think to close this portal, and I was right. This is a win. This is a win." He repeated the last words in the hope that all was not lost. To cement his self-convincing rhetoric, he slid down the slick boulder, grabbing his pack in one fluid swipe, and set about building a camp.

22

THREE WAYS

"Ha!" Lucifer shouted. The portal was open. He had tried and failed to open the portal night after long night, icy rain and bitter cold wind providing a constant assault on his body. In fitful moments of stolen sleep, he dreamed of Raphael, laughing and joking, eating, and enjoying the fruits of Heaven. The dreams ended abruptly with a shadow forming over Raphael's face, his laughter replaced by fear, and a trickle of blood appeared, running down his face. Lucifer always awoke with a start at the same moment of this dream, sweat breaking out, the back of his neck prickling. He harnessed these feelings, the fear, the anger, the injustice, and he channeled them toward the portal. Mixing his heightened emotions with his desire to open the portal allowed him to focus, eventually succeeding.

Lucifer felt the wash of achievement. He hopped around the plain of Hell. He waved his hands in the air, grabbing a long piece of red weed, holding it close to his body, whirling around as if he were twirling in the sand with Raphael. He stopped and looked around. What if someone saw him?

He scoffed and shook his head, heart sinking. No one would see, he was alone here.

"Am I alone?" he said aloud before letting out a full laugh. Perhaps it was truly time to question his sanity.

"I would rather not think about it," he said. "Anyway, what should I do now?"

His plan had been to get back through the portal and confront Alpha. But it was only at this moment he realized what this really meant. He would have to kill.

Lucifer's face fell as he realized his plan was not flawless. How was he going to make sure Alpha was dead? How was he going to make sure humans remained after he was dead? What was even going on in Heaven? He climbed back to the boulder, staring at the portal he had worked so hard to open, feeling hopeless.

LUCIFER SAW MOVEMENT. His eyes widened, breath stopped midway between mouth and lungs.

There was a man, a human man. Lucifer's eyebrows nearly met his hairline.

Peering deep into the portal, Lucifer felt a spark ignite. He knew this man. He was Alpha's pick, his first perfect human. He was wandering, fruit in hand, taking mindless chunks from it every few paces. Lucifer's mouth watered at the sight of the fruit, a dull yellow skin with orange flesh. The man held it loosely, expertly biting away skin to get to the sweet juicy flesh beneath. The juice ran down his chin unchecked. The man's pace slowed, he had seen something out of Lucifer's view. Lucifer worked hard to manipulate the portal as he had seen Alpha do many times. He zoomed in on a woman, sitting on the ground, cradling her knees to her chest, staring.

Lucifer gasped. "Only two," he said as he watched the man whose eyes were alight, a mischievous grin plastered on his face. He must have been moving silently, the woman did not turn to face him. His feet were padding carefully along the moss before he took three quick steps, grabbing her hair and yanking it hard enough that her head snapped back and she was dragged to her feet. The man held her at arm's length, laughing.

Lucifer's chest tightened. Destined to do nothing for these people, he fought the urge to jump through the portal and beat the man into a bloody mess. As the flow of empathetic pain subsided, confusion took its place.

If they were in Heaven, then they were slaves, mindless bodies to do Alpha's bidding. But these two seemed to have plenty of personality remaining within their skin, even if that personality was repulsive.

"I can't blame you," said Lucifer, addressing the man through the portal. "I have no doubt that Alpha made you this way."

Lucifer scoffed at the thought. This man was the epitome of what Alpha considered perfection, inside and out.

Lucifer surveyed the surrounding area, confusion growing within him. Everything looked like Heaven, but the life had gone out of it. Everything fragile, dull.

"Earth," whispered Lucifer. "I'm looking at Earth."

LUCIFER GAZED IN THE DARK, the portal had closed. Yet to discover the power to keep it open, he preferred not to try, he didn't want Alpha to know he had found another portal.

A portal to Earth, but Lucifer knew Earth time moved faster than in Heaven.

"How am I seeing Alpha's first perfect human? Surely he would be dead by now." Lucifer murmured aloud. With no idea how long he had been in Hell, he didn't know if the man should be dead or not. All he knew, was that it felt like he should be.

Lucifer brought his hands up in front of his face, appraising. He twisted them around, front to back. Other than the damage caused by climbing and the deep marks left by pulling up the tough red weed, they remained the same. Youthful.

Lucifer placed his hands close together on the ground and closed his eyes, concentrating. Making something from nothing, pulling particles from Hell, binding them together in one useful item. The object appeared. Grabbing the reflective shard from the ground, he swiftly raised it to his face before he could change his mind.

His skin was weathered, cracked from constant exposure to wind, rain, and storms. He had grown little hair on his face, and his lank, dark greasy hair remained slightly past his shoulders.

Since Alpha had invented scissors and knives, Raphael had always given Lucifer's hair a tidy up. He said it made him look "cleaner," but it had always been cut slightly above his shoulders.

The memory of Raphael running his gentle fingers through Lucifer's hair, pouring cascades of sun-warmed water over him to allow for easy cutting. He was back there in Heaven with Raphael. A close clap of thunder snapped him back to Hell, the place he now called home.

"Daydreaming will get you nowhere," he scolded. "Get on with it."

Lucifer reopened the portal. The man and woman were still there, moving and talking at a normal pace.

"Wait," he said aloud, a sudden rush of shock coursing up his body. "Can they see me?" he said, shuffling as close to the portal as he dared.

"Hello?" he called. Nothing. A small sigh escaped his lips. Torn as to whether this was good or bad.

Lucifer moved the portal a little, recentering on the humans. All breath left his lungs. Someone else was there. The woman's face visible above the long gray hair.

Lucifer couldn't tell if the figure was a man or woman. He couldn't hear them, but he saw the human woman's lips moving, asking a question, and upon receiving a reply, she quirked up her mouth in a gesture that made Lucifer smile. She had character, the disdain for this person was written plainly on her face. Then, as quick as it had appeared, it was wiped away by a vicious slap across the cheek. Lucifer's hand clapped to his mouth, his eyes widened. Time stood still as the feeling crept from his heart to his chest down to his fingertips, seeping into the marrow of his bones. Recognition.

Following the vicious assault on the woman, the figure turned. Lucifer could see him, long gray hair streaked with strands of white, unkempt and frizzy, the only thing stopping its curls from forming a perfect bird's nest was its extreme length. The billows of fuzzy hair flowed into a mangled beard, hiding the man's mouth, ending midchest in a dirty tip.

Lucifer's eyes opened so wide that he felt his eyelids may separate entirely.

With swirls of hair whipping around the body, the figure

snapped away from the two humans. Lucifer saw his eyes: small, black, and smug with the power of assimilated souls. It was him.

Alpha sprang into some nearby bushes. Lucifer lost control of the portal as it returned to its default view. And there he was, Alpha, at the portal. So close to Lucifer, he could touch him. Lucifer tightened his grip on the shard of glass in his hand. Right at this moment, he could reach through and cut Alpha's throat.

Questions ran through his head. Could he be seen? What was Alpha doing? Why was he so old? Every one remained unanswered.

Alpha was face-to-face with Lucifer. He raised his hands, and Lucifer's portal shuddered, a savage wind swirling around him in Hell.

Alpha took a purposeful step. "He's coming through," said Lucifer as he darted to the side, ready to strike upon Alpha's entrance.

But Alpha did not come through. Lucifer peeked back to the portal, trying to stay hidden. Alpha was still there, through the portal. He was fuzzy, like an apparition gliding over the land. Lucifer watched him walk to a chair, *his* chair.

Lucifer's neurons fired so fast, he was unaware of his comprehension. He could see Alpha in Heaven, overlaid on Earth. Lucifer's discovery may mean everything for him, potentially changing his chances. It was a three-way portal. He could see both Heaven and Earth. Lucifer had been pushed through a portal, at a specific place in Heaven, and moved through to Hell. He had seen Alpha work through a portal in a specific place in Heaven that led to Earth. What Lucifer could see now, was the overlap of the three worlds, all ultimately controlled by Alpha.

Alpha had gone back to Heaven, he had left the humans.

Lucifer watched the ghostlike image of Alpha slump in the chair, placing his face in his hands, uncontrollably shaking.

Alpha was crying. For a fleeting moment, Lucifer's heart broke. He remembered Alpha when they first met, tormented by Gabriel and Michael, sniffling in his sleep, face stained with tears. The memories playing in his mind darkened, all the things Alpha had done drowned Lucifer in anger. A scowl spread across Lucifer's face. He had to get through the portal.

GOD'S SHOCK departure left Adam mute, his mouth hanging open. He stared at the empty path before him, and shook his head, attempting to defragment his thoughts. The shards coming together to form clear and present anger.

"What did you *do*?" he yelled at Eve, giving her a shove on the shoulders.

"I didn't do anything. I just asked what was outside of Eden."

Adam screamed, bringing his hands up to his head and bunching his fists into the tufts of hair that curled at the side of his head. "Stupid, stupid," he repeated rhythmically, banging the ball of his palm against his temple, eyes scrunched tight. He hoped when he reopened them, God would be there.

"That is not going to happen, thanks to the stupid woman," he thought.

Adam worked to calm himself as God had taught him. He took slow deep breaths and relaxed every muscle one by one. A wave spread down his body as he loosened each muscle. Once the tenseness in his fingers had receded, he opened his eyes, ready to give Eve a piece of his mind. She was gone.

"She will not get away with this," he thought, hands retwisting into fists. He would punish her, and he knew God would approve. He didn't need to ask him, he would show God that he cared for him over all else. God's absence left a void in Adam's chest. He no longer felt whole. He had to get him back.

Adam's jaw clenched as he charged with a gait of purpose. He would find her. She would get what she deserved.

EVE SNUCK THROUGH THE UNDERGROWTH, moving quietly, careful not to disturb the plant fronds or branches. She chose soft areas of moss or hard rock to make her footfalls, hoping Adam would not be skilled enough to follow. She needed to escape, his moods were something Eve found hard to handle, tempers that God fed incessantly.

Eve knew God was like Adam, he said himself he had made him in God's own image. The way they jumped from good mood to bad and changed their minds without warning or reason made for an unstable existence where everything could go wrong at any moment.

Eve had been on the brink for a long time. Her life felt empty with only Adam and God to share it. She knew she had a purpose beyond Eden, beyond being in the service of Adam, as God told her she was meant to be. With rising unhappiness with the way things were, she took her chance, getting away from Adam and God for the first time. She was alone, enjoying her solitude.

Eve knew she could not avoid Adam forever. Losing her

bearings from her purposefully erratic route, she stopped and listened. Nothing other than the chirping of birds and the soft rustle of critters on the forest floor. Good. She nodded, still alone.

She turned in a slow circle, pivoting her bare feet on the smooth rock. Slowly, searching for a landmark, doubt sprang in her mind, she recognized nothing. She had never been allowed to explore on her own. Adam always guided her excursions, carefully managing her discoveries.

She saw it. The tallest tree in Eden, poking out above the canopy. Its golden leaves sparkled in the sun, a contrast to the deep black of the gnarled branches. Adam had told her of this tree once when he was in a stupor brought on by excess food. But she had never seen it. Her hand raised to the place where God's hand had stung her skin. She set off toward the golden fronds, seeking the truth.

LUCIFER'S HEAD HURT. He hadn't felt such pain since his fall from the coconut tree back in Heaven. But now he found it easier, his body acclimatized to agony. A grunt came from deep within his throat. Pain had become a normal part of his existence.

Sprawled in front of the portal, the physical memory was not available to him. Judging by his smarting tailbone and throbbing head, he had bounced from the portal. He had tried and failed to get through.

"Why can't I do it?" he asked the portal. Had the power gained from Raphael diminished? Or was it just different going from Hell to Earth as it was from Heaven to Hell?

Lucifer got up with a groan, his whole body ached. He stepped to the portal and searched for the humans. He saw movement, just the slight rustle of a palm frond. It may have been his overactive imagination or the knock to the head. The woman appeared. She peeked through the fronds, eyes darting from side to side, instincts assessing danger.

She gingerly stepped into the small clearing, staring. Wonderment was rife on her face. Lucifer saw so many emotions hiding within her: fear, awe, and suspicion all rolled together. He maneuvered to see what she had encountered.

The tree sat in the center of the clearing, commanding its surroundings, dwarfing all its fellow plant life, its shining leaves making everything in the near vicinity look like a dull copy. Lucifer knew this tree. He recognized its beauty, the way it seemed alive with a faint thrumming on the breeze. This was a Heaven tree.

"How did he do it?" Lucifer said, biting his lower lip in thought. This tree had a darkness about it, a menacing undertone running through the branches of the spectacular monument to Heaven on Earth.

Alpha had manipulated it, added something. The tree, laden with fruits from Lucifer's old life, led his mind straight to food, and his stomach rumbled. He ate only to preserve life now; nothing would make him eat the red weed except impending death.

Lucifer pulled himself from his thoughts. The woman was standing, still and quiet, contemplating the tree. She seemed entranced by it. He wondered if she could feel its power, or that as a creation of Alpha and nonresident of Heaven, she could feel nothing at all.

She moved close to the tree, touching one of the low hanging fruit. She explored, hand running lightly over the fuzzy skin, unsure of what it might be or the power it might hold. Gradually gaining more confidence, the woman moved her whole hand around the fruit. Lucifer, holding his breath, willed her to take it. "Do it; do it," he muttered rhythmically, sending all his positive thought through to her, hoping it would give her the courage to take the fruit and take a bite. Perhaps a taste of Heaven fruit was all they needed to understand what Alpha was. Captor, not savior.

An uneasy thought struck Lucifer. Why would Alpha put this tree on Earth? Was it to let them eat it and document the effects it had? Was it to kill them? Or to test them? Lucifer didn't even try to analyze Alpha's actions, he was so inconsistent it was pointless.

The woman tightened her grip, tensed her muscles, and moved her arm. It would take just one quick flick of the wrist to dislodge the fruit.

She jerked her hand away and spun on her heel, long hair flying in a train behind her. She backed up toward the trunk of the tree as the man strode toward her, a mean grin on his face that reminded Lucifer of Alpha. A shiver ran down his spine. The man grabbed the woman roughly around the wrists. The fruit swung above their heads.

"You thought you could get away from me?" growled Adam, his cheek touching hers, his mouth so close to her ear that his lips brushed it as he spoke. She felt rather than heard his sneer as his lips parted, teeth scraping the lobe of her ear. An icicle ran down her spine, rough bark scratching her back. Adam had both her slender wrists firmly grasped in one hand. She was pinioned to the tree, helpless.

Adam smashed her hands above her head, her thumbs crushed against the jagged bark. He shoved his knee between her legs, staring into her face. He had a plan, and nothing would stop him.

Eve tried to stop herself from trembling. She swallowed hard, trying to get words out of her dry mouth.

"Adam," she croaked. "I...I..." Stumbling, she paused, collecting herself. She needed to appear strong. "I didn't mean to run away, I just thought you needed some time on your own"—she paused—"to calm down."

Eve wheezed, doubled over. The blow landed right in her side, just below her ribs. Gasping for breath, she writhed to escape Adam's sturdy grip, the bones in her wrist grated. Adam yanked her upright and slammed her back against the tree. Her head jolted against the solid trunk, snapping forward, hair cascading over her face.

Adam smoothed her hair back, straightening her neck with a tight grip around her chin. Eve gradually opened her eyes. Adam was jeering, his eyes alight with trouble. The icicle crept further down Eve's spine and made it to her stomach, enhancing the pain from the blow.

"You will learn what it is to serve me and to serve God. You will never question me or God again," said Adam, authority absolute.

Eve's naivety let her down. She did not fully understand what may happen, but she had instincts.

One last attempt to stop him, stop his rage and his desire to possess and control. There was only one way she could do that. He didn't care for anything in this world, not her, not Eden. These were things only there to serve him and give him a contented existence. The only thing she could draw on was his love for God.

"God told you not to touch me," Eve said, mustering all the strength she could to sound in control.

Adam tipped his head back and laughed. The boom

made her ears ring. He stopped and brought his hardened eyes level with hers.

"God isn't here," he snarled before rearing back and driving his skull into Eve's nose, using the full force of his muscled neck.

Eve couldn't make a sound, the pain erupted in her face with the crack and scrape of bone and cartilage. In a haze, she was aware but behind a cloud. Blood dripped in her mouth, the metallic tang of the warm liquid covered her tongue. Her head raised, pulled by the hair. Adam spoke as if from far away. She felt his body close to hers.

"Not so pretty now," he said, clicking his tongue. "Shame, shame." He paused. She tried to open her eyes. Adam was swimming in a field of dots, his image pulsing from blackness. She could feel her head lull. He tightened the grip on her hair, pulling her face right up to his. "Never mind," he said with slight shrug. "It's not your face I really need."

Adam let go of Eve. She couldn't stand alone. She collapsed to the ground, retching from the pain. He grabbed her by the shoulders, pushing her to the ground. Her head crashed into the spongy earth, patches reappearing before her eyes. Her limbs were frozen, her thoughts not speaking to her body, her arms and legs ignoring the urgent messages from her brain, they had given in. Any struggle was in vain, he was too strong. She felt Adam's weight on top of her. She scrunched her eyes and waited.

23

THE SERPENT

Lucifer wiped the tears from his face, the rough back of his hand scratching his skin. He sniffed. It had grown cold in Hell; sharp icicles rained down from the sky. He didn't care. Thoughts of his own comfort were far from his mind, the sting of icy rain and damp that made his bones ache pushed aside, making room for the pain of another. All he cared for was the woman, beaten and taken forcibly by a brute who had no care or love for her as a fellow human. A man who thought of her as nothing but a toy. His likeness to Alpha was striking.

She was still lying by the tree, bleeding, shaking. Curled into a ball, she stared at nothing. Lucifer was staring back at her now, trying to tell her he was here. She was not alone. She hadn't wept, she hadn't screamed. She had disappeared within herself, hiding in a sanctuary she had built to survive her life in Eden. A place that would keep her sanity safe through any ordeal, a feeling Lucifer understood well.

"No," Lucifer said into the portal. "No, I will not sit back and watch this." His renewed sense of purpose caused him to rise to his feet and move to his nearby shelter. He sat cross-legged next to his supply of red weed and water. He would not move until he found a way to help her.

GOD HAD NOT STOPPED WATCHING. Seeing Adam deal with the insolence of his woman helped to heal the wounds slashed across his battered soul. He felt loved again.

Adam was brutal, and he liked that. He wasn't even angry that he touched her, despite this having been forbidden throughout previous conversations.

"Well done, my son," he said, proud that Adam's chosen punishment had worked to hurt Eve and establish a power she would not easily break. God had succeeded, he had built a man in his own image.

Adam had left Eve in the clearing. God wanted badly to return to Earth to congratulate him, but he lacked strength to go through the portal again so quickly. He zoomed in on Adam's face, standing so close that if he were in Heaven, he would be able to smell his sweet fruit-laden breath. God closed his eyes, hovering his hands in front of Adam's head. "You did well, my son. Rest now," he whispered, channeling his words directly into Adam's thoughts.

Adam stopped and looked around. God repeated, "You did well my son. Rest now. I am watching over you."

Adam beamed, face upturned to the sky, hands held up, palms flat. He was copying God's creation gesture, worshiping his father, accepting him and his power.

God smiled, his broken heart mending.

LUCIFER ALLOWED himself time to think and to work out how

to get to the woman. His inability to get through the portal did not to quell his persistence. He tried multiple times, checking the alignment and current coming from the portal, testing each potential issue. Each time, he awoke on the ground, having lost a few seconds. A faint current dissipated through his limbs.

There must be another way. Lucifer tried to channel Raphael and his power to help him. He could feel Raphael somewhere deep inside him, life force providing him with the will to help. But the force was quiet, lost in the deep recesses of Lucifer's soul, pulled more to Alpha.

Lucifer continued to check in on Earth, opening the portal and locating the woman, checking she was still alive. It could be any day the man went too far with his beatings and violent sexual appetite.

The woman had no choice but to stay in his company. He had ultimate control over their environment, and without help, she had no escape. The constant threat of violence was enough cause for even the most intelligent and vibrant of humans to retract, to hide within their flesh and bones to cope as best they can.

Lucifer's affinity to the woman grew. The power lorded over her, the way the man manipulated her, was learned from Alpha. Lucifer himself had been treated this way as Alpha took advantage of his grief, his drive to discover, and his fascination with humans to blind him to the truth. To alter his perspective of life.

Given the chance for self-reflection, Lucifer could see it now, what Alpha had always been like. How he had worked to separate everyone in Heaven, controlling them each in a different but equally destructive way. It was only Raphael who had truly seen through him.

Watching Earth, Lucifer realized that for the first time,

he felt free from the power of Alpha. Even before his acqui-
sition of powers, he had been manipulated. Alpha had been
planning, plotting, and twisting the truth. Playing back
moments from his life in Heaven, Lucifer saw things differently and understood Alpha in a way he had not seen at the
time. Lucifer saw all this within the man through the portal.
Alpha had little need for violence, the threat of force was
present in every word he uttered. A trait passed to his
progeny that was compounded by his consistent use of
violence.

The man was talking. Lucifer thought he was giving one
of his long-winded sermons on the merits of Alpha and how
the woman had spoiled it all for him. She was just sitting,
face blank, eyes empty. She was elsewhere.

Lucifer zoomed the portal close to the man. He closed
his eyes, sending every shard of energy to his ears.

Yes! He could hear the man faintly. With great concentration and straining, he could hear.

Lucifer listened carefully, his summation of the conversation had been accurate.

"God is still here," the man said, gesticulating wildly. "I
heard God's voice come into my head. He told me I had
done a good job and that he wasn't angry with me. He said
he would watch over me."

Lucifer's eyes widened. They were calling him God! And
either he had fabricated this experience to keep the fear ripe
in the woman's mind, or he had really heard Alpha speak to
him through the portal? Lucifer suspected the latter,
knowing this was the kind of thing Alpha would say to his
perfect human. God, the master manipulator, creating
control from praise as well as control from violence.

Lucifer's mounting disgust dispersed as he played the
man's speech back in his mind. If the man had truly heard

Alpha through the portal, then his voice could enter without his physical body.

Lucifer's brain sparked. He had a rescue plan. Unable to rescue her physically, he would do it through persuasion.

He continued to listen to the man, holding out for more information.

"Eve!" Adam shouted at the woman. "Are you listening to me?"

She gave a small nod of the head and a faint smile that did not reach her eyes. She now had a name. Eve.

EVE PUT herself wherever she could to be away from Adam, the sight of him making her sick, her stomach tying in knots. A jolt of real pain ran through her as her brain recounted Adam's abuses. The visions came in flashes, segmented but real. All of them painful, none of them nice. At least for her.

Eve was aimless. Adam was less particular regarding her whereabouts these days, knowing she couldn't escape and knowing she valued her own life enough not to stop him from fulfilling his needs. Usually he was busy kneeling by the camp, hands together and body swaying in his prayers to God. Asking for him to return to Eden so he could become whole again.

She thought about that day, that awful day when he had changed her so quickly. The person she was, gone in an instant, replaced by a broken version of herself. The woman who carefully managed Adam and God, who let her wit and intelligence simmer just below the surface, was gone. Now she felt like nothing but a bag of skin containing a sloshing bowl of pain.

Unaware of the path she was taking, she arrived at the tree. It was unchanged, the fruit, the golden leaves, the black trunk and branches, the ground rock covered by patchy soft moss. But the place had changed. Desperation and sadness clung to the air. She held back tears.

She moved to the tree, examining the fruit. She lightly touched the same fruit she had on that day that felt so long ago. It was soft, with a fuzzy outer skin, juicy, and inviting. She craved to bite the flesh, to take the sweet pith, and inhale the tangy aroma deep into her nostrils. To investigate what made this fruit different, what made it thrum with life itself.

She let out a deep breath, reluctantly letting go of the fruit. As she was preparing to return to camp for another night of brutality, her ears pricked.

"Hello," she heard, a mere whisper, spoken slowly and deliberately as if with effort. She jerked to the trunk of the tree, flattening herself against it. Her head spun wildly, trying to locate the threat.

It wasn't Adam, it didn't sound like God, was there someone else here? She unfolded from the trunk slowly and ran her hand along the lowest dark limb.

"Eve," the voiced whispered again. She stared at the tree. Could it be?

"Is that you, tree?" Eve said out loud, too intrigued to feel stupid. A small cackle that may have been a laugh erupted just above her.

"No, look skyward," said the voice, with a pronounced lisp on the "s," Lucifer doing his best to get his strangled words past the forked, flipping snake tongue.

Eve raised her eyes, stepping back a pace.

A fleck hid among shining gold leaves, a bright green tail hanging down into forking branches at the heart of the tree.

Breathing heavily, Eve pushed back the ticket of golden leaves to find a snake of brilliant green nestled in the tree, head raised, tongue flicking in and out of its mouth. Its knowing golden eyes looked straight at her, penetrating deep into her soul.

Eve froze, fear rising within her. This snake was the most brilliant creature she had ever seen, of such vibrant green that a halo of light appeared around its coiled body.

Her fear subsided when she looked deep into the snake's eyes. Unable to look away, entranced.

"My name is Lucifer," hissed the snake. "I am here to help you."

LUCIFER STOOD AT THE PORTAL, eyes closed, arms out stretched, feet planted wide for balance, channeling his thoughts into the snake. In his head, he could see Eve through slitted eyes.

Lucifer had been determined to find another way. Using his enhanced skills to his benefit, he worked at thinking differently. With no clues as to why he couldn't get through, he tackled the problem from another perspective. God's voice carried through the portal, perhaps he could do the same.

He tried speaking into the portal. It was possible he could be heard, there was a correlation between his speaking and a start from the inhabitants. To beat God at his own game, he needed to communicate.

God had built a stunning garden for his perfect humans. Full of colorful creatures, the aesthetics of the place rivaled Heaven. God had always put importance on aesthetics. With so many creatures around, perhaps he could control them through the portal? Perhaps if he couldn't communicate directly, he could communicate through something. He experimented, letting his mind drift through the portal while his physical body remained in Hell, connected back to his soul only by the thin strand of the dimensional gateway. Manipulating a lesser creature should be easy, it was what God had done his whole life.

He tried and failed to inhabit the brains of many creatures in Eden. The snake was easiest, its cold blood allowing him greater control. The brain, when starved of sunlight, worked slowly, allowing Lucifer to overpower the natural and rudimentary thought processes. The snake's consciousness was responsible for nothing but breathing, pushed down to the base of the brain.

Lucifer saw Eve just as a snake would. Her form was blurry, but he picked up the aura her body emitted. He could see her fear just as clearly as he saw her bruised face.

Eve had healed somewhat, her broken nose forever disfigured, sporting a smattering of shaded bruises. She was staring, mesmerized by a talking animal. Lucifer had better explain, or she would stand there until the end of the world.

"My name is Lucifer," he repeated. "I know God, and I have seen what Adam has done to you. I want to help you." Lucifer's words did nothing to stop her staring. Finally, a wave of suspicion replaced her stare, doing nothing to appease Lucifer's tight stomach.

"You know God?" she asked. "How? From when? I've never seen you here."

Lucifer took in a deep breath, ready to explain as best he could in a way she would understand.

"God is not from here, he created you and this place. God is from a place that looks like this but is more beautiful, a place where he holds great power. I was also from that place."

Eve was nodding. "God said he was from a different place that was many times better than here. He said one day, we would get to go there. Are there more people there?"

"No," said Lucifer. "Not during my time there. I am not there anymore." His explanation, uttered out loud, caused a greater tightness in his chest, a stone settling in his throat.

"Why?" said Eve abruptly, not thinking of anything past her own curiosity. Lucifer, taken aback by her bluntness, took a moment to respond.

Honesty was best.

"I lived in that place with God. He was called Alpha then. There were five of us. He killed one of us and made two more into mindless servants. Then, when I gained the courage to stand up to him, he banished me to a place that is worse than anything in your world. I am there now, stuck for eternity to suffer at the hands of a self-proclaimed God."

Eve looked horrified. Lucifer continued, his powers of persuasion all he had to convince her.

"God killed the man I loved, used his soul to increase his own strength, and then banished me to Hell, where I exist on nothing but weeds and water. It is cold and wet, and I am alone."

"Cold?" said Eve. Lucifer rolled his eyes behind his closed lids. Out of everything he said, she cared about the fact it was cold in Hell. Perhaps she was more superficial than he thought.

"Are you a man?" Eve asked. "Like Adam?"

"In a way," said Lucifer. It was strange making this categorization of himself. "Not quite like Adam. I am like God. God made Adam in his image, but they are not the same in every way. But both God and I are *more* like Adam than we are like you." Eve was nodding, her brain showing outward signs of comprehension. "Encouraging," Lucifer thought.

"God said that about Adam being in his image and all that. He said he created us, too," she paused, brow furrowed, thinking. "If you are a man, how can you be in love with a man? I don't understand how that works." Eve said this with so much sincerity, it almost made Lucifer laugh before his anger and frustration took hold. She may be the smartest person on Earth, but there was still a significant gap between God's "perfect" creations and his own mental agility.

"I really thought you would be more interested in the fact that God is bad and has a bad plan for you and that I am willing to help you get away from Adam," Lucifer snapped.

Eve's eyes widened, too curious to be angry. "What do you mean, God is bad? He says he made us and loves us. He says we are perfect, that is why we have the perfect garden to live in and why he will take us back to his place when we have proven that we are good enough."

Lucifer sighed. Absolute indoctrination from the foundation of living memory is hard to break.

"Eve," Lucifer said. "God does want to bring you back to his place, but he only wants your soul to fill a space in Heaven as a servant."

"Yes," she said, smiling. "Yes, that's right. We are to serve him; that is why he created us. We have to believe in him so that we can join him."

Lucifer shook his head. "The service is bad, Eve, he is using you for his own gain. Just like Adam uses you to get what he wants." This time it hit the mark. Her face dropped, and she gripped both elbows, arms folded across her middle. "Is that what you want to happen to you for an eternity, Eve?"

She shook her head. Lucifer could see she understood the similarities between Adam and God.

"How do I know to trust you? How do I know you are telling the truth?" she said, eyes pleading.

"You don't," answered Lucifer immediately. "But you will have to."

LUCIFER AND EVE talked for as long as he could keep up the energy to possess the snake through the portal. He told Eve his story, her told her of Raphael, Gabriel, and Michael. He told her of Alpha's tempers, mood swings, and proclivity for wide-scale destruction. The more he told her, the more she believed him. She would sit cross-legged in front of the tree, listening and asking questions for as long as she could before Adam would come looking for her. Lucifer used the name God with Eve, it was what she knew. He used it so much even he began to think of Alpha as God.

"Do you know anything about this tree?" Lucifer asked.

"God told us that we had to stay away from it. I have always wanted to eat the fruit, it looks tasty, and I like the little buzz it gives off in your hand," Eve said.

"Interesting," thought Lucifer. "She can feel something."

Eve continued. "But Adam said God told him if we ate it, we would die. And I know he meant it. Adam said that is the only time God raised a hand to him. It was important."

"Did God say why you would die?" asked Lucifer, probing further.

Eve shook her head and shrugged. "I'm not about to test it."

Every human wants to protect their own life, no matter how pointless that life is. She wouldn't understand that. The minds of these humans were too small to think beyond themselves.

"It won't kill you," Lucifer said with kindness, laced with as much authority as he could.

Eve leaned forward, eyes wide.

"It won't?" she said, a little breathlessly.

"No, this is God's way to test and control you. He brought this tree from Heaven. It is a magic tree. If you eat the fruit, it will do nothing to harm you, only help you. There is no plant in Heaven that will kill anything, so I know this one is safe for you to eat." Lucifer paused. He didn't know, but his assumption seemed reasonable. The benefit of providing Eve with greater insight greatly outweighed the risk of killing her. Lucifer hoped that upon ingesting the flesh, Eve's abilities would grow, and she would understand her world with greater clarity.

"God isn't here, he can't control you," Lucifer said. "Take a bite. It will bring you power over Eden, and over Adam."

Eve shuddered. She took a deep breath, rose to her feet, and in one swift movement, strode to the tree, picked the low-hanging fruit, and without hesitation, took a bite.

Pounding. Eve shut her eyes against the piercing light of Eden, willing her head to stop throbbing. Everything was sharp, dormant parts of her mind forming thoughts that came together in a rush of understanding. The truth of Lucifer's story hit her. It was logical and sensible. Everything fit into place, her swollen brain believing it as truth. She had once believed God's version of the truth. But there was so much hidden from her, so much unexplained she could not take his side. Lucifer was the one who would save her, who would take her away.

"Wow." She shook her head, a lifetime of fog burning from her brain. She drank in her surroundings, seeing everything from a new angle and with a new light. She brought her hands up to her face and inspected herself. She understood her makeup, why God had created her in such a way. Looking down the length of her body, her head snapped up to meet the snake's gaze.

"I need to hide," said Eve.

"What do you mean?" said Lucifer.

"I don't want Adam to see me. I think it will be better if I cover myself up. Perhaps it might stop him from wanting me all the time."

Lucifer laughed. "You really think so? I don't know anything will stop that."

Eve's eyes narrowed. "I think he is a simple brute who only sees what is right in front of his nose. If I take away my body, he has one less control over me."

"Interesting," said Lucifer. "You can make something to wear from the tree leaves." Eve nodded and scampered off into the brush.

EVE RETURNED, somewhat covered. It made no difference to Lucifer. Clothed or not, she was still the same.

"All right," she said, hands on hips. "What do we do about God and Adam then? I can probably kill Adam in his sleep, but I don't think I could get God. And I have no idea where he is and how to get there," she said with sincerity. Lucifer lost concentration, becoming disconnected from the snake. The shock of her homicidal thought jarred him. Lucifer blinked in the darkness of Hell, hoping that she had not stormed off with a club, ready to bash Adam's meaty head in the intervening minutes.

"No," Lucifer shouted as soon as he regained possession. "No, we can't do that."

Eve's shoulders slumped, her lips moving into a full pout. "I know what he did to me was horrible, he deserves to die for it."

"That may be so," said Lucifer, not in the mood to argue, "but if we are going to defeat God, we need Adam on our side. God is strong. We are going to need all the help we can get, and even then, it will take a long time to plan. We will only have one chance to get it right."

"Point taken," said Eve, her improved vocabulary, reasoning skills, and directness immediately obvious. "What are you proposing?"

Lucifer took a breath. She would not like it. "We need to give Adam the fruit."

"What? No! Absolutely not! That man is stupid, and I don't want to be around him ever again. If you said God is bad, then Adam is bad, too, and we can't risk giving him more power," Eve shouted, terse anger punctured with wavering fear.

"If we give him the fruit," Lucifer said, remaining calm, "he will get smarter, he'll have more knowledge. He should be able to see through God just as you do. And besides, smart and knowledgeable people should have more reasoning power to not beat up their companions." Lucifer skipped over the lie. "We need him to trick God. God loves him most of all, we both know you will never be favorite. He will never like a woman enough to make her favorite."

"True," said Eve, dejected. "But how are we going to do

it? He won't eat the fruit, and if he knows I have eaten it, he will be *very* mad."

Lucifer thought for a moment. "Wait until he is asleep, chew up the fruit, and then put it into his mouth. He should swallow without realizing."

Eve nodded, the plan set.

EVE STOOD OVER ADAM, glaring. She hated him, possibly more than before. She was shocked that there was room for so much hatred inside her body. The immediate pain of his physical beatings no longer present, she felt a much deeper and more solid wound deep inside her soul.

She inserted the piece of fruit into her mouth and chewed, sweet flesh rolling over her tongue. Small pops spread out all over her skin.

Eve looked down the length of Adam's body. She was in charge now. She could not only take charge of her own modesty, but she didn't have to look at him, either. Fashioning a covering, she hid him.

Kneeling beside Adam's sleeping form, she spat the mush into her cupped hand. He was on his back, mouth slightly open, snoring. One arm was strewn across his chest, the other placed protectively between his legs. Eve moved the mush close to Adam's mouth, wrenched down his chin, and threw the handful into his mouth, scampering a few steps back, out of his immediate vicinity.

Adam coughed and spluttered, twisting onto his hands and knees, red in the face. He didn't stop choking on the fruit.

Eve was hit by the immediate force of true temptation.

She hesitated, watching his skin turn ashen and his eyes bulge in his head. This could all be over.

Body and brain battling, she rolled her eyes and strode to his side, patting him firmly on the back. Adam let in a roaring breath.

"What was that?" he gasped. Before Eve could make something up, his eyes rolled back in his head, and he collapsed face-first on the ground. She knew she had succeeded.

ADAM SAT. He couldn't move his body, his brain taking every piece of energy. He couldn't believe Eve would do such a thing. She had forced him to defy God. God would not be pleased this time.

Adam understood now. Everything made sense. He had a new feeling, a pull deep within his body. Questions and doubts were fighting each other, a constant turn of truth. He craved more knowledge and desired the secrets of Eden and beyond. The guilt was rotting in his bones, the feelings scratching at his love for God. Thrust suddenly and deeply into this new world, he had no chance of reconciling with the old.

Adam's ability to reason had eaten away at his ability to speak. Forming words in his head with the utmost clarity but unable to move them through his mouth and into existence, he had everything and nothing to say.

Eve was still there, standing a short distance away. She hadn't moved, neither coming for his comfort nor running for her own. He tilted his head up, peering up through heavy lids. Her face was blank, masked, waiting to read him before she gave herself away.

He tried to play the game, failing. Eve's head snapped, her stance adjusted. Her muscles tensed, feet lightened on the ground, and a soft ripple of tightening flesh traveled across her body.

Adam felt it, his own skin prickling, exploding from the center of his body, rippling to his extremities. He was lightly on his feet before he realized what he had heard, a rustling in the trees.

It was gentle, its movement smooth, the sound barely audible. Adam met Eve's eyes, a moment of wordless communication leading to all past events being temporarily forgotten. They were bound like tree and vine over their sudden and immediate fear of God.

In a synchronized movement, they ran as fast and quietly as they could. Their sudden worldly knowledge told them to run. Entwined by common terror.

They made it to the tree, hands on their knees, silently catching their breath. Adam came back into himself, having surrendered to the animal within. He was washed over by a wholly unpleasant and unfamiliar feeling.

Eve's cold eyes locked on him, unrelenting deep-seated hatred shining through.

∽

"SNAKE!" hissed Eve. "Snake! Where are you?"

Adam gave her a quizzical look. Determined not to let the situation or company get the better of her, she waved a hand.

"A snake lives here, in this tree. He told me to eat the fruit. He is the one who told me God was not what he seemed and that I should take initiative for myself and make my own decisions. I did as he told me and ate the fruit. The snake will know what to do."

Adam closed his eyes and shook his head. "Wait, just a minute," he said, holding a hand up, pleading for patience to let his brain catch up with the speed of recent events. "You decided God wasn't to be trusted, all on the word of a *snake?*"

Eve nodded, her eyes wide.

Adam continued. "He told you make your own decisions, so you did what he told you to?"

Eve, taken aback by this frank assessment, opened her mouth to speak, closing it firmly when his point settled in her brain. This stupid man, who could do nothing but to think with his favorite appendage and take what he wanted when he wanted with no care for consequence, was right. She gave a small shrug. "Well, I wasn't like this then, was I?"

"Eve! What have you done? Snakes don't even talk!" Adam groaned, hands curling in his hair.

"Adam." They heard the name from above and turned on their heels toward the gentle hiss of the name. "Adam, welcome. I am here to help you. Now that you have the knowledge, I can help you be free of God. We can defeat him."

Adam was in a trance. There *was* a snake, it *was* talking, and it was the most brilliant green with the deepest eyes he had ever seen. At first, he nodded with an open mouth before his brain fired into action.

"Defeat?" he said, turning to Eve, meeting her eyes. "What do you mean, *defeat*?"

"Yes," said a voice, suddenly appearing beside them. "What do you mean, defeat? What are you doing here? And why on Earth are you wearing plants?" asked God.

Eve took a deep breath, squared her shoulders, and looked into God's eyes.

"Yes, defeat. We know what your real intentions are. These are not *plants*, they are modesty garments because no one should have to be exposed to the constant belittling and disgusting ogling of a man. Adam is here because he followed me, and I am here because I want the snake to help me. He will know what to do to let us be free of you and your supposed *love.*"

Eve's heartfelt monologue hung in the air, stagnating between them. God flicked his gaze to Adam, whose eyes had dropped to his feet.

God's head flew back, laughing. He slapped his hand on his knees, bending forward when breath became hard to draw. Eve stood her ground. Adam continued to stare.

God's laughter halted. His eyes narrowed. Voice dropping, he drew so close to Eve she could feel his breath on her face and hear the sharp edges of his teeth grind together.

"You have no idea what you have done," God snarled as he raised a chubby hand and clasped Eve's neck. He added the other hand to reinforce his grip.

"You will never defy me," he jeered into her face. "You are mine, you will love me, and you will like it."

Spots were forming before Eve's eyes, red patches overtaking her field of vision. She attempted to draw breath, her fingernails clawing at God's fingers, desperate for space.

Her eyes rolled, she saw a green flick. She tumbled, God's grip falling away.

LUCIFER CHARGED. Seizing the moment, he channeled all his strength to spring the snake's body from the tree, jaw wide, aiming to land a bite square on the pulse on God's neck, throbbing so violently, it was visible behind his bushy beard.

God was fast and batted at the snake's body. The fang scraped down his neck, inflicting no real damage.

As the snake's body hit the ground, Lucifer felt a burst of pain ripple through him. His vision blurred as he lost his connection through the portal. He couldn't give up, he had to get back through. Ignoring the pain that seared through his veins and covered him down to the tips of his hair, he reconnected with the portal.

Disorientated, he felt weightless. He looked around furiously, trying to get his bearings, tapping into his available serpentine senses. He saw the ripples of heat, tasting the fear in the air. Lucifer came face-to-face with the pair of dark eyes he knew to the depths of their black soul.

"Lucifer," God growled. He heard the rumble loud in his ears. God was holding the snake up to his face.

"I see you. I see your eyes. I cannot believe you would do such a thing! Turn my own creations against me! You will never see! You will never leave me alone!" he shouted in a strangled, choked cry.

"I will save them," was all Lucifer got out before he was hurled against the tree. He lost all connection with those he wished to save from the wrath of God.

24

ORIGINAL SIN

"Tell me the meaning of this." God waved his hand over Eve's covered genitals and breasts, his eyes narrowed to slits, harboring an inky blackness.

Eve opened her mouth. But before words would form in her throat, Adam blurted.

"It was her," he said, turning, raising his finger, menacing blame. "She made me do it. She made me eat it, and then I felt exposed, shameful. Please, God, please forgive me. She tricked me, she made me do it. I would never have defied you." Adam had bent to his knees in front of God. All Eve could do was stand, open-mouthed. She was not shocked, Adam had forsaken her, all hopes he would change with the fruit dashed.

Adam crouched, grasping at God's ankles. He rocked back and forth with "I'm sorry" rhythmically escaping his lips in nothing more than a whisper.

God stood for a while, his expression blank, taking in Adam's worshipful remorse, before rolling his eyes, grabbing Adam by his chestnut hair, and pushing him away. Adam fell, sobbing in the moss, clutching his knees.

God snapped his head to Eve, eyes narrowing, intensifying the storm that lay between his narrow eyelids. He took one long step and reached her, his small hand wrapping around her throat, and as he pushed her to the tree, his strength amplified, fueled by anger.

Violently, he brought his flat palm up to her cheek and pushed her head to the side, her ear flush with the black bark. Eyes adjusting, she saw the limp and lifeless body of the snake, pinioned to the tree by God's force. God was telling her, without words, that she would soon suffer a similar fate.

"He tricked me," she blurted. God wrenched her head back, so she was staring right into his face. She felt his stale breath on her, his eyes sucking her into hopelessness. Desperation to protect herself was the only way to claw herself out.

"He told me that he would help me, that he would stop Adam from touching me again, and I believed him. Now I know this is not true." Eve finished her plea in a whisper.

God slammed her head violently against the tree before letting go. Eve slumped to the ground.

"You defied me. You deliberately went against me. This is why I needed to test you, to assure your loyalty. I made you, and look how you repaid me. You deserve what Adam did to you. You have always been defiant, you have always been a problem," God yelled, body jittering with rage. Eve could hear him, but the words were muffled as if she were underwater and he was yelling at her from the surface. He bent over her, talking through gritted teeth. He waved flat palms over her body before stopping on her lower abdomen.

"To punish you and all like you for eternity, I will make your reproduction painful and dangerous. I always knew you were inferior to my perfect specimen, but I needed you, and I still do. And because I need you, I will punish you and all your kind. You will listen to Adam in all things, you will never defy him or any other male again. They are above your station. You are only here to provide children to ensure my race of perfect humans continues, so I can have the Heaven I truly desire, filled with souls to serve me."

Eve lay motionless, flicking a brief glance to Adam, who was sitting on his haunches, cowering from God, the remnants of sobs still racking his body.

"And you," God turned to Adam, "you should have known better." Adam only sniffled and nodded, offering nothing further.

Eve was regaining her wits, her brain working again. She had forgotten how easily things came to her. Eve had nothing to lose, she had nothing to begin with. Her very existence, according to God, was useless. She took a stand.

"No," she said quietly.

God swished back to her in a fluid movement of stubby limbs, his long hair whipping.

"What did you say?" said God, having heard her perfectly well.

"No," she said again louder, swallowing deeply. "He shouldn't have known better. He is a stupid, violent brute who only cares about his own sick personal pleasures. He doesn't care how much he hurts people, he wants power, to please, and be pleased."

God's eye twitched. He remained still, brimming with anger. Eve awaited the eruption of hate.

Eventually it came, but even she did not anticipate God's actions. God was even more volatile than she thought, and she knew that Lucifer had been right. He was dead. She had betrayed him to save her own life. All that remained of the one who would be her savior was hanging lifeless from the trunk of the tree, reminding her of what he had sacrificed and what could have been.

God crouched down and whispered into her ear, "I created you. I decide your purpose. Insolence is unacceptable. You will be punished."

Eve awaited the blow. She had been punished before and expected hard and fast physical torture. She felt her body rise high above the ground, stiff, limbs flopping down by her sides. Adam floated by her side, a fear shining from his eyes that was born of naivety to God's true character.

Eve saw Eden disappear. God stood in the center, arms raised, moving them farther and farther away.

GOD STOOD BY THE TREE. He was perfectly still, fingernails digging into his palms. His perfect creations turned against him, led astray by Lucifer. God should have killed him. If God had not convinced himself that banishment was worse punishment for Lucifer, that he could feel pain and suffering every single day, none of this would have happened.

But death was too easy. The same could be said for Adam and Eve.

If he was to forgive them and bring them to Heaven, they would have to pay for entrance with the same hard life of those inferior humans who still walked the Earth.

He had dumped them some distance away in the desert. Inspired by his banishment of Lucifer, he had chosen an inhospitable environment in the hope they might harden up and truly understand their actions. He was not to be questioned.

God grunted. "It worked for Lucifer." Lucifer would never have outright attacked God in Heaven, fear of power constraining his hand.

A shockwave went through God's body. What if Lucifer had developed additional powers? God knew he was the special one, so he didn't think Lucifer would be powerful like him, but doubt crept into the dark crevices of his mind.

Lucifer had shown his cunning possessing the body of the snake. God could see how a snake worked well, cold blood with a brain structure that was easy to compartmentalize. God needed to do something to stop future meddling. He still did not want to kill Lucifer; he was too wedded to Lucifer's personalized punishment of eternal damnation, grief, and torture.

God stared at the limp form of the snake, stuck to the tree with invisible nails. He had a brilliant solution. If the snake was the easiest creature to possess, he would make sure the humans ran from it by instinct.

"Easy." He nodded to himself with satisfaction. "I will just make sure a snake kills one of Eve's children. She will never be sure if it was him or not."

"And I will make sure you never get through here again," God said, addressing the lifeless snake.

God rose above the ground, leaving Eden far below. Forming a fireball in his hand, he dropped it squarely on the tree. He burned his utopia to the ground as though it were nothing.

Adam and Eve would never see Eden again, but this was punishment enough. God had not finished, he could still not let them die. They will soon see others. If Eve thought Adam was rough, she should wait until she encountered the tribe. They were something she would never have conjured in her wildest dreams.

LUCIFER BLINKED. Hell, dark, portal closed. He opened and closed the fists that had formed by his sides. The mud squelched between his fingers. He had failed again. He moved to get up but couldn't. The only movement he could muster was squelching his fingers and lifting his head. The rest of his body defying his demands, he lay there in the filth of Hell.

It was where he belonged. He had failed the humans. They were now at the mercy of God.

25

SONS

The atrocity of childbirth.

Each time Eve made it to this point in pregnancy, her heart sank, prickles of sweat breaking out all over her body. The instinct to run away hit her hard. But she could not. She had to face it, there was no backing out now.

It started with a small quiver, a tensing that waved over her belly, its vicious fingers curling around her, digging into her lower back, clawing at the skin, trying to rip her spine from her body.

She had done this enough, she learned from experience and mistakes. She took herself away from the hut, squatting against a scarce tree in the barren lands they now called home. Staring across the flat plain of scrub and dirt, she focused on the mountains rising in the distance, peaks topped in white, catching the sun.

Taking herself away from her body, her mind elsewhere, she remembered the beauty of Eden. She tried to remember happy times in her life. There were none.

She pushed. The pressure within her body released. A thud in the dirt.

This one was a boy. "Would he live?" Eve wondered. All other children died at birth or shortly after, her milk supply lacking. The shriveled skeleton children dying in the night.

Discarded by God, Adam and Eve had learned to fend for themselves as best they could. There was not much food. Adam went on long walks to forage what he could from sparse plants, digging roots from the ground. They pulverized them into a gritty mush. With little to sustain her own body, Eve failed to sustain the bodies of her offspring.

One of her children, a girl, had lived a short while, long enough to look her mother in the face, showing a smile of recognition. Eve had called her Evette, the only creativity she could show in a name, taking her own for inspiration.

But Eve woke to a cold body lying close on her straw mat. Evette's little leg was swollen to twice its size, dancing with a vibrant mix of purples, reds, and yellows. It reminded Eve of the sun setting over Eden. Visible at the child's upper leg were two puncture marks, sharp stabs deep in the roll of flesh that protected the baby from the cold.

Eve knew what this was. A serpent bite. What she would never know was why. Was this an accident, or was it her punishment from God? Or from Lucifer? She had forsaken them both.

She held the latest baby in her arms. He was large and strong. His birth had been an easy one, her muscles stretched from multiple siblings before him. She cradled him. The cord connected him to her, pulsating. The baby took its first worldly breath.

"You are the one," she whispered. "You are the one who will live."

"PAPA," Abel said, crouching at Adam's feet, eagerly watching him skin a deer. The knife he used was the only thing God gave him for life in the desert, a Heavenly object that Adam treated as a true relic of God. Hunting luck was rare. The beast's appearance was a blessing, topping up his dwindling pool of faith. "If God created us and loves us, why are things so hard?"

Adam sighed. Always with the questions.

"Your mother did something bad, we had to be punished. Just like when you hurt your brother, I punish you."

Abel nodded and looked over to Cain, who sat in brooding silence.

"But," Adam continued, anticipating the next question, "if we prove to God that we are resilient and continue to live well in his name, he will still take us up to Heaven. We have to prove we are worthy of him." The deep hole that had grown in his chest the day he was cast out of Eden had never been filled. Speaking to his son about God rose the black pit to the surface. "Heaven is a beautiful place where we will want for nothing, but we must earn the right to enjoy it. But look, Abel." Adam sought to change the subject. "God is looking after us, he sent us this deer. And tonight we will eat fresh meat."

His attempt to sideline the conversation failed.

"How do you know what Heaven is like, Papa?" Abel questioned, the look of a disbeliever in his eye far too pronounced for one so young.

Adam and Eve waged an endless battle over God. It seemed to Adam that no matter how much he told her the truth, she would not believe it. She insisted on confusing their sons with stories of God's harsh treatment, leaving Adam to continually counter with the truth. That she deserved it.

"Because God told me," he said, standing swiftly. "Come on, both of you. Let's cook up our feast."

~

FORCED into reality with insufficient food, shelter, and skill, Adam and Eve never heard from God or Lucifer.

As the boys grew, Eve would spend long hours grinding grain to make bread, the rhythmic pulse lulling her brain into a place outside this world. Her thoughts often returned to her last days in Eden. Having lost her chance at salvation, she would never truly know who was right. Should she have followed God or Lucifer? Constant doubt filled her mind.

Time drifted. Each day, the same routine of chores was required to stay alive. Time ravaged the two perfect humans. The torture of pregnancy marked Eve's body. Adam's once taught body was sagged and flabby, a ring of fat was ever present around his middle, despite the scarcity of food.

Adam and Eve had no choice. To survive in the harsh wilderness, they needed strength, they had to stick together. Living with two surviving sons in a hut perched at the base of the rocky mountain, overlooking a vast desolate plain dotted with shrubbery, they survived. Eve always turned to the mountains in the distance, dreaming of more, knowing it would never come.

The children became Eve's focus, how to raise them and what to tell them. She had never done this before and had no one to learn from. But, the one thing that made the deepest impression on the boys, was Adam and Eve's simmering hatred for each other.

CAIN TOWERED OVER HIS MOTHER. Whenever he saw her, he always looked down.

He watched her grind the flour. She was always grinding flour. The crunching sound of the stone, the dust that spat off his mother's hands, dancing in the dank air, put him on edge. His hands balled to fists, anger rising.

He strode, snatching the smaller stone from Eve's hand, throwing it heavily across the room, where it added to the existing dents in the wall of the hut.

"Stop that," he growled.

"If you don't like it, Cain, don't come in here," said Eve, eyes focused on the ground, unmoving.

Cain stood beside his mother, breathing heavily. The grinding bothered him, anything would set him off. He rested his hand on his mother's head, smoothing over her straggly hair, which he then grabbed violently at the back of her neck, yanking so her face turned up to his.

"I do what I want, Mother," he snarled through gritted teeth, eyes roaming down her body.

Eve held his gaze "Not quite," she spat. "Remember, God is watching."

Cain grinned, dropping her hair. She always used God against him. Cain believed with all his heart he was meant for more than a hard life in the desert of scrub. God would come to save him and take him to Heaven.

"I will be able to do completely as I please, one day soon," he said through his grin, lumbering toward the door, rising to full height outside. He looked back through the door; Eve returned to her task. He bristled, every muscle on his bulky arms tensing. She would get what she deserved.

∽

ABEL PERCHED ON A ROCK. His toes dug in the dirt, elbows balanced on his knees to support his chin, cradled in his hands. Still. Growing from the dirt near his feet was a singular flower. Its long green stem ended in a puff of white spores, a perfectly formed circle. Perched lightly on this flower was a creature of such magnificence that Abel's breath escaped him. The long, thin body supported pointed wings of various browns. Its tiny arms busily worked on the spores.

He felt a tickle in his nose. Panic rushed through him, trying to suppress the sneeze. Failure struck, and the creature flew away. There were no other flowers.

As the younger brother, Abel had been at the whim of Cain's anger his whole life, feeling the physical effects of his muscular frame. Abel removed himself as much as possible.

Abel understood life in their small family. Cain had the muscles and the looks. He was "God's perfect human," according to their father. Abel was on the edge of the family, deafness in one ear making communication difficult. Cain flew into a rage when Abel failed to hear a comment.

But Abel saw Cain for what he was, a man of broken mind. What made Abel so astute was that he also possessed the skill of seeing himself for what he was. A man of broken body. Along with his deafness, Abel possessed a profoundly protruding lower jaw that made it difficult to eat. The rest of his body remained skin and bone, weak.

Abel had one thing to save him. God.

Neither Abel nor Cain had ever met God. They heard stories from their father, placing him on a reverent pedestal.

Abel had been schooled on the events that led to their current circumstance, particularly his mother's transgressions. Their father treated her poorly, which was acceptable if she had gotten them thrown out of their home and made the great creator turn his back on them.

Cain believed what his father told him; God was still out there, and once they did their time of suffering, they would be let back into Eden and eventually taken to Heaven. Cain, devoted to the idea this life was never meant for him, would speak to God, explaining how he was helping the family return to his good graces. This mostly included beating his mother to remind her of the mistake she made, flouting God's rules.

Abel questioned. He questioned his father, who clipped him over the ear for any question that may dig into the truth about God.

He would ask the same questions of his mother. Her answers were more coherent but equally reticent.

ABEL LOOKED across the valley from his vantage point on the hill. He could see his flock grazing on the mountainside, finding pockets of grass between the rocks. Abel had found this place on one of his secret expeditions away from home, its discovery dragging his family from near starvation. It was the greenest he had ever seen. Determined to find Eden, he would walk in a different direction every day as far as he could until he had to turn back. On one of these days, he found a sheep. He stood there, still, looking it in the eye. It eyed him right back, its continuously moving mouth silent, glassy eyes staring right into his soul, a battle of the wills. Abel lunged, grabbing the sheep around the neck, shifting his body on top of it. The sheep bucked, his weight was too much. He wrestled the sheep to a grassy patch. It munched, distracted by its stomach. He fashioned a rough rope from flax and led it back to camp. The sheep caused great interest among his family. Cain and Adam immediately wished to kill and eat the animal. Eve tactfully pointed out that there was movement from within the sheep and that she would soon give birth, at which point there would be milk to drink, and if they were lucky and she birthed a male ewe, they could breed to make a flock.

A shiver ran through Abel. This was the first time he had realized his similarity to that of an animal. A strange desire surfaced in a manner he did not expect. He ran away before anyone would notice. He had seen his mother and father copulate many times, sometimes willingly, sometimes not. They knew he watched, Eve would lock eyes with Abel in a pleading stare before shutting hers and traveling to another place. No babies had resulted from his parents' fornication since him.

Abel smiled down at his flock. He had bred and managed the sheep for many years, now allowing the family to have a healthy supply of meat and milk. They had wool to make warm garments and skins to enhance their huts. Abel's ability to figure out uses for things kept him in good favor, a place he needed to remain.

Abel trotted down the mountainside. He was adept at negotiating the large rocks and steep inclines with specifically fashioned cloth to pad his knees and elbows, a long stick held in his hand for balance.

Halfway down the mountain, he saw smoke rising from the gap in the roof of the large central hut. His mother was cooking, it must have been later than he thought. He struggled to tell the time of day, clouds obstructed his view of the sun.

In answer to the silent curse he placed on the weather,

drops of rain spattered the ground. He sighed, picked up his pace, and wished he had brought his wool garment to repel the rain.

Abel hovered at the small arched opening of the hut. His mother squatted at the central fire, cooking yams and the remnants of mutton from their harvested sheep. His father was not there, having left the day before to forage for fruits. He said he might be days.

Abel stayed away for two nights with the sheep, leaving his mother and Cain alone. A frown came over Abel's face, and a spark of jealously leapt from his heart to mouth.

Cain crouched behind his mother, his eyes running up and down her skin, evaluating. The smooth olive skin of her arms and her matted hair were visible outside of the large hide she wore for warmth. Cain's hand moved to the back of his mother's neck, moving her hair aside, exposing her skin. Abel held his breath. Eve swatted Cain's hand away without looking up. She was still uninterested in him. Abel let out his breath and cleared his throat, walking into the room.

"Where is Father?" he asked, giving Eve a fright, receiving a stare that chastised him for his stealthy entrance, followed by a look of guilt as she realized Cain was still crouching right behind her.

"He hasn't come back," she said, turning back to her cooking. "He said he might be a while." Abel nodded, not caring enough to question why it took so long to collect berries. He had gone on many long foraging trips, always returning with a good bounty to enhance their pantry.

But the major advantage of his father's absence was that his mother was alone. His father had not forced himself on her for quite some time. Abel felt that Eve was better for it. She had to deal with Cain, but she was strong, he would not get the better of her.

"Dinner is almost ready. Get ready to eat, both of you."

They ate in silence with occasional punctuations by Cain gloating about the new field of corn he had sown and what a wonderful crop it would be. Abel remained quiet, knowing his contribution to the family was much more important, but he didn't feel the need to gloat.

"How were your sheep, Abel? Did they show you love today?" Cain asked with a snicker.

Abel remained stone-faced, a well-practiced maneuver. He could not let Cain get to him.

"When should we kill the next sheep, Mother? Are we running out of meat yet?" said Abel, never taking his eyes from Cain, whose mouth only twitched at the jab. Abel knew his crops were doing poorly. All they had for the table were a few blighted pieces of corn every day.

"In a few days perhaps, Abel," said Eve, distracted.

"We will need to wait for Father to get back. He needs to kill the beast. He is the only one who God has blessed to take the lives of animals," Cain said.

Abel rolled his eyes, letting out a small grunt. Cain scowled.

"He is the only one!" Cain said between gritted teeth. "I will not go against God, he is the only way I am going to get out of this miserable hole. I want back into Eden, and doing as God wants is the only way I am going to get there." Cain was gesticulating wildly, ending his rant by slamming a fist on the ground.

Abel allowed himself an inward smile. That probably hurt.

He was sick of the talk. Doing the right thing in the eyes of God while being aggressive and violent was the worst.

"That is just something Father made up so he gets to kill everything! God is not here, God has gone! I get that he made us, but he also abandoned us. There will be no salvation for you. This is your life. Nothing will change unless you change it."

Cain flung himself at Abel, pushing him to the ground. The two men wrestled, Abel subdued.

"Stop it," Eve said. Neither heard her. "Stop!" she shrieked. The men disentangled themselves and sat upright, both in shock at the vehemence that exited their mother's mouth.

"This is why neither of you are fit to be with me. You are both little boys who are weak and pathetic. No matter how much you beg," she said, looking straight at Abel, "or sneak," she added, shifting her gaze to Cain, "neither of you will have the pleasure of bedding me until you show you are men. I know this is what you want, what you have been fighting over. Do you think I am stupid and don't know how you look at me?"

This is the moment they had been waiting for; they had a chance to bed Eve for their pleasure. It was a competition, each set against the other to prove themselves as worthy of their mother's attentions.

Cain turned to Abel. "I want to prove God to you, I want to get him down here. I will offer my crops and give it all to God to prove how much I love him, and he will come down. My faith in God will prove to Mother I am strong enough." Cain's eyes traveled down Eve's body.

Abel sighed and shrugged his shoulders. "Well then, I'll kill a lamb. From what I have heard of God, he will much prefer that than a bunch of blighted stinking corn."

Cain stared angrily. "Deal," he said through tight lips.

26

OFFERINGS

G od sat on his throne.

It was a piece of art. He designed the shimmering substance to catch the light. It let him shine at the true center of Heaven.

He sat directly in front of the space where the portal to Earth should have been. He drummed his fingers on the cool arm of the throne, the metal tinkling below his long nails. He had closed the portal; it was too painful to look down on Earth. He fought himself, pain and boredom wrestling for supremacy. He was done with Heaven, he needed to reopen the portal for something to do.

Camp had moved from the beach to the portal plain. Surrounding trees cleared to make room for his pattern of shining buildings, ready to be filled. God utilized Gabriel and Michael for the heavy lifting, stepping in when they couldn't get it right. God sat in the center with the portal, the remaining buildings arranged around his central buildings in ever-increasing concentric circles, each ring accessible by paths radiating from God's regal dais.

God was alone. His current slaves were not enough. He

needed a servant who would also offer him some mental stimulation. Adam was his perfect choice. Adam loved him, always would. God had told him of his plan for a life in Heaven from the day of Adam's first memory. It was part of his soul, he could never shake it. Adam would have to prove he learned from his mistake.

Toe tapping, fingers twitching, God opened the portal.

GOD LIKED THE BROTHERS. The simultaneous love and hate they felt for each other, similar yet competitive in every way.

He felt an unfamiliar pang in his chest. He missed Lucifer, the competition and comradery. God shook the thought out of his head, he had long ago destroyed any chance with Lucifer; killing and eating his lover and banishing him to a place of nightmares were not likely forgiven.

"Anyway," God said to himself. "Doesn't matter. I'll get someone else."

God pulled out of his reverie, stretching, readying to retrieve food from the large pile at the foot of his throne.

A flicker from the portal. A ferocious orange inferno. Flames engulfed Cain's cornfield. God stared, how did this happen? No fire nearby, no lightning (not lightning he had sent, anyway). Cain stood by the edge of the blaze, arms held high into the sky, yelling something into the air. God tuned in to Cain's words.

"Hear me, God, I make this offering to you. This proves how I love you and that I would burn all my crops. I am worthy of your greatness. Come down to us from your mighty place in Heaven. I beg you."

"Huh," said God, delighted at Cain's apparent devotion.

He had never spoken to him personally. An interesting trait in his creations shone through this action: gullibility. They would believe what they were told from a person in authority, taking that experience on as their own. His creation of faith and belief had worked. He would soon have a never-ending supply of souls for Heaven.

God searched for Abel. Much more like his mother, independent and smart, he was not God's favorite. He thought for himself and asked too many questions.

God scoffed. Even now, his failure to calculate the level of Eve's brain function plagued him. "I should have made her more stupid," he said, shaking his head.

God manipulated the portal with deft fingers, finding Abel on the mountainside where he grazed his sheep, a testament to his ability to make the most of a situation.

"Shame," said God, tutting. "Your brain would make an excellent slave. It is a shame you won't accept me. Shame for you. I will just have to make you."

Abel stood astride a beast. God gasped as he zoomed in on the creature.

There was a knife to its throat, the killing knife. It was the only thing God had left with Adam when he thrust him out of Eden. Abel was outwardly thwarting God's law, as he had been told it by Adam. Abel was disobeying his father and his God. Adam had made up the rule about the knife to increase his own importance. But Abel was going against what he had been told. Thinking for himself.

God watched Abel pull the blade across the animal's throbbing neck, warm red blood washing over his arms, dripping down to his feet. Life drained from the beast. God's whole body quivered, the rush he felt at the ultimate end of life returning to his body as strongly as if he were doing the killing himself. But there was something else, a new thrill. One of his creations was killing for him. Not for nourishment, not for his own amusement, but for him. God felt the power surge in his chest, success and power mingling in an unstoppable haze.

Abel spoke. "I am doing this to show Cain that he is wrong. He is wrong about crops, and he is wrong about you. You do not care about us, but nor do you care about a field of burned corn."

"The cheek of the boy," said God. "I will show him." God raised his hands to portal, and grabbing both Cain and Abel, he raised them from the ground and carried them back to their house. Eve was not there.

ABEL OPENED HIS EYES, he was looking at the sky. Gray clouds hovered overhead, the rest of the sky a perfect blue. He sat up, head throbbing. Cain was next to him, eyes closed, unmoving. Maybe he was dead. Abel had never seen a dead person but lots of dead sheep. Cain did not seem drained of life.

Looking farther around him, Abel saw the hut. He was home. The last he remembered, he had been sacrificing the sheep on the mountaintop.

"Abel," said a booming voice, coming from everywhere and nowhere.

Abel stared, mouth dropping open. He was frozen in place, not sure what he had heard, who it was, or whether he had heard it at all.

"Abel, you flout my law and disbelieve in me and my powers," said the voice. Abel quickly rose to his knees and bowed his head. "But you have given me a great sacrifice.

The sacrifice of a life is of great significance. You have done well, son."

Abel was far gone with shock, the throbbing in his head intensifying, heartbeat fast and shallow in his ears. He shook Cain, whose eyes eventually opened with a sheen of pain.

"Get up," Abel hissed.

"Huh?" said Cain.

"Get up," Abel continued to hiss. "It's God; it's God."

Cain snapped to life and scrambled to his knees, bending his head. "Mighty God, thank you for the gift of your presence."

"Quiet," said God's booming voice.

"What?" said Cain, disbelief rife in his voice. His head snapped to meet Abel's glance. Abel shrugged in response.

"Just be quiet. I have something to say to you." Cain bowed his head, waiting.

"You show great devotion, but you lack understanding of what I want. You thought I would be proud of a burned crop of corn. I do not care for crispy vegetables. You failed to show me respect by not taking a life, and for that I am angry with you."

"B-b-but," stuttered Cain. "I didn't want to flout your law of Father being the only one to kill animals, and I burned all my work for you."

"No law was flouted, it was made here on Earth and therefore unimportant. What is important to me is that you give me the gift of life through death."

Abel looked over to Cain, he clearly didn't understand. Abel understood perfectly. God was a bloodthirsty voyeur who liked suffering and death. Abel knew this from what his mother had said, it was why they were here. God was also volatile and changed his mind frequently. But Abel also knew that all God wanted, was to be known and loved.

"Abel has my blessing as the first son of this family, he is the provider for them and the closest to God."

Cain screamed, punched Abel in the side of the head, and ran off toward his smoldering fields.

Abel fell to the ground, spots forming before his eyes, and a small trickle of blood ran from his ear, mixing with the dirt on his skin.

Eve ran from behind the house, cradling Abel's head in her lap.

"There, my son, you are all right. You did well, you did well," Eve took Abel's hand, pressing it to her lips, ignoring the dried lamb's blood. Abel's dilated pupils stared into her face, expressionless, still as a tree with no wind.

Eve glared to the clouds in the sky but said nothing.

GOD CLAPPED his hands together and laughed. Job well done. He realized he forgot to eat. Slouched in his chair, he munched into the dried leg of a waterfowl.

27

THE LOST TRIBE

Adam trudged along the dusty path, his bronzed shoulders hunched. Each step was harder than the last.

His family was a constant reminder of what he had lost through no fault of his own. Their grating personalities added to his distaste for home.

Adam stopped and stared toward the mountains. A fine mist hung around the tree-covered face, the peak visible above a straight layer of cloud. It was bright up the mountain. Adam's heart thumped. Perhaps God was up there. Perhaps that is why it was so bright and beautiful up on that mountain peak.

Adam shook his head, scolding himself for his errant thoughts. Shoulders rehunched, he continued the trudge back to his modest compound. He had given up getting back into God's good graces, and almost given up on God altogether. But deep down, there was a genuine love sown into his heart, and it was as much a piece of him as the organ itself. But there was another feeling that clung to the back of this enduring love. Guilt. Like light and dark, where there was one, the other was not far away. He tried to move on. He should think of something else.

Adam allowed a small inward smile, which slowly broadened at the memory playing in his head. He chuckled. Startled by his own emotional response, he stopped, reminding himself he was going home and that he should always adopt the appropriate air. He could not afford to let his family suspect anything. They couldn't find out about the others.

ADAM HAD FOUND them one day while foraging. He had gone quite some way to find the wild yams Eve liked to cook. Cain had tried to grow them from cuttings in rows near the house, but the dust had taken them, nothing would grow.

Adam had been searching, stopping, hacking at the ground, wrenching the beastly yams from the deep until they sprang free. He chopped off the roots, brushed off the dirt, and added them to his sack.

Adam was hacking at a particularly stubborn yam. He stopped to wipe the mixture of sweat and dirt from his forehead. He sat back on his haunches, eyes closed. He heard a rustle.

Adam's eyes snapped open, darting back and forth across the scrubland. Nothing. He let out a slow breath and closed his eyes, he must be tired. Time to eat and rest. He only ever ate yams on these trips, catching or gathering any other food was impossible. There was no time, he was too old to successfully catch large animals. His speed and agility were leaving him as his hair grew long and skin wrinkled, patched with dark spots from years in the sun.

He stood to heave the sack, groaning loudly as he swung it over his shoulder.

This time a giggle, two giggles. Adam dropped the sack, grabbing for the knife hanging from the belt at his waist. He drew the knife, his legs spread wide, knees bent ready to strike. Still nothing.

Slowly, as if emerging from a thick fog, he saw them. Blurry at first, blending with their surroundings, two girls appeared from the vegetation. They were dark-skinned with large, gleaming eyes, hair down to their waists clumped together in large sections, covered with clay. They wore grass skirts that did nothing to cover their slender, shiny bodies. The two girls stood together, one taller than other, her arm draped across the shorter one's shoulder. The other's hand sat lightly on the taller girl's hip. They cocked their heads in the same manner. The shorter girl said something in a strange tongue made up of a series of clicks.

Adam could do nothing but stand still, his mouth agape, fingers twitching slightly, other parts of his body following. He had not seen beauty like this in the world before, not even in Eden.

Adam stared. They were looking at him, assessing, as amazed as he was. They stared at his wrinkly body as he stared at the brush of curly hair visible beneath their skirts.

The silent assessment continued. The taller girl's nipples hardened. This was enough. Adam ripped off his tunic and pounced toward the girls. They shrieked in shock and delight, running. Darting through the scrub, playing the game. Adam was built to play this game. Excitement coursed through his body. He thought he might burst, crashing through the thickets, not caring for damage or noise. Using his old hunting skills, he found a line through the scrub to capture the shorter girl.

He was panting heavily, his libido overwhelming his old age. The girl turned to smile at him. He seized the moment. Taking advantage of his taller stature and superior gate, he pounced, grabbing her by the arm. She giggled, playfully writhing, acting innocent.

Adam felt in his bones that this would be different to his previous experience. The girl giving him all he desired and getting what she wanted in return without sharing a single word. They had come to a standstill under a small cluster of trees. Grinning at the fine specimen of humanity before him, he grabbed the girl by the waist, lifted her, pushing her back into the soft bark of the tree. Her legs rose instinctively, enveloping him around his waist. Pinioning her between his body and the tree, he entered with one quick thrust. He pumped her slowly, biting her neck, collarbone, and down to her shoulder with every movement. Her fingers clawed his back as their bodies warmed together. An entanglement of light and dark.

Adam had never felt this before, someone who wanted him. This girl was participating, she knew what she was doing. He was on the edge of ecstasy with every fine movement of her hips. Engrossed, he did not hear the taller girl approach. She slinked up behind him like snake through grass, giving him a firm slap on the behind.

He cried out, on the edge of climax.

He lost his balance. The girl steadied herself on his shoulders. Adam stopped, staring at the newcomer, excitement growing from reading her face.

The girl rested against the wide trunk of the tree. Her hand slowly moved to the shorter girl's face and traced a line from her cheek, moving along her collarbone before reaching her breast, cupping it with her full hand. Her other hand rested against Adam's chest. He felt an electricity run from her to the girl, they were a unit. The taller girl tweaked the shorter girl's nipple, and she gasped in pleasure. Smiling at this noise, still massaging the nipple of her friend, she moved her hand through the strands of her grass skirt, each touch answered by a moan.

Adam watched her, remaining still inside the shorter girl, entranced by the practices of these dark humans. He felt the touch of the tall girl through the body of the short one. He exited, lowering the girl to her feet. Both girls stood against the tree, both panting, both flushed. All for him.

He moved to the taller girl. She put a hand up to his chest, pushing him back slowly. He staggered backward, his eyes not breaking with hers. Hands now gripping his shoulders, he let himself be pushed to a rock, cold on his bare behind. The tall girl walked languidly back to the short girl, still resting against the tree. The taller girl touched the shorter girl, a trail of bumps left behind on her skin.

Teasing became too much. The shorter girl, who had been on the brink with Adam, violently grabbed the taller girl and kissed her hard, raising her leg around her waist, inviting, pleading.

Adam's world had shrunk. He was in a bubble of light. The only things on this Earth, were here. He watched in amazement as the taller girl obliged. They were moving together, moving as one. The shorter girl was lost in ecstasy. The taller girl's eyes locked on Adam. The shorter girl let out a high-pitched yelp. Her body shuddered, and her face relaxed. She leant back against the tree, panting.

Adam had never seen this before, he was awestruck. The taller girl had not taken her eyes from Adam. Knowing what he was meant to do, he stood and walked over. She grabbed his arms and licked her lower lip with a seductive, mischievous grin. Unable to take it any longer, he pushed her to the ground, holding her legs high. She wrestled; her legs were kicking, his entry thwarted. With a swift and practiced movement, she flipped Adam onto his back. She sat on top of him, expertly settling herself. The feeling was exquisite, he was deep inside her, the pressure of her body on his hips adding to the pleasure. Resting her hands on his chest, she moved. The world swam in front of Adam's eyes.

The shorter girl came to kneel between them, stroking both of their bodies. Adam was struggling to maintain himself, bombarded by sensation. The heat of bodies, the feelings of skin, two beautiful girls. He let go, letting the girl continue to ride him until she shivered and groaned. They fell in a heap on the ground. Cradled between the two girls, Adam fell into the deepest sleep since Eden.

When Adam awoke, the two girls looked down at him, bright teeth shining through soft brown lips. Adam smiled back. They looked to each other, conversing in their strange tongue. Adam lay there, watching, listening. This is what it sounded like to grow away from God, free of his rules and issues. Their language fluid and carefree as their actions. After a few more words of clicking and tutting, they seemed to reach a decision. They each held a hand to Adam, who took them to hoist himself up, his old bones groaning at the strain of the encounter. The girls led him through the brush. They soon reached a wide dirt path. Adam did not recognize it. He hadn't come this far before, and tried hard to get his bearings.

Adam followed the two stunning creatures. He said nothing, trusting them. The sun dipped on the horizon. They came over a rise, and he saw a bustling town of stick huts, fires, and busy people, all clad in the same grass skirts. Each one as beautifully dark as the next.

The girls led him through the outer huts to the center of

camp. As people saw him, they stopped, their mouths agape at the olive-skinned human walking among them. Some of them bowed their heads, some of them stared, and some of them gave him a look of desire that made his spine shiver.

ADAM RECOUNTED and relived his memories of the girls and the town, a place where he could do as he pleased and have whomever he wanted, and although not faithful to his two original findings, he went back to them more often than not. The only thing he had left when he clawed himself away to go home, to his wife and sons, was the thought that he would soon be back in the embraces he truly desired.

Adam's thoughts drifted. God had never told him of these people. God had told him he was the only one, he was special, and God had made him in his image to serve him in Heaven. Adam's emotions ran wild, he felt guilt about doing things that God would not approve of, copulating with others, those that weren't God's perfection, like him and Eve. The guilt merged into anger; he had been abandoned.

28

GOD'S CHOSEN

Cain burst into his burned field. Black, hot. The acrid smell of char reached into his nostrils.

The whole crop was gone. Gone for a God who had shown his true self. He had dismissed Cain and all he had done to serve him. The picture he had of God all his life had been wrong. What his father had told him, he had believed without question. He no longer knew what to do. His only quest in life burned and fizzled into a black mess just like his crop.

He clenched and unclenched his fists, attempting to release the aggression building up inside of him. His brain worked as fast as it could, his mind trying to make sense of his feelings.

He still felt a deep guilt. He was angry with God.

"But it is not God," he shouted to the land in cinders. "It is Abel."

Abel had to pay. The time of smugness and constant pushing back was over. It was time for Cain to teach him a lesson.

~

CAIN APPROACHED THE MAIN HUT. It was quiet, still. A few lambs were milling outside, chewing on bunches of grass. Abel must be near.

There was no grass where their huts were situated. Abel had argued for relocation to the mountains, but Cain had refused, all his crops were here, and he was not willing to change. Abel had said some of the crops would do well in the lush area where he kept his sheep, but Cain refused to acknowledge anything Abel had to say.

Eve would know where he was, she kept a close eye on him. Perhaps he had always been the favorite. The thought sent a fresh wave of anger through Cain's body. He reached the door to the hut and stopped, still.

There were faint noises, whispers, and grunts. Cain edged to the door and peeked through the opening. In the middle of the room, next to the fire pit, Cain saw a tangle of legs and hair, clothing hitched up to the waist of his mother, who was lying beneath his brother. He was clumsily pumping her. She was smiling and whispering encouragement into his ear. He was getting faster.

Anger rose like a sea of fire rising from his feet to the tips of his ears. Abel gave a big thrust, his groan followed by a look of surprise on his face, his eyes wide open with something that was almost disbelief. Enough. Cain could and would not contain himself. He let out a primal noise, anger and frustration combining to take over his actions.

Eve and Abel's heads shot toward the door. They said nothing, frozen, Abel still inside his mother. Cain reached the coupled pair in a few strides. He grabbed Abel by the neck and threw him across the room. Abel crashed into the wall on the far side of the hut. Eve sat, fear in her eyes.

"Cain," she said. "Cain, please," she repeated, her eyes pleading. She knew his strength was too much for her.

"No." Cain spoke through clenched teeth, standing over Eve. "You will never tell me what to do. You will take nothing away from me ever again."

Cain knelt in front of Eve. A single tear ran down her cheek. She cleared her throat, closed her eyes. They reopened full of anger.

"I will give and take what I like from those who deserve it," Eve said in a flat tone.

Without hesitation, Cain punched her in the jaw. Her hands reached for her face, an instinct to protect herself from harm. Taking advantage of the unguarded moment, Cain pushed her back to the ground. She was writhing beneath him, kicking, trying to throw him off. He grabbed her wrists with one hand and held them above her head. She was coughing and spluttering through the mixture of blood and mucus streaming down her face. She looked him in the eyes.

"You will never have me the way your brother did. One day you will understand that."

"Shut up, bitch," Cain grunted, poking around between his mother's legs until he found the opening. Pinioning her legs wide, he ground her into the dirt, pleasure and power mixing, forming a thrum through his body. He thrust hard. Eve stopped writhing, giving in. A few seconds later, Cain felt a shiver, a powerful emission, pouring himself into his mother. Panting, he collapsed on top of her before rolling off to the side, smirking.

"I hope you think that was worth it because it will never happen again," said Eve, each word laced with bitterness.

He laughed. "I get what I want, Mother. From you, from Abel, and from God, I will get what I want."

∽

ABEL CAME TO. His head hurt, his memory blank. Pieces came back to him. The shock of Cain's arrival, being thrown against the wall, blackness. The fragments of his encounter with his mother surfaced. She had been an excellent mentor, she had explained to him how things worked and what he needed to do. On top of his mother's teachings and encouragement, he had instincts.

With Cain and Eve gone, Abel adjusted his clothes and went outside, blinking in the sunlight. His lambs were gone, too. A trickle of fear ran down his spine. Cain would be angry.

Abel ran behind the huts in search of his precious baby lambs, gripped by fear for his life's work and ticket to freedom. His heart beat in his ears. Abel approached the fields. Two figures stood, surrounded by ash, wisps of smoke curling around their legs. Eve was shrunken, Cain lording over her, demanding.

"What happened?" muttered Abel. Lambs forgotten, he ran to help his mother, to save her from the brute that was his brother.

Abel approached, hands outstretched. He came in peace. Coming up from behind Cain, he hoped Eve would get the first hint of his presence. She stiffened, and Cain immediately gave a laugh.

"Hello, little brother," he said without turning, disdain dripping from his voice.

"I was just having a talk with our Mother here," said Cain. "I was trying to get her to admit which one of us she liked best."

Abel closed his eyes. Cain must have taken her by force. She would never let him otherwise. She made it clear to him he was the only one. Adam had lost his right, no longer the head of the family. Abel's mind flashed to Eve looking at him while his father took her. Her eyes were pleading for help, but Abel was helpless to intervene. She had endured it all again with her eldest son.

"How dare you," Abel hissed. Eyes drilling into the back of Cain's head, he moved closer, itching for a fight.

"How dare I?" yelled Cain. "How dare you! You took what was mine! Both my rightful place with God and with our mother."

"You deserve nothing," Abel spat, stepping closer.

"I deserve everything," Cain yelled.

Cain swung around on his heel. The large wooden club was nestled in his strong hand; it was used to stun the sheep before a kill. Abel wrenched his gaze from the club to the horror etched on Eve's face.

Cain turned the club toward his brother. No hesitation. He cried, the anger of his life flowing out his lungs. He raised the club, swinging it deftly, a slow arc forming through the air. A delicate dance of blood left Abel's head an empty mess, his body crumpled on the ground.

CAIN TURNED TO EVE, her face splattered with blood. The joy he felt was clear on his face, his eyes burning with power and satisfaction.

"See, Mother, I do what I want," Cain said through his smug and bloody grin.

Eve remained calm. Her insides churned, sweat prickled her brow. The desires to fight and flee colliding within her. She narrowed her eyes and stepped toward Cain.

"You will never have what you want. God will see what

you have done, and you will be punished. I was punished for gaining intellect, thrown from Eden to exist in this horrible place. Just imagine what he will do to you for killing his favorite son," she said, each word spitting out of her mouth.

The veneer of control slipped from Cain's face. He swallowed audibly before replacing his mask of evil.

"God doesn't care about us; God only cares about himself. He is not the God I thought he was."

"He is definitely the God I have always known," said Eve, not breaking eye contact, trying to look strong.

"You know nothing, Mother," sneered Cain.

He grabbed her by the shoulders and roughly pushed her down to the ground so she was lying beside the bashed in head of her youngest son and recent lover. Cain climbed on top of her, she didn't bother to fight. Cain entered her with a hard shove, the power readying his body. Eve jolted on the burned ground, sharp prickles dug into her skin.

"Look at him. Look to see what I am capable of," Cain grunted between thrusts. He pushed her head to the side, face-to-face with death. "I control you," he said as he finished. She lay, squeezing her eyes tight against the sight of Abel's mangled head.

Quick footsteps. She rolled, jumping to her feet as fast as her aged bones would allow.

She saw Adam holding Cain's woolen tunic scrunched in his fist.

"What have you done, boy?" Adam growled. Cain said nothing, eyes downcast. Adam turned to Eve. "And you, woman, what have you done? How dare you let your son copulate with you!" he spat.

Eve spat at the feet of both men "I didn't *let* him; he

forced himself on me," she said, adding with a sneer, "I wonder where he got that idea from."

"Enough!" Adam shouted. "My life was perfect. I had everything. And then *you*"—he sneered, pointing a finger at Eve—"ruined everything. After all I have done for you, keeping you alive in this wasteland, this is how you repay me? Letting one son be killed while copulating with another? I am done! Done!" He stamped his foot like a child. "See you in the next life, if you make it. God may not want either of you."

He walked off, stopped, and turned, returning to stand over Abel's body.

"Go with God, son, you will have a better life with him in Heaven." His back turned, he trudged away, empty-handed. Eve's emotions ran, she would never see Adam again. Fear quickly ran over her as she realized that no matter how awful Adam was, he was the only thing protecting her from Cain. She screeched after him to stop. He continued to walk.

Eve turned to Cain. "You are being dishonest with yourself if you think God won't punish you."

"No, Mother, God won't punish me. I am all he has. Without me, he will not have any humans to serve him."

Eve's face fell. He was right. For the first time in her life, she raised her head to the sky and silently implored God for help.

GOD WAS EATING a meal of fish and vegetables prepared by Michael the slave. Meals tasted best when prepared by a slave. God was glad he had kept some of his minor talents after being tortured to a catatonic state. A whisper entered his head. God stopped mid-mouthful. What was this? Who was this? He dropped his spoon with a clatter, closing his eyes to concentrate. He heard it again.

"Stop rustling, you fools," he yelled into Heaven, pieces of flesh flying from his mouth, lodging in his beard. All movement stopped.

He scrunched his eyes. There it was, a whisper, a woman's voice. He couldn't make out all the words. "Please" and "God" were the main ones. God's brain worked, trying to place the voice. His eyes shot open. It was Eve. She had never spoken to him like this before, not even in Eden. Something must be wrong. He sprang up from the table. It overturned, his stew hit the floor, splattering like blood.

God ran to the portal. He saw Eve kneeling below Cain, old blood crusting on her face. Cain was grinning at a mangled body on the burned-out field, pointing and laughing.

"Abel," said God in disbelief.

"Abel!" he screamed.

29

THE FIRST ENTRANT

God leapt into action. He had always planned to take the consciousness of Adam, Eve, and their family to serve him in Heaven. But he made no preparations, he had planned on taking their lives himself when he was ready. Cain had ruined all this for him.

God had no practice at moving a soul through the portal. He had to create a body, the humans could not come over intact. He had hoped to practice, to try it out on the tribe. No loss would be sustained if his efforts resulted in failure. But his chosen ones were important.

Even though Adam and Eve had betrayed him in Eden, he had bred them to be the perfect humans for this purpose. Thanks to Lucifer, they were smarter than he had hoped, but he could work around this minor issue with a little extra work. Lucifer's interference would not delay his ultimate plan.

God had to work quickly, not knowing how long he had to extract a human's consciousness from their body or if it would work. He had no choice. Abel had pleased him greatly, and he sorely wanted him in service.

God closed his eyes and created an empty shell of a body. He tried to make it look like Abel without the unfortunate features he had somehow inherited from both his attractive parents. God faced the portal and zoomed in on Abel's body. His skull was crushed, hopefully serious brain damage wouldn't stop God from getting what he needed. God himself was amazed at the ability of the human brain, evolving slowly over time had given the humans a multilayered functioning system that he could not have created. God did not understand the life force of a person; now was the moment he might understand the residence of the soul.

God zoomed to the remnants of Abel's face. Closing his eyes, he mentally stripped back the layers of the brain, taking aim at the epicenter. God raised his hands, pulling the essence from the brain. It hovered above Abel's body, a small ball of light. God was sweating, losing energy through the portal, the effort of containing the essence of a human extraordinary. With one final grunt, he wrenched the ball through the portal and smashed it into the awaiting body.

Sparks flew, the body shuddered and collapsed. God lost control, falling to the ground.

∾

EVE BLOCKED out Cain's rant about power and indestructibility. He was spouting that God would not mess with him, he was too important.

Eve was in a haze of grief. She was mercy to Cain's every whim, and her Abel, the son with the beautiful soul, was gone.

Cain stopped talking. Eve turned her head slowly. Her face was blank, no emotion registered, grief had cut off her brain. Cain's mouth was agape, staring at the body.

Following the line of Cain's gaze, Eve gasped. A ball of light hovered above the bloody head before shooting into the sky with a power beyond anything Eve had ever seen.

Eve bowed her head. "Go with God, my son. Good luck with him."

∾

GOD STOOD OVER ABEL. He had not woken up. God had shaken, slapped, and kicked with no response. Exhausted, God slumped into a nearby chair and entered a fitful sleep brought on by pure exhaustion.

∾

GOD AWOKE WITH A START. He had a strange feeling, something he had never felt before in all his time in Heaven and Earth. The memory of his dash to save Abel came back to him, and he abruptly stood. The place where Abel's body had been was nothing but flattened moss. God spun around and gasped. His heart jumped into his mouth as he came face-to-face with Abel.

"Abel!" God cried, clutching his chest. "Don't sneak up on me like that! I am not used to it."

Abel stood, staring. God waved a hand in front of his eyes. Nothing but a blink.

God kicked over the chair. "It didn't work! Why didn't it work?" God paced in circles in front of the portal. He pumped his fists to calm himself, his brain turning fast, trying to assess the situation.

God stopped, closed his eyes, and took a practiced deep breath, an action born of realization that his penchant for destroying things just made more work for him in the long run, especially in an empty Heaven.

God spoke to himself. "It is all right. Abel is not right, but he can be used with Michael and Gabriel for the tasks that require no real skill. Shame though, he had pleased me greatly. It would have been good to have him as my first real slave."

God walked back to Abel. Taking his chin between thumb and forefinger, he kissed him lightly on the lips, and resting his forehead gently against Abel's, he said, "I will punish him." With a swift turn back toward the portal, God readied himself for justice.

30

BAD SON

E ve's skin grated against the stony ground. Strips of flesh were torn, small rocks lodged in her back. Her hair pulled on her scalp, long ends balled in Cain's fist, each strand wrenching slowly from her sensitive skin. A door swung. Eve's head bounced as she hit the floor.

"I am hungry," said Cain. "I have worked up an appetite today, make me a good meal. You know what will happen if you don't."

Head down, she moved about the hut, gathering items for the meal. She couldn't bear to meet his gaze. The club, crusted with Abel's remains, crashed down on the ground. Eve's wound-up nerves betrayed her, the thud causing an involuntary leap.

"Faster," Cain growled. This was her life now.

Eve tried to block the events of the day from her mind. Her family's rapid destruction had been a simmering pot for years, and in keeping with a common pattern, the end had come swiftly. Her life moved from normal to extreme in the space of one rise and fall of the sun.

Eve placed boiled yams and salted mutton on two plates. At least Adam had left the yams.

Bringing the plates over to the sitting area, she flicked her eyes to Cain, who was cleaning blood from his nails with a knife. She raised the plate. He hurled it into the dank corner of the hut. Chunks dropped down the wall to form a mound on the dirt floor.

Eve flinched again at the sound. "You eat there," said Cain, snatching the other plate from Eve's hand. "You eat in the corner like an animal. That is what you are."

Eve stood still, her face expressionless.

"Go on then," said Cain, pointing to the corner with his knife before stabbing a yam and stuffing it into his mouth.

Eve moved to the corner. Her brain dead, she did not know what to do except obey, her body could not bear much more. She sat cross-legged, taking a piece of yam from the dirt with shaking hands.

Cain watched. "I don't think animals eat that way. Get on all fours and eat off the ground like a sheep."

Eve glared at Cain. His knife waved in response. The unspoken threat was enough. She got on all fours, taking a timid bite of salt mutton, yam, and dirt. She dared not look at him; she dared not stop.

Eve heard the rustling of clothes and the clattering of the earthenware plate. She felt the point of the knife running down her back, she held her breath.

"You know something, Mother," said Cain, his voice dripping with power. "Sheep don't wear clothes, either." Cain ran the knife down her tunic, ripping the rags from her body. "Sheep are there to serve their masters," he said, grabbing her by the hips. Eve shut her eyes tightly, ready for another assault.

Cain positioned himself. There was a rumble in the

distance. He hesitated. The roof of the hut flew off into the sky. The walls collapsed outward in a delicate fan.

Eve was naked on all fours, when God appeared before them.

God shouted, buzzing with energy. "I had forgotten how good it feels to destroy things," he said, panting, brushing dust from his shoulders.

Cain scrambled to his feet, staggered the few steps, falling at God's feet.

"Mighty God," said Cain into the ground.

"Cain," said God, still brushing. "I don't want to hear from you." Cain attempted to continue his speech.

God raising a hand, stepping back a pace. "Not only did you burn a field and insult me with such a meaningless sacrifice, you killed you brother, who was my chosen one. It also looks to me like you are torturing your mother." God gave Eve a quick glance as she struggled to her haunches, covering herself with the rags of her tunic. "I know she is a woman, but don't you think this is a bit too much?"

Cain kept his head down, spoken to like a child.

"You have put my plan in a precarious situation, Cain. I would be inclined just to kill you for what you have done, but as I have heard you gloat, I need you. As unfortunate as that may be, it is the truth."

Cain stiffened. God grabbed him by the arms and physically hauled him to his feet. Cain's head swam, looking into the eyes of God.

God moved his mouth to Cain's ear, breathing heavily. "I banish you to wander for the rest of your life. No one will take you in, no one will accept you. Your children will not care for you, they will only be made to serve me," he whispered, stepping back to appraise the prickles of fear-induced tears swelling in Cain's eyes.

"Good," said God. He threw Cain with all his force out toward the desert of nothingness beyond, just as he had thrust Eve from Eden long ago. But this time, he had less thought about where Cain would land.

"Good," he repeated, clapping his hands together.

He nodded to Eve, who was still sitting, dumbstruck.

"I'll be back for you one day soon, Eve. You may have caused me great trouble, but I can still salvage this. I will use you in Heaven."

Eve had no reply. God was gone. She was alone.

"No, no, no," God said. "It goes over there. I have shown you so many times!" he continued in frustration.

Abel moved slowly, dumping his coconut fibers on the existing pile in plain sight within the storage room.

God collapsed on the chair. Abel was hard work. For such a resourceful human, he was not a good Heavenly servant. God had tried to think of why this might have been. Was it the brain damage suffered in Cain's assault? Was it that God had left it too long from his moment of death to retrieving his consciousness? Or was it God's worst-case scenario, was this just what happened when the little ball of light, the human soul, came through the portal? God rubbed his hand across his brow.

"I hope not," he said to himself. "I will just have to try again to be sure."

God tried to train Abel. But he was just a skin, reverted to absolute basic human needs. He ate, slept, and wanted to copulate with anything and everything like a randy animal. Trees, food, and the other inhabitants of Heaven were victims if God didn't stop him. God heard a rustling of coconut fibers. Abel was going at it again, humping a pile of what God planned to get his slaves to make into beds.

God rolled his eyes. "Right," he said. "That is enough." He pulled Abel to his feet and pushed him out of the storage hut. "We will take care of this once and for all," he said, pushing Abel gently along the path toward the portal. "If it doesn't work, I will bear the consequences."

God reached the portal and stood Abel off to the side. "Let's get this out of your system," he said. God searched Earth through the portal. There were several people occupying the world now, they were far from as perfect as his own creations. But due to the series of unfortunate events, he would have to use them, his supply of potential souls running low.

Once he had taken Adam and Eve, Cain's offspring would be next. Halfway to perfection was better than nothing. He had made the heartbreaking decision that because Cain had shown such disrespect, he would not be entering Heaven, no matter how desperate he was.

"Perfect," said God. He had found a lone woman foraging for berries just outside a town.

"OK, Abel, here you go. There is a woman down there who I'm sure won't mind you getting some of your natural urges out of your system." God pushed Abel through the portal and watched. Waiting for an answer, he breathed.

Abel survived, quickly moving toward the woman. A normal human body couldn't move between the portals, but a being made by God in Heaven seemed to have the ability. God didn't know why, even he didn't question everything. There were things he did not want to know.

The woman was screaming. Abel used his size advantage to pinion her easily to the ground. God watched. Women had issues about copulation. He didn't understand why, it was what they were made to do. But women were strange creatures.

Abel finished. God dragged him back to Heaven through the portal.

"Better?" asked God. He received no reply. God shrugged and turned Abel back toward the work huts.

31

ALONE

E ve knew she was pregnant. With Cain banished, Adam gone, and Abel dead, she was alone. But she felt a presence, a hint she was not abandoned. The thought of running anything sharp along her wrist was settled by the tiny beating of a soul deep within her belly.

It could be anyone's child. Cain and Abel were both sure contenders; it was unlikely Adam's. But she blocked her rare wifely duties from her mind with such practiced proficiency, that it was possible. She hoped Abel's seed would win the race. A child to remind her of her darling boy, to keep her company and care for her until her time came.

Her hope built, calming plans of renewed motherhood laid. Then it was gone. Blood seeped down her legs, signaling the end of life and the end to her reasons to live.

ALONE WAS a word Eve no longer thought as a concept of its own. Alone was part of her, filling every moment of her existence. It seeped into her bones, as much part of her as the blood that pumped through her veins. She often looked to the hills where Abel had tended his sheep, quashing the urge to wander up there and yell to God from the highest peak. She wanted him to take her, pleading to be reunited with her son.

Late at night, more than once, she lay on her sleeping mat, knife poised. Despair could be over; she could be with Abel in Heaven. One thing stopped her.

She could end her life. She had the courage. But what if God did not choose her? What if God was angry at her for beating him to the end? She would never see Abel again, that was too much to bear. The only choice was to go on. To exist alone, hoping that at the end of her life, God would see fit to give her what she wanted for the first time in her life.

Eve lived an automatic life. The only way she could survive her desire to die was to wake, eat, forage, sleep. She was a shell of a human. She no longer counted the days, the long wait to the end of her life unbearable with the slow passing of time.

EVE BENT, yam held firmly in one hand, stick digging to release her only sustenance. She had ventured a distance from the huts. Running out of food and water, she meandered farther away day by day. She slept in the dirt for nights at a time, not caring if a beast took her.

With a sack of hard-earned yams slung over her shoulder, she scuffed her dirty feet along the ground, kicking rocks. They skittered across the earth, finding their resting places alone, just like her.

A little overzealous with a particularly large pebble, she

yelped as her toe crushed into the side of the rock. Grabbing her foot, balance lost, she crashed to the ground, the yams spilling across the dirt, rolling away.

She heard a deep thud, a strange sound she had not heard in many years, but one that would stick with her forever. The sound of flesh indented by force, the squelch of skin and blood.

She turned toward the sound. A nearby dusty mound was the obvious source. Scrambling to her feet, she trod gingerly, each step forcing her body to go against its instincts to run. Her memory of imploding flesh was pulled to the front of her mind. Her brain froze, not allowing her to process effectively. What she saw was something new. A body, freshly dead, blood seeping from a substantial head wound. The blood did not shock her. She had seen her share of it, and the sight of death did not perturb her, her life was filled with it.

It was the body itself. She reached out to brush the thin layer of dust. She gasped, her hand pulling back out of instinct. The body was black, matte skin perfectly taught, almost as perfect as if it were still living. Dark, but human.

God had told her they were the only ones. The perfect humans for him to use in Heaven. Her brain ran, replaying her long-faded memories of Lucifer and what he had told her. At the time, she did not know who to believe and had no courage to take a side.

Eve's head snapped. A movement. The flat plain of the desert gave way to a shimmering line of distant trees. She saw a man. Rubbing her eyes, she squinted. A man, strong, tall. Animal skin was wrapped around his waist, a club dangling carelessly from his hand. Cain.

Eve scrambled to her feet, desperately seeking a sparse

tree for shelter. Her panic subsided when her rational mind took over. He was gone, if he had ever been there at all.

Again, God had lied, he had not punished Cain. He may have abandoned him, but he wandered the Earth as he pleased. Cain's treatment was no different from her own. It was time for her to make her own destiny.

32

NEW LIFE

E ve decided. She had enough of being told what to do. Enough of being alone, scratching out a living on the land with her basic talents. Doing something for herself, it was time to walk, explore.

Packing a modest bag of supplies, she set out in a random direction, keeping away from the grassy mountainous region to avoid the feral sheep.

Eve wandered. Memories of lost children were following, chasing her with every step.

EVE HAPPENED UPON A CREATURE. It took her a while to realize that what she saw was, in fact, human. A man was butchering the carcass of an animal, skinning its pelt and slicing the meat into manageable chunks. She had seen one such man before, but never a live one. The man was so dark, she could barely see him against the black pelt of the animal. He was an amazing specimen, strong and lean with skin so shiny she could see the sun bounce off it. He heard her and turned, the knife butted to his chest for quick self-defense. Eve stood still. She didn't want to appear a threat; she didn't want the knife transferring to her own chest. She knew enough about the instincts of men.

The man lowered the knife, his pure white teeth splitting his black skin. He said something she didn't understand. She gestured. He sprang to his feet and came close to her, inspecting her hair and face, then the rest of her body. He stepped back, eyes wide. He gestured for her to wait. Throwing the pelt over his shoulders, balancing large armfuls of meat, he motioned for her to follow.

SHE FOLLOWED the man through a maze of stick huts. Smoke curled from central holes. There was a smell of meat cooking. Eve held her head high, the man hadn't hurt her. The best way to preserve her life was to act with confidence, hiding the chattering of her teeth and wobbling of her knees.

The people stopped their chores, staring and whispering. An eerie hush fell over the bustling town, every eye on her.

Weaving through huts, people bowed from their path. Finally, they stopped at the door to the expertly built central hut.

The room was dark, a small central fire the only light. Eve's eyes adjusted, she made out opulent furnishings. It was the most beautiful room she had ever seen. Colorful woolen hangings lined the walls, and wooden objects decorated every surface. At the far side of the room, a pile of soft cushions was swarming with movement.

The swarm of black bodies hovered over a central figure.

A large man, propped in a sitting position, supported by rolls of fat covered by light olive skin. He was not copulating with anyone, but he was touching and being touched, watching a variety of sexual activities going on around him.

Eve stared at the scene, she had seen nothing like it. So many bodies writhing gave her an ill feeling in the pit of her stomach. The feeling overpowered the skills of recognition. Finally, she placed him. Adam.

He had grown old and fat. She walked as close to the throng as she dared, and stood, waiting for him to see her.

A beautiful woman, older than the others, held a wooden cup to his mouth. She poured a golden liquid down his throat, which spilled down his chin and past the nipples that had grown to look like breasts. He gave her a lascivious smile, which she returned. Eve's stomach turned in knots. Had he been living this way all this time? Leaving her in the desert?

He clawed his eyes from the woman; he saw her. His mouth hung open. He held his hand up, clicking his fingers. The people disengaged and wandered out of the hut, some ran hand in hand to find a better place to continue their activities.

Only two women remained.

"What are you doing here, Eve?" asked Adam, anger simmering.

"I am alone now, Adam. Abel is dead, and God banished Cain to wander the desert. He came down to do it personally."

Adam's eyes narrowed.

"I grew tired of scratching out a life for myself in that awful place, so I left and have been wandering. I found a man today, he brought me here."

"And what do you want?" scoffed Adam.

"I want a good life, if anyone deserves it, I do. I have been through a lot, Adam, some at your hands, some at the hands of your sons."

Adam shook his head. "I owe you nothing," he sneered. He took a deep breath, the shadow of guilt creeping over his face. "You can have a small hut on the outskirts of town, so long as you promise you will never come near to me again."

"Why do you hate me so much?" Eve asked, anger rising in her own voice.

Adam thought for a moment. "You remind me of my previous life. I am God here, this is my life now."

Eve's brain ticked. Did she want to live near Adam and never see him? Knowing of his hatred?

She jumped. A beautiful, honey-colored girl appeared next to her with a tray of food and drink. Eve took it gladly, looking the girl in the eyes, she turned back to Adam and the two black princesses beside him.

"She is yours?" Eve asked.

"Yes, one of many. The skin color of my children is highly sought after, and I am generally only too happy to oblige on the say-so of my wives here. My children here will amount to something, Eve. They are made of my flesh. That makes them the flesh of God. I spread the word in this village. God has bestowed great power in me for doing so, giving me a life of luxury. I have given him a great many followers. They believe in God, and I am his delegate." Adam's eyes narrowed.

"Bestowed great power on you, has he?" said Eve, eyebrow raised. "Spoken to you lately, has he?"

Adam's mouth twitched. Eve grinned. He was just as alone as she was. "I will take up your offer, Adam, and I promise to stay out of your way."

Adam nodded, his muscles relaxing in relief.

"But I require one thing from you," she added.

Adam raised an eyebrow.

"I want you to give me a son," said Eve, head held high.

Adam spluttered his latest mouthful. "What?" he said, a look of shock coming across his face. "Why?"

"I am alone; my children are dead, or dead to me. I want someone to keep me company and provide me with what I need."

"You know, here they frown upon copulation between parents and children." said Adam.

"I don't care. I want a son, and if you don't give me one, I will remain your enemy. I will never leave you alone." Eve kept her voice calm and steady.

"I can arrange for plenty of other people to give you a child, Eve."

"No, that won't do; I want him to look like me. Nothing else will do."

Adam sighed. "All right then."

"Good," said Eve. "Now."

"Now?" Adam yelped.

"Now I am ripe, I know it."

"I don't even get time?"

"Now," repeated Eve forcefully.

Adam leaned to his wives, saying something to them she couldn't hear, the faint clicks touching her ears. The women rose, giving practiced disapproving looks as they passed.

Eve climbed the dais, picking her way across cushions, nestling beside Adam. They were soft and warm, her first comfort since Eden.

She lifted a hand to touch his flabby arm. He grabbed her by the wrist.

"No, I will not enjoy forced copulation," Adam growled.

"That is how I have felt all my life," Eve said, meeting his eyes. She saw his rage bubble to the surface.

He pulled her wrist, flipping her facedown, and entered her with the force of the large man he had become. Eve's face smashed against the pillows, the colors blurring as she went to the place outside her body. He finished quickly, forcing himself to the end.

He got off her immediately. "Now get out."

She didn't argue. She left the hut.

As the child grew, he resembled Adam more and more. She vowed to learn from her mistakes, this son would not mistreat her. The power would be hers.

She kept him inside, away from humans, tied to a support post if she went out to retrieve food or indulge her social needs. She would then come back to the child. He had enough to eat, he had games and could create art with colored wool. He had never seen the outside. Eve told him she was keeping him safe and that he must never go outside. Every night she would school him in the art of copulation. She was building herself a slave.

33

SLAVE TO MAN

E ve stretched on her cushioned bed, her smallest toe brushing skin. He didn't move.

She turned her head to her son. He stared at the ceiling, thick hair shining in the light of the central fire. His skin, never touched by sunlight, was translucent, reflecting the glowing flicker bouncing off the cabin walls.

Eve had trained him well, he was born to please her. She controlled his indoor exercise regime carefully. He was just strong enough to undertake his duties but not strong enough to overpower her and escape. The careful balance of strength was just precaution, she knew he would never leave. He knew nothing of the world. He faced no hardship, and he believed what he was told with no reason to question.

As she was aware, being told something from a person's first memories did not always keep the questions at bay, but she had been careful. She inflicted the perfect measure of pain, taking it away with the perfect measure of pleasure. Her life was balanced; everything had its place.

She was no longer the victim, she would forget her past by forging a new future. A future where she was in control.

She moved her hand to Seth's chest, which was gently rising and falling, its dark hairs springing between her fingers. He had one solitary mole above his left nipple, otherwise he was blemish-less.

"There seems a lot of noise today," he said, eyes sticking to the ceiling.

"Yes, there would be."

Seth turned his head, face neutral, eyes questioning.

"I was told of another attack in a village not far from here. The people are scared, they most likely think they will be here soon to burn the houses to the ground," she said. "This is why we stay here, Seth, you know I will always keep you safe."

He turned to his side, taking both of her hands in his.

"What if they come? What if they come while you are out getting food?"

"Don't worry," she said, a smile dancing on her lips. She moved her hands to the outside of the grip, running her thumbs along his knuckles. "I can handle them."

"And there is God," she added, taking advantage of the natural segue to a lesson in Seth's history.

"What would God do?" asked Seth.

"He would save you, darling boy," Eve said as she reached out, stroking his hair from his eyes. "God would not let you come to harm."

"But why? Sometimes when you talk of him, you sound so angry. But then you tell me that I must believe in him with all my heart."

Eve propped up on her elbow, holding Seth firmly by the chin, looking him square in the eye. "You must believe in him with all your heart. It is the only way we will get to be together forever." She relaxed, allowing a smile to break her stern face. "He will like you, Seth, you are everything he ever wanted. One day you will be his, but for now you are mine."

He nodded, flopping to his back, letting out a sigh. Bending at the waist, he maneuvered to shuffle off the end of the bed. Eve's heart thumped as it did every time he went to disengage from her. She rolled, placing a bent leg over his thighs.

"I need the pot," he said, not meeting her eyes. She rolled back, watching his porcelain back move to the corner of the hut.

"You trust me, don't you, Seth? You know I will never let you come to harm," said Eve, keeping the pleading edge from her voice.

Twisting at the waist, he looked back to her, his small nod and smile giving her what she needed.

PART III

***

HELL

One of the saddest lessons of history is this: If we've been bamboozled long enough, we tend to reject any evidence of the bamboozle. We're no longer interested in finding out the truth. The bamboozle has captured us. It's simply too painful to acknowledge, even to ourselves, that we've been taken. Once you give a charlatan power over you, you almost never get it back.

—Carl Sagan, *The Demon-Haunted World: Science as a Candle in the Dark*

34

THE FILLING OF HEAVEN

God stared through his portal. It was now or never. Since the Abel incident, he worried about bringing another soul to Heaven. An empty Heaven left his plan balancing on the edge of failure. Success was all that mattered now. It was time to try again.

God craved to reign over his subservient race. Although God still liked to smite a village of the imperfect ones every now and then, satisfying his bloodlust and his constant need for destruction, it was no substitute for wielding power over every moment in his own world. God could not deny his needs had an impact on Heaven, and he had learned from his mistakes. Once, Michael served a bowl of soup that was so bland, God's mouth felt like a senseless void. He held the soup in his cupped palm, and aiming carefully, he hurled the bowl at Michael's head. Aim not careful enough, strength underestimated; the bowl smashed into the wall, the resulting hole collapsing half the kitchen. This mistake, he rebuilt himself, but on Earth, that was not his worry. Once God had his fun, humans would rebuild or move on somewhere else. For all their flaws, they were adaptable.

God watched Adam. Brittle bones had collapsed his spine to a short hump, and spots of age covered his body; his head was shinier than that of a newborn baby. Bald at the start, bald at the end. Adam had lived much longer than the other humans. God believed it must have been his adjustments. Adam had been true perfection.

After considerable thought, God took Adam, fresh and quick. He was on one of his rare trips outside. He was so old he was no longer virile, most of the interested women had left him, only his two wives staying by his side. His sons were now in high demand for copulation, those with honey-colored skin were the first choice for all the town's women. His recent lack of virility had taken some of his God-like shine. God could not be angry, although he did not like Adam acting as God, he had been chosen by God, and he spread the word. These people followed what he said, lacking the skill to analyze life any other way.

God watched Adam sit on an outside bench, his aged body heaving with exertion. Now was a good time to go. Through the portal, God raised his hand and held it to Adam's chest. Adam took one sharp breath.

"God?" It was his final word. He collapsed, heart stopped.

God went immediately to work, dragging Adam's life force from his brain.

"This is a good sign," God grunted. "This feels heavier, more vibrant." God continued his monologue internally, hopeful that in Heaven, Adam would make a better specimen than his son. Wrenching the ball of energy free of the Earthly plain, God smashed the light into the awaiting body.

In Heaven, he was well made, God had the time to ensure he got it right. The process was easier when God chose the time and place of death.

Adam spluttered. "God?" he asked again. God smiled, he had done it.

GOD SEARCHED EVE'S FACE. They were standing nose to nose through the portal. Her face was expressionless, concentrating on her task of cooking slop on an open fire. God had not watched Eve closely for some time, but he knew the slop was not for her. Her days of eating slop were far behind her. He discovered her living nearby with another son, one who could only be born of her and Adam. She had forced him somehow, she was a wily one.

God's mouth tipped at the corners, he realized he was smiling. He forced his upper lip to curl. His feelings for women were unchanged, he didn't like her. But even God must eat his words. Eve had proven her resilience and developed an intriguing, controlling nature.

God turned his head to Adam in Heaven, who was slowly hammering nails into planks to make seating for camp. God's snarl did not decrease, Adam was making a mess of the furniture making.

"But what is the point of having a Heaven full of slaves if I have to do all the work?" he muttered to himself, sighing heavily, his body slumping as the air exited his lungs. His plans for domination and slavery were slow, rife with difficulties.

Adam was clumsy, getting used to his new body. But it wasn't Adam's base ability that was a concern. It was his fire, the lack of *himself*.

God thought back to when he took Adam from Earth, dragging his essence through the portal into Heaven. He had felt a strong life force, much more intense than he felt with Abel, but Adam was dull, his strength not surviving the journey to Heaven.

God sighed, he would bring Eve over in the spirit of the experiment. He didn't like her, didn't trust her, but even God shows compassion, and that poor boy of hers needed time out in the open in his life. All God could hope, was that he could control Eve in his own domain. Desperation was mounting. He was running out of souls.

35

SLAVE TO GOD

Something switched in Seth's head. For the first time in his life, he needed fresh air. He did not know where this need came from, but it was as strong as his need to breathe or eat, or to ensure his mother did not fly into a rage.

She had gone out. It was food day. The only way he kept track of time was where she went. The only way to tell the time of day was the appearance or absence of light peeking through the cracks in the hut. At least he was no longer bound. Left free inside the hut, he was under no illusion what could happen if he snuck outside.

"Perhaps just for a moment," he said, talking to himself, the best way to pass the time. He shuffled toward the door, his hand outstretched, rapid heart beating through his chest. Just one little push and he could see outside. His fingertips brushed the rough wood.

The door swung open. Eve jumped back, startled by Seth's presence by the door. Expecting him on the bed, waiting for her.

"What are you doing?" she growled, shoving him back into the hut.

"Just waiting for you, Mother. I missed you," he said, words dripping with innocence. The scowl on her face vanished, swept away by the perceived sincerity.

"Well," she said, brushing her hand down the length of his arm. "I am back now, and we have some lovely food for supper."

They ate in silence. The pleasantries finished, they both concentrated on their meal.

"Be a good boy, and put the plates by the door," Eve said. "Then go to bed." Seth's heart sank. Events had become intense, his mother demanding he perform acts that did not feel right. Whenever he tensed or shied from her, she explained that he was ridiculous and that everyone on the outside does these things.

Once, he had replied, "Well, let me go to the outside and meet some of these people." For that remark, he had received swift punishment. His wrists were tied to his ankles, and he was left to sit in his own filth for days in the corner of the hut.

Learning from this experience, he did as he was told. He placed the plates by the door and sat on the bed. His heart raced as she turned.

"You know what to do," she said calmly. Seth lay on the bed, closing his eyes, taking in the last ray of sunlight slipping between the cracks in the walls.

He heard voices. Alone again, he pressed his ear to the wall. High-pitched talking and giggles. He didn't understand the words. He pushed his eye against the crack, the tiny part of the world he could see taken up by a pair of slender black legs. A smile broke his face, he wanted to invite them in.

A faint gasp, the legs ran away. Shoulders hunched, he slunk back to the bed. He sat on the edge, wringing his hands. He so wanted to meet the people. He examined his hands, translucently white with tiny blue lines spidering across the muscle and bone. The people were different. His mother had never said this. His brain went to the dark place he tried to avoid. What else was she not saying?

He heard the door. Eve had fresh wool to weave into a new blanket. He gave her a smile.

SETH STRUGGLED TO STAY INSIDE. He heard more voices and caught glimpses of feet and hair as they swished by his hut. No one ever came near when his mother was at home.

His desires were irresistible, causing him to twitch. He wanted to touch the them and feel their difference. He wanted to cut them to see if their blood was the same as his. He wasn't sure if they were human.

Eve had just left the hut. It was food day again, she would be gone for some time. He pressed his ear to the wall, waiting for the voices to appear. He heard them, giggling, walking so close to the hut that he heard their hair flick the wooden beams.

"They must be tall," he said. The giggling abruptly stopped. One of them asked a question. Feet came back to his crack.

A dark eye appeared at the outside of the crack. Seth squealed, pushing himself back from the wall, breathing heavily. He raced to the door, and before he could hesitate yanked it open, stepping into the outside world, shrieking as the full light hit his unaccustomed eyes. He fell to his knees.

A hand on his shoulder. Rough and warm. Darkness surrounded him. He blinked slowly. First, he saw the knees, brown and covered with dust from kneeling. The girl's body was blocking the sun, providing him with some shade. Cupping his hand around his eyes, he let them drift upward. Her beautifully round breast was peeking beneath layers of colored necklaces. She had a fine face with black hair sprouting from the scalp in curls. His eyes drifted back to the breasts, high and unmarked, unlike his mother's. He reached out to cup one in his hand.

The girl slapped his hand away and shuffled back, yelling something at him and calling to the distance. Blinded by her disappearing shadow, he covered his eyes.

More footsteps, more yelling. He scrabbled in the dirt, trying to get back to the house. He felt a tight grip on his arm. He was yanked to his feet and dragged inside to darkness.

He blinked, eyes teeming with dots. A figure stood above him. His mother's face was red, jittering with anger.

"How could you do this to me?" she erupted. "What have I ever done to you? I have protected you from the harsh world, and this is how you repay me?" She stomped, grabbing a fistful of his hair, yanking his head back and peering down into his semiblinded eyes.

"You will be punished for this," she growled.

Seth whirled saliva in his mouth, the urge to spit at her close to overwhelming his better senses.

She let go. A sudden fear was on her face. She stumbled back, holding her chest with both hands, her eyes wide, breathing halted.

"Help" came from her strangled mouth. He stood,

unmoving. She reached out to him, red patches creeping across widened eyes. Collapsing on the ground with fear still plain on her face, a large breath wheezed from her body, empty lungs collapsing in her chest. Seth had never seen death, but he knew this was it, his mother was gone.

Shock took him. It slowly thawed as a smile crept across his face. Every one of his internal desires had been recognized. Every silent plea to explore and every doubt that his mother was his salvation. His sudden opportunity made it clear what his mother had kept from him all his life.

"Freedom," he said, pushing the guilt far down. "You cannot control me any longer, Mother. I will take from you what you have always taken from me."

He moved down to her, pushing her legs wide. He dominated her body; it was his turn. He did what he pleased, not caring for inflicting pain or suffering. She was dead.

Seth flopped back against the wall, breathing hard. How wonderful it was to be in charge, to perform the act that had been part of his life since his first memory, but with a body who bent to his every whim, one that had no soul of its own.

The wall behind him shuddered, light angled through the cracks. The door burst off its hinges. A radiant man filled the doorway, beard swaying with his movement. Seth stared, the most beautiful thing he had ever seen was standing right before him.

"God?" Seth squeezed the word from his open mouth.

"You are magnificent," God said, his voice kept low in the confines of the hut. Seth scrambled to his knees and bent his head. His mother had never told him what to do if God came to him. "I have taken your mother, Seth," said God, stating facts with no emotion. Seth nodded, his head remaining bent, not daring to look his creator in the eye.

"You can get up," said God, waving a hand. Seth scrambled to his feet. "It is time for you to live your life." Seth's mouth was agape. The black eyes peering out from the gap between God's hair and beard seemed to eat into his body, driving his soul into a swirling torrent. "But I need you to do something for me."

Seth swallowed hard. "Anything," he croaked. The awe of being in God's presence was overwhelming.

"I need people, Seth. More people like you. I need you to go out into the world and multiply for me." Seth tried to understand what God was saying, but his head was swimming. His disconnected thoughts translated into a puzzled look on his face. God gave an impatient sigh.

"I suppose you may not know," God muttered to himself. "You know how to do it, Seth, I just saw you. What you did to your Mother, and what she has done to you for your whole life, has another purpose. If you do that to as many women as possible, they will beget your children. That is the true purpose of this act. You do that for me, and I will take you to Heaven when you have produced enough heirs."

Seth nodded, speech evading him. God nodded back. A wordless communication was all that was required to ensure they understood each other. God hovered by the doorway, turning back to Seth, who was still frozen to the ground.

"And Seth," he said. Seth's eager eyes found his. "Just make sure they are alive when you do it, or it won't work." Seth nodded, alone again.

He sprang to his feet, energized by the inducement from God. Buzzing from the meeting, he gathered his mother's knives and rope into a leather sack. With the sack slung over his shoulder, he left the hut, sauntering out into the sunlight.

∼

SETH CROUCHED BEHIND A LOW BUSH, watching the women grinding corn, talking and laughing as they worked. He waited patiently for his moment. The women scooped the meal into large clay urns, which they carried with them back to the central hut, balanced skillfully on their heads. A group of women rose to leave, a straggler was still filling her urn. She gestured that she would catch up. Ensuring enough space between the group and his lone victim, Seth pounced from behind the bush, clasping a strong hand over the girl's mouth before she could make a sound. Her eyes were wild, darting across his face. Her nostrils flared above his hand, air whistling over his fingers. He had to move fast before the others realized she was gone. Unfastening his small club from the belt around his waist, he gave the girl a swift knock to the base of the head, letting her limp body crash to the ground. He grabbed a fistful of her thick hair and dragged her into the scrub.

He watched her lying unconscious, breathing as peacefully as if she were asleep. Crouching at her feet, Seth waited. Her eyes flickered. Memory returned quickly, she scrabbled backward. Seth pounced, grabbing her by the wrists, overpowering her struggles.

"The power," he said, taking a sharp breath through his nose, "is now all mine." He leered at the girl as he wrestled her to her back. Clambering on top of her, he did God's bidding. He was the dominant one now, and he would get what he wanted.

36

PRISON

Pacing. This had become Lucifer's life. He grunted.

"A life, hardly." He spoke confidently to himself. He had no other soul to engage, not to watch, not to listen, not to speak to. He was alone again and spoke aloud, practicing in case he forgot how.

His mind drifted back to Eve. He was at his happiest then, since Raphael. He had a purpose, helping Eve to reach her enlightenment, trying to make her see who God really was. Lucifer knew that if she stuck by God, things would not end well for her. Things would never end well for anyone who needed to fill the void of his or her creation through worship of the unknown.

"It just seems strange, doesn't it?" Lucifer asked himself. "Humans can't possibly know where they came from. They know they are more important than other animals, they feel they are destined for something." He paused, thinking. Talking to himself served a higher purpose, helping him to order his frantic thoughts.

"Arrogant," he said. "And so needy. I would hate to think

what would happen if they thought God had abandoned them," he concluded, shrugging.

Lucifer stood up, stretching his long arms high into the air. He paced in a small circle and lifted his face to the sky. Giving a silent curse to God, he sat down again.

This was now Lucifer's life. God had seen to him, he had seen to him well.

"I hate you right now, God. You certainly thought hard about keeping me here this time," Lucifer muttered.

Lucifer stretched his arms out to the side at full length, his fingertips brushed the walls. A crackle ran down his arms, jolting his system. God's expert force field made sure Lucifer could not escape.

It felt like a dozen lifetimes since Lucifer had awoken, curled on the ground with dusty earth covering his body, creeping into his mouth. Face down in the dirt. God had attacked him through the body of the snake, he was lucky to survive. Or unlucky to survive. Why had God not killed him? Awake but trapped in a broken shell that was once his body. He lay silently, still, unable to do anything but think.

His chest heaved, sweat prickled his brow. He thought he would die, paralyzed in Hell. Powerless to stop God. Needless death and continuous pain would be all he ever knew. God would enslave and destroy humanity.

He finally managed to move by concentrating on one muscle at a time, hoping for a response. Was it real? Twitching the muscle, he tried again. Cold, wet, and parched, he worked each toe, one by one.

After many nights, he flipped onto his back. It was raining, he caught the droplets on his tongue. He felt liquid life drip down his throat. It clawed him away from death, giving him the strength to stretch.

His knees were bent, flopping to the side. He focused on one leg, trying to straighten it. He moved, a thud reverberated down his leg and lodged in his twisted hips.

Again, thud, crackle. He wiggled, switching his arms.

He felt it. A wall. An imperceptible barrier, the crackling presence of the force field coursing through his body. The hair on his neck stood on end as if something were watching, waiting.

His fingers found a small piece of weed resting on the dirt, it had drifted in when the wind picked up. The rain wet his cheeks.

The only way to survive was to make small goals, each one more difficult than the last. Breaking up this task the only way he felt he could handle it.

First, he must stand.

Success came with great pain, which was kept at bay by his internal fire. Reaching his hands high above his head, he traced around his prison, a tube that ran high into the sky, far higher than his reach could tell him.

Resting every few minutes to recover from activity, he tried to dig below with bare hands, his nails tearing in the dirt. He tried to make something, a stool, a trowel, anything he could use to get over or under the force field. Every attempt fizzled to a spark. Too weak to escape, too strong to die.

He sat on the muddy ground, warm tears streaming down his face, an unstoppable well of despair. "What is the point?" he said aloud through the tears. "The only thing I want is to stop God, but I can't escape. It's useless." His fire left him, replaced with despair's black ink, its tendrils creeping to every corner of his body.

Lucifer spiraled into a dark pit he couldn't claw out of alone. Wasting away, he would die soon, this would all be over. Moments from death, he felt a kick in his chest, his eyes sprang open. Nothing. Perhaps it was just his heart stopping.

He felt it again. "Dig." He heard a voice. Lucifer's eyes widened, he knew that voice.

"Dig," it repeated, both near and far, appearing in his head through a murky film of distance.

"I have dug; I just can't," he said, broken voice quiet through welling tears.

"Center, not edge." The voice was having difficulty stringing words together.

"What?" Lucifer was getting frustrated. This made no sense.

"Dig in the center of the circle? That will not get me out."

"Do it," the disembodied voice said, an angry tone creeping into the strangled words.

Lucifer sighed and dropped his shoulders.

"All right, I think I am truly going mad now. I am not only talking to myself, but to someone else." This thought made his chuckle; it was the first laughter he felt for what seemed an eternity. Laughter with Raphael in another time and another place came to the surface of his memory. Struck with a wave of desire to live, the memories of Raphael, and what God had done to him, reignited the fire in the pit of Lucifer's belly. What did he have to lose? He was starving, freezing, and mad. If this killed him, so be it. Wrenched to his knees, he crouched in the center of the circle. He dug into the hard ground. His nails broken and bloody, he eventually came across a weed.

"Red weed! There is red weed under the ground!"

Lucifer clawed at the rubbery plant, ripping thick segments from the ground, covered in dirt and mud. He ate, chewing furiously to drain it of its nutrients. It tasted terrible. He didn't care, it was enough to keep him alive. Faced with losing everything, the smallest of things can become a marvel.

Energy flowed, the surge returning some of his abilities. Lucifer tried everything. He dug with a trowel he made, he climbed with a ladder. The cylindrical walls, sheer and high, buzzed with energy. He could not get traction to climb. Lucifer was losing heart, he would never get out. Collapsing yet again, the voice came to him.

"All you have to do is wait," it said.

"Wait to die," Lucifer grunted.

"I did not die for nothing." said the voice. "Wait."

Lucifer's head snapped up. "Raphael?" he whispered. But the voice was gone. He broke down. Suffering, loss, and torment flooded out.

WAITING WAS LUCIFER'S LIFE. The unknown was becoming too much. Not know what he was waiting for, or how long the torment would continue drove him closer to madness.

Lucifer felt it: a giant droplet.

He looked to the sky. It was an ominous mix of gray swirling clouds punctuated by flashes of lightning high in the haze. It had not rained in a long time. But maybe it had. He didn't trust his senses, not knowing the true passage of time.

Lucifer waited. Each droplet tormented him, hinting at the possibility of what was to come. With a sudden snap, the sky opened in a deluge that assaulted every inch of his skin.

The rain filled his tubular prison, he let himself float as the water reached his head. Slowly creeping up the tube, Lucifer let the water carry his body. Suspended in a perfect cylinder of water, he waited. The rain eased. He felt around the tube, no end was in sight. He opened his arms as wide as he could, closed his eyes, and visualized the water in his mind. It was made up of millions of small components. He concentrated on expanding the smallest parts, expanding them all, bigger and bigger. The volume of water increased, pushing him upward through the tube. Higher and higher he went, the force of the water beneath him increasing with every passing moment as more particles enlarged. Lucifer closed his eyes and held his breath.

He was no longer ascending. Hurtling back towards the surface of Hell. Free! But the fall would kill him. Bracing for inevitable impact, he closed his eyes, not wanting to see the final moment of his death.

"No," yelled the voice in his head. "Powers."

Lucifer, facing imminent death, had forgotten his powers. Stretching out to the approaching ground, he created himself a landing.

37

DESCENDANTS

God sat back on his throne, a smile brushing his lips. Watching the Heavenly bustling below, he was in his rightful place, above all inhabitants of Heaven and Earth. He finally felt fulfilled in a perfect place where he could be free. He was on top, where he belonged.

God had nearly perfected the transfer of souls from Earth. He still had to create the bodies, a taxing process, but worth the final product. He could have the stunning bodies of youth rather than those that were old, wrinkly, and fat. The way they wobbled as they worked set his teeth on edge.

The inner circles of Heaven were filled with slaves. After the disaster with Abel and the slightly less extreme disaster of Adam, God experimented with the best souls to take.

In the throng of people, God found Eve, standing ahead of the crowd, her tall, lean, bronzed body shimmering in the sunlight. He had taken her from within her own home. He struck her down in front of her slave son, working quickly to take her soul before it was too late. It pained him to admit it, she made an excellent servant. Lumbering in the background, in stark contrast to Eve, were his original slaves.

Gabriel and Michael shuffled, creased skin falling from their bones. Their feet and hands were deeply calloused from continuous slow, menial labor. Always together, their vacant minds degraded with time, their only use was to carry heavy objects under the supervision of another slave.

Through trial and error, God discovered the perfect categories for slaves. First, the soul must be taken from the body as close to the moment of death as possible. The best souls were from those he killed himself, rather from those killed by accident, illness, or murdered by a fellow human.

Second, the humans with stronger personalities transferred with greater success. With quite some loss of fidelity of the soul in the transfer process, the stronger the individual in mind, the more intact they remained when transplanted into their Heavenly body.

Third was blind belief. The people of Earth who believed in him wholeheartedly, those who believed they would go to Heaven for a happy and eternal afterlife, were the ones who transitioned the best. There was something about the expectations lodged in their brains and how that transferred to the new world. The expectations of the soul.

God's first choice had always been for believers. Loving him in their earthly lives made them worthy. They would do anything in his name, anything to get themselves a place in what they believed the ultimate luxury.

Luckily for God, Adam's philandering ways had allowed him to spread the word, his rarity and knowledge leading him to hold high office among the savages, almost a God himself. At first, God felt a jealousy rise from the locked portion of his soul, something he had not felt since the time before humans. When many of the natives converted to the beliefs of Adam's constant speeches, the jealousy dissipated; it was him they loved after all. The savages were far from perfect, but they were tough. He made tweaks to appearances, since the devastation of the brothers, he didn't have much of a choice but to gain perfection where he could. They were a means to an end, a resource he had no choice but to utilize. He successfully deluded himself. They were perfect so long as he didn't think too much.

God abandoned the nonbelievers. He tried to bring some through the portal to boost his population, but they did not make the journey well. Their brains were not prepared, they did not take to the bodies, and all they did once they gained their Heavenly consciousness was scream.

If there was one thing God loved on Earth, it was the screams of those in turmoil, watching them run, fear alight on their face. The instinct to survive jumped from the dormant parts of their brains, leading to horrendously selfish acts. But Heaven was his peaceful place, there was no place for that here. He gave them swift blows to the head with a heavy club and directed the other slaves to bury the bodies deep in the uncleared section of Heaven. God did not dwell on these souls, but sometimes he felt the prickle of something nearby. He shook it off and went about his daily business. He had work to do, an empire of passive and loyal individuals to rule.

God heard a rustle from a tree to his left. Snapping out of his deep mediation, he startled, his hand jumping to his chest to stop his heart escaping through his ribs and forming its final beats on the dusty ground at his feet.

"Seth," God panted. "You startled me."

Seth stood, his head cocked at an angle, straight mouth somewhere between a smile and a frown.

"Come and sit by me, my son," God said, waving his hand to the foot of his throne. Seth obediently climbed the two steps and nestled at God's feet.

"You always know when I need company. It is like you feel it in your bones." Seth said nothing. With his head leaning softly against God's knee, he let God stroke his mane of thick brown hair.

"My favorite boy, we need to think about our future," God said. He loved Seth's company. A life of abuse by his mother, set free by God. He lived many years and turned predator himself, recreating the only life he knew. An interesting life made an interesting soul.

Most of Heaven's quality servants were down to this boy. Eve's need for a slave had worked well for God, finally she had done something worthwhile for him. Seth's widespread predation had ended in many children. Seth had chosen well, leaving the women of the believing tribes alive after his assaults, stalking them to ensure the delivery of a healthy child. If the woman was a nonbeliever, he stole the child to deposit it with those who would instill the correct beliefs into them, otherwise they would be useless to God. Predation for God's purpose. The children lived average lives. Growing up in isolation of their father's predatory traits allowed most of them to flourish without the inheritance of Seth's more controversial tastes.

In a careful balance of fulfilling his own desires and also obeying God's will, Seth chose his true victims carefully. Those with their fruitful years behind them or those who did not need to live. He had one enduring taste, older women with graying brown hair. He kept them prisoner, using their living bodies as long as he cared before ending their lives and moving on when he was ready.

Seth was passive, but God knew he listened. It fulfilled God's need for companionship while still allowing him total control.

"We have taken nearly all your descendants," God said

pensively, rhythmically stroking Seth's hair. "I need more people in Heaven, and my believers are thinning out. I took your sons, I took your daughters, and now they have run out. I don't have a great man on Earth to spread my word. I can't do that and manage things here in Heaven."

Seth nodded. "How many people do you need, God?" he asked without moving his head from its resting place.

God smiled. Seth was not a mute, but each question came with a great thought.

"As many as I can, Seth, as many as I can," God repeated. "I want Heaven to be a great kingdom. I want Heaven to flourish and for me to live in luxury for all eternity."

Seth nodded again. Suddenly he straightened, twisting to look up at God with large black eyes. God's breath caught in his throat, he was a beautiful specimen. God was proud and awed at his own ability, feeling a pang to reconnect physical contact with Seth as soon as he broke away from him.

"Can we make people here in Heaven?" asked Seth, his large eyes not breaking contact.

God's mouth dropped open, astounded at Seth's audacity and his ability to think so laterally since his movement through the portal.

God swooped down, crouching close to Seth, grabbing him by both hands. He moved his face so close he could feel Seth's breath. A shudder moved through Seth's body as his breathing picked up slightly.

"Darling boy. You are right. Very clever, very clever indeed," God said, releasing one hand, gently stroking Seth's cheek.

Seth did not move, his expression passive, never breaking eye contact from God. Black eyes staring into black eyes. God chewed his lower lip, thinking, letting his brain run with the idea Seth had implanted. He looked back, eyes burning with an idea for success.

"I have a job for you, Seth. I want you to find two strong slaves, ones who are in some of my better bodies, and get them to copulate."

Seth rose. "I will not disappoint you, God."

God smiled. A possible way forward. Quickly, his thoughts grew dark, a strange feeling sending a dagger to his heart.

"Seth?" he called out after the boy, voice broken. Seth turned at the sound of his name.

"Just not you; I don't want it to be you." Seth gave a small nod, and without speaking, returned to his task. Jealousy was something God could not handle. Seth was his.

GOD STARED THROUGH THE PORTAL. His stress rose, his hands tightened. The urge to hit something was overwhelming. He had learned to control his temper successfully in Heaven, not wanting to ruin his perfect paradise, but he still used Earth to release his pent-up frustration. God raised his hands, concentrating on the large mountain in his sight. Moving his hands in continued upward motions, he made the mountain explode in a brilliant spectacle of molten rock and ash, spewing high into the sky, lava running down the side in hot rivers of pain. Fingers of lava crept toward the nearest village.

"Excellent," God said to himself, feeling better at his small burst of destruction. The urge to use his powers regularly overwhelmed him. He felt he must continue to use them, ensuring his strength remained to benefit his life in Heaven.

Things had not been going well. Seth's copulation project had not worked, natural impregnation simply did not happen. God had attempted to get involved on a molecular level and failed. After several disasters and dissecting his slaves to find the cause of the problem, he gave up. He still did not have a total understanding of his own creations. Not wishing to dwell on his own shortcomings, he turned to Earth for answers.

Looking through the portal, his mood was not improving. He wanted more slaves, *needed* more. What he had was not enough. He was not great enough until he had covered Heaven with his empire.

God felt a hand touch his pumping fist and relaxed a little, allowing his shoulders to droop and his chest to expand with a deep breath.

"They are all terrible, Seth," said God, dejected. "There are no more candidates for Heaven. They either don't believe in me, or they are so insipid, they will be no good. There is only one decent believer left, and look at him."

Good moved the portal. The man, of decently advanced age, had the ugliest face God had ever witnessed in his living memory.

The small hum emitting from Seth's tight lips told God he understood.

"God?" said Seth, turning toward him. God turned slightly, giving Seth a raised eyebrow.

"Start afresh?" Seth said, returning the raised eyebrow.

God was stunned. Another true thought from his favorite Heavenly being. Seth's perfect mix of obedience and lively spark allowed him to be God's true companion. His upbringing led to an excellent view of humanity. He believed that they were all for God, and anything else was unnecessary. He also had a streak that God recognized. He enjoyed the carnage and destruction, he enjoyed watching the lowly people suffer.

"This could work; this could work indeed," he said to himself. Snapping out of thought, he raised a hand and ruffled Seth's hair. "Clever boy, now we need to start from somewhere. I can't afford the time to start from bacteria again. We have this one, he is as good as we are going to get." Seth leaned his head against God's arm. They stood together, staring through the portal.

38

NOAH

Noah was reeling. He sat stone-faced on the simple wooden chair in his rudimentary hut. The only thing he could do was stare at the dirt floor, making small circular patterns with his feet.

Noah had received a visit from God and had not quite recovered. Noah believed in God, of course, as his creator. But he led a solitary life, never speaking of such nebulous ideas as life after death.

The few devout people he had known were dead. He was the only one, his feelings of solitude reiterated by God, who told him he was the last valued person on Earth.

Noah had been so shocked by God's presence that all he could do was stare. Most of what God had said in his rant to Noah had made no sense. Something about evil and stupid people, something about gene pools and his family, what-ever a gene pool was, he had never seen one of those. What-ever it had to do with him, he did not understand. All he had picked up from his conversation with God was that everyone would die except for him. This had yet to sink in.

Noah looked up from his chair to see his wife of many

unhappy years enter the room. She stopped short, eyeing him. She knew something was wrong.

"What?" she asked, eyes wide, questioning bluntly. Friendliness was a waste of time.

Noah took a deep breath, speaking rapidly, words escaping in a monotone waterfall of barely constructed sentences.

"God came here. Everyone bad. Or stupid. Or something. Going to kill them all. I am the only one. I will be saved. We must rebuild. Water will come. We must save the animals. We will be saved." Noah let out a breath, his eyes glazed, staring at the corner of the room.

Naamah collapsed into roaring laughter. "Well, is that all?" she said between heaving ribs. "How about you tell me that again?"

$\approx$

LUCIFER DRAGGED himself to the portal.

Bruised from the fall, he chewed on red weed, collecting the never-ending icy cold rainwater to gain strength as his bones healed.

Stumbling to the portal, delirious and disorientated, he lost his way several times, but the imaginary voice led him back to the right path. The voice was Raphael's. Lucifer was sure of that now. A cruel way for his mind to deal with loneliness, a construction of the one he missed the most.

Anger bubbled to the surface. Lucifer pulled his hair and fell to the ground in fits of sobbing. Every bone ached, his skin was raw from Hell. He was angry at God for so many things, he could no longer contain it.

Raising a weathered hand to open the portal took every drop of energy he had. He hesitated, what had happened?

Did he want to know? Looking over the plain brimming with lightning, he imagined himself walking to the high peak, standing, waiting for the sharp rod to pierce his body, alighting the deep lines in his face.

"No, too much at stake," he said, trying to calm his heart.

Struggling, he raised his head to see the strange double world before him.

God was sitting on an ornate throne, raised on a dais, built right beside the portal. His small black eyes were lost in a mash of hair and beard. His skin sagged, deep crevices lining his visible skin. Lucifer swallowed audibly. He was staring right into the portal, looking straight through, as if nothing was there. At God's feet sat an attractive young man, brown hair and bronzed skin reflecting the bright Heaven light. His long nose melded seamlessly into high forehead, and sharp cheekbones framed his symmetrical face.

A flash invaded Lucifer's brain. Eve, he looked just like her. God had begun to take his slaves from the descendants of his first humans. They had survived God's wrath in Eden only to face slavery.

Lucifer explored, working hard to discern Heaven from the hazy view. God had built a paradise. Buzzing with activity, slaves undertook chores, cooking, cleaning, and fashioning furniture, all for God. But how was he progressing with his plan? Did he have enough slaves? Would he ever have enough? And would he destroy the Earth to move onto something better once Heaven was perfected?

God was watching something. Lucifer panned, following God's gaze to Earth.

An old man, three younger men, and a group of women were lugging timber to a building site.

He felt a chill. God was overseeing an Earthly project personally. It must be important.

The muddy three-way portal was difficult. He couldn't discern the events, his broken brain doing nothing to help him.

A memory surfaced. His fall to Hell, being pushed to a wasteland that almost claimed his life. Lucifer gasped as his brain fired, pieces of information formed into understanding. Three dimensions, connected by portals. The central three-way hub was the connection point, the worlds folded to meet at additional points. Hell was not only intrinsically linked to Heaven, but also to Earth. He must find the other portal. It would lead him straight to Earth.

Lucifer trudged across the difficult terrain. The pain no longer bothered him. Blood welled in his fingertips as he grabbed the next jagged rock. His hands turned black. With no fingernails to lose, his fingers large and hardened, he could barely feel them.

The buzzing filled his ears, electricity danced on his skin. He was in the right place. Opening the portal, he searched for the work site.

There was wood, rope, and sticky black slop painted into cracks of timber. Work was frantic. The site buzzed with stress, laced with the taste of fear.

All hairs on his body were standing on end. Danger was prickling, willing him to run.

"Find out," the voice echoed in his head. Lucifer nodded, drew in a great breath, and concentrated on the portal. The last time he had done this, he failed and nearly died. He hesitated, forcing his actions to overcome his instinct to preserve his own life.

"You have to, no choice," the voice echoed again. He

knew this, the voice always told him what he already knew. It was his own head, after all. He shook the thoughts of death and failure from his mind. He shook his hands, springing up and down on his toes, psyching himself to make the leap to his possible death.

Lucifer closed his eyes and stepped up to the portal. He steeled his mind to leave his body and inhabit another. He had no choice, he could either die himself or watch the humans die. He did not know which was worse.

Lucifer opened his eyes a crack. A bright blue in every direction. The strange sensation of looking through the eyes of a different species brought forth memories of the snake.

But this was no snake. The colors were bright, and he could see a long way. Bright blue sky stretched over the horizon, green fields below, getting closer. Fear gripped him, awareness grew. He was falling. The ground was far below him. His breaths came heavily. He tried to move his head. Out of the corner of his eye, he saw a feather.

"A bird!" he gasped, his talking restricted through what could only be a beak.

"Flap or die," the faraway voice hissed. Lucifer attempted to flap the wings, it was difficult to get the feelings of a new animal so quickly. He closed his eyes, blocking out the rising ground. If he was too slow, he would die. He would rather not know it.

Concentrating hard, he found the mechanism to flap his wings. Maneuvering his new body to take advantage of the air flow, he pulled into a glide and let out a breath. He was alive.

"How did I end up all the way up here?" Lucifer said aloud to himself. Having only possessed a creature once before, he didn't know. He did not have time to ask questions of the world. Lucifer concentrated on flying, thinking of the positives. Using the bird's view, he located the building site. Gliding down, he perched on a nearby branch.

Lucifer watched. The old man was the leader, but he did not lead well, there was no respect from his entourage. Yelling an order to quicken the pace, he was ignored. The pace of the site remained at its constant speed, sons and daughters going about their tasks.

"What to do?" Lucifer chirped, settling to approach the wife of the old man.

NAAMAH STOPPED SHORT, wiping her brow. It was a hot day; the bucket of tar was heavy. Her hands quivered. The long walk to the fire and the constant stripping of bark made her tired to the bone. The bucket slopped. A splash of hot tar dripped to her bare ankle.

Crashing the bucket to the ground, she quickly wiped the spot from her skin with the cloth that protected her hand, stopping the bucket handle from painfully digging into her flesh. A large red welt appeared, adding to the collection of wounds on her arms and legs.

Hands on her hips, steeling herself to pick up the bucket, now half-full, she heard a chirpy whisper.

"Hello."

She looked around, a bird was perched on a branch. She heard the sound again. Shaking her head, she stooped for the bucket. She had been working too hard, all to enact her husband's, and God's, crazy plan. She had told herself it was worth it anyway, as if something happened, she would live on the ark, and if nothing happened, she would just continue living at home. The work was hard, but she had no choice but to obey her husband. Or at least appear to obey him.

Shifting the weight of the bucket, Naamah continued her journey.

"Don't go."

She snapped her head up and stared right at the bird.

"Yes, it is me," it said.

"I have been working too hard," she said straight to the bird's face, dropping hard to the ground.

NAAMAH CAME TO. Her tar had spilled in a big black splash. With her head turned to the side, she lost her bearings. What had happened? Moving her head straight, she yelped, the bird sat on her chest.

"Good, you are awake," said the bird. All Naamah could do was stare, no words would form.

"I need you to tell me what is going on here," the bird said.

"W-what? I didn't just imagine you? How can you talk?"

"My name is Lucifer. I am just using the body of this bird to reach you." Naamah stared, she did not understand.

"I am from where God is from," said the bird.

"Oh," she said, trying to collect her thoughts. "Well, I guess you can probably do what you want then."

"What is going on here?" the bird pushed again.

"We are building a boat," she said, nothing else forming in her mind. She was talking to a bird.

"Why?" the bird pushed.

"Why? Why so many questions? You are a bird," she said disdainfully. The bird flapped its wings in return.

"All right," she said, bringing her hands up to hide her

face. "God came and said we must build a boat, and then he would send all his animals. He is going to destroy everyone and everything in the world because everyone except us is bad."

The bird cheeped uncontrollably. One word emerged from the outburst.

"When?" it said. "When, when, when?" it repeated frantically.

"I don't know!" Naamah yelled to stop the noise. "Anytime from when we have finished, I suppose."

"When will you finish?"

"We are finishing our tar coat and the final wooden ramp for the animals," she said, flustered.

"You are in great danger, woman. You must not listen to God. He will only use you," said the bird.

"Why should I listen to you? Even if God and my husband are a pair of crazy old men, if I get on the ark, I live whether God destroys everything or not," she said.

The bird flapped, digging its talons into her chest to spring into the air. Naamah lay still.

LUCIFER FLEW AWAY.

"Intolerable woman," he muttered. The wind whipped past as he circled above the building site. He could see she was right, the ark was close to completion. God could enact his plan for destruction at any time. Lucifer couldn't think, he had no time to plan and no time to waste with Noah and his family. There was no point in trying to get through to a group that cared only for themselves and nothing for others who had no hope.

He needed to stop God and save humans, but how?

Could he do both? Which was more important? He could stay on Earth and tell all the others to build boats. No, God would just kill them another way. He could go back to Heaven to deal with God in person, but he didn't know how. And God had a legion of slaves to protect him now.

"But I can," Lucifer said, realization dawning. "The Hell-Heaven portal is sealed, but the Earth-Heaven portal must be open." He had to get through or every living thing on Earth would die.

Assessing his surroundings, he tried to remember Earth's layout from what he had seen during his time in Heaven. Where was the portal? How far away was he? Using the enhanced direction-finding skills of his host body, he ascertained his position. It was a long distance to the site of the portal. But he had wings to fly.

LUCIFER FLEW. Unsure of how many days and nights passed, he flew without stopping until he reached the portal, hungry and exhausted.

The portal was open. He flew to it, he couldn't see anything from this side. In a way he could not explain, Lucifer felt that disaster was imminent. He was out of time, he had to act now. He didn't know if he could even get through, could the bird get through? Would he be thrown back? Or would he die? He had no choice. He had to confront God now, he had to reason with him, and if he failed, he would have to kill, even if it meant dying himself. His life for millions, an impossible measurement.

Lucifer heard a noise, a rushing noise. He flew in a wide circle, assessing the area. Water was creeping from the horizon, crashing over plants and trees, relentlessly engulfing the landscape. This was God, he knew it. Lucifer had manipulated water to escape his tubular prison. God's power, advanced beyond Lucifer's abilities to a level he could not comprehend, would spell disaster.

"Now or never," Lucifer breathed. He positioned himself ahead of the portal, diving, flattening his wings against his body, gaining speed, aiming for the center of the open portal to Heaven. Closer, faster, lunging to his destiny.

Lucifer braced himself to collide with the portal, pushing the unknowns from his mind. With the shimmering surface moments from his face, a figure appeared at the portal, a ghostly apparition, its hand outstretched to Lucifer.

"You can't," said the apparition. Lucifer spun up into the air away from the portal, crashing to the ground in a slop of salty water.

Lucifer lay stunned, wings useless in the encroaching deluge. He had failed to get to God. Lucifer was engulfed, lying helpless, drowning like the rest of the world.

He could see the portal crackling. Under the water, he could see through. God was on his throne, surrounded by slaves. People serving him were beaten down, broken. He could not let go. He could not die. He would not give up.

39

FLOOD

He was crushed. the weight of the water restricted his chest. He had been here before. Underwater, breathless, afraid.

His life played before his eyes. Happiness with Raphael, fear of God, pain for humanity. His mind drew back to his first near drowning. His circle of failure was complete. He had achieved nothing. The fall into the water had started it all. Perhaps he should have died there. Now it was truly time to die. His physical body was still in Hell, his mind trapped in the bird. He tried to disengage, not knowing if his mind would die along with the host body.

As he was ready to take his deathly last breath, the image of the slaves burst back into his head. How could he abandon them? In the familiar moment of clarity that appeared before death, he understood his purpose. He had to stop God, he needed to fight. His closeness to death renewing his senses, he struggled. With his brain screaming, he forced his mind into action.

~

HE OPENED HIS EYES. He was floating with no sensation of up or down. He felt himself moving, carried up through the water to what he hoped was the surface. Looking around wildly, he strained his eyes, wishing to see anything that would give him a clue. He couldn't be dead, he hurt too much.

Deep under water, he tried to yell for help. A strange tone emitted from his throat. It lit a path before him in a bright glow, a beacon. He was not breathing nor gasping for breath. He took in his newly alighted surroundings.

"How did I get here?" he thought to himself. The last action of his dying mind was to jump to another creature. Feeling alive again, it all began to make sense. His determination overtaking his weakness.

Lucifer's flipper brushed something soft. He maneuvered his body, he could see lighter blue, the surface within reach.

The sun peeked through the dense ocean, the water above him oddly mottled. He saw something in his peripheral vision, flicking the end of his flipper. He felt a softness. With a precise bash, the thing drifted into his field of vision.

He let out an underwater scream. Swimming through a field of lifeless bodies, he tried to cover his face, but his flipper did not reach. Motionless eyes were staring at him, coldly judging him on his failure. He continued to rise.

He broke the surface and took the deepest breath, letting out a screech of anguish. He twisted around, breathing heavily. His eyes were wide with exhaustion and fear. He was kicking his tail below the surface, pushing parts of human beings. In every direction he looked, there was nothing but floating bodies. Just like the ocean, the weight of his failure crushed him.

40

SUCCESS

God clapped Seth on the shoulder, squeezing tight. "We did it," he said. "We have a fresh start, we can build up a perfect race of believers again. I will improve them this time, too," God added in a quieter tone. As much as it hurt him to admit his mistakes, he needed to embrace this opportunity.

It was difficult to see Noah and the ark through the water-obstructed view. God had created enough water to cover Earth entirely, just enough to cover every mountain peak to make sure no one could sneak up to survive. The last thing he wanted were pockets of humanity he couldn't control. That would never happen again. He could start afresh with his chosen collection.

Noah was dull and ugly, but he would serve his purpose perfectly. He could also instill in all his children and grand-children that the only reason they survived the great flood was because God chose them. God knew humans. They would love being *chosen*.

God added a note to his mental list, he would speak to

Noah's family when the flood receded and tell them what to say to the coming generations.

God had been admiring his handiwork for most of the evening. He enjoyed perusing his water-logged planet. There was a beauty to the water, and everywhere he looked, there were pockets of death. But the thing he found the most beautiful was the haze that had collected at the outer atmosphere of the world, a miasma of suffering. A blanket of souls.

So many people had died. He could clearly make out their collective souls, roaming free of bodies, barely clinging to the world they had called home. God closed his eyes and drew a sharp breath through his nostrils. Yes, he could hear it. He could hear their wails, the sound of souls with no purpose.

It was late, it had been a big day. Committing genocide against most of humanity would take it out of anyone. He spun this over in his head, telling himself he was not weak. Turning from the portal, stretching his arms and giving a loud yawn, he stopped.

"What was that?" he said aloud. No response.

A garbled sound, half-singing. God moved back to the portal. He zoomed the view toward the noise, visibility was low.

A whale was bellowing in the sea of bodies, nuzzling the dead with its head in a gesture that could only be mourning.

God had never seen such actions. He watched the whale for some time, a mournful dance, showing care for a species not even its own.

"Wait," said God, peering as close as he could see through the murky, body-ridden water. He saw a familiar look in the eyes, a presence beyond that of the body.

"That slippery little fool escaped my tube?" God shouted into the portal. The whale startled.

"Hey Lucifer!" God snickered. "I know that is you! Get back to where you belong." God felt the laughter rising in his belly. He couldn't hold it in, he bellowed through the portal.

"How can you laugh? You killed everyone," the whale sang. "I thought even you would feel some pain."

"Pain?" he said, laughter replaced with a sneer. "I feel no pain, I inflict pain. And I vow to maintain your pain for the rest of your life. I will never halt your suffering by killing you. You will see me do what I please to the humans, you will watch them die, you are helpless. You will never stop me. *I* am the almighty, *I* am God. *I* choose who lives and who dies. You will live, for that is your true path to suffering."

God's final word hung in the air. "Suffering," he repeated quietly, clicking his tongue, a thought forming in his mind. He turned back to his view, searching for the Hell-Earth portal. He lifted his arms, swirling the atmosphere into a screaming vortex of souls. He cleared a path through the water, funneling the whirlwind of souls through to Hell. God would miss their beautiful sound, but that was a sound that would place pain and suffering directly into the fiber of Lucifer's being for the rest of his life in Hell.

41

THE ATMOSPHERE OF HELL

Lucifer lay curled on his side, back in his own body, knees bent, his hands over his ears. The frightful screams seeped into his bones. The lost souls formed a thick blanket over Hell. The temperature had risen, constant storms turned to wet steam. He had lost. He failed humanity, and now he had the never-ending torment of shrieks to remind him.

"Damn you," he muttered under his breath. "Why did you stop me? How did you stop me?" he said more loudly, anger bubbling out with every word.

"I had to," came a voice, resonating in his head. The air pulsed. Lucifer squinted. A faint apparition formed. Lucifer rubbed his eyes. It was still there, an apparition of the thing he wanted most. Raphael. Not knowing if it was truly Raphael, his own madness, or a cruel trick from God, his anxiety escaped in waterfalls of tears.

"Why did you stop me?" Lucifer said once he had calmed enough to speak.

"I had to," said the voice, disembodied from the vision. "If you went through the portal, God would have defeated you, and you are the only hope for these people. I couldn't allow him to win."

"But I failed anyway," said Lucifer, smashing his fist on the ground. "They are all dead, and they are all here, screaming at me. My eternal punishment for failure," Lucifer said, voice breaking. "I should have died there, underwater, with everyone else."

"No," said the voice, quiet but full of vehemence. "God will pay for what he has done. He will pay for what he did to me, to you, to the souls enslaved in Heaven, and to the millions of souls here in Hell. This rests with you, you must stop him when the time is right and when you know you have a chance."

Lucifer nodded, hands clenched in the dirt. "But how did you stop me? How can you do anything? You are dead."

"What we must do now is work to open the eyes of future humans to what God really is, we need to work out how to use the souls against him. We will work it out, Lucifer; we will get him. But for now, I must go. Remember, I am always with you."

Lucifer was alone except for the company of a million wailing souls. Or perhaps he always had been, the vision nothing but a mixture of memory and desire. He sat on the ground, staring at the spot where Raphael had been moments ago. The burden of lost souls, the slaves in Heaven, and the need to avenge Raphael was too much. The responsibility of saving future mankind from God's increasing madness was a weight he could not bear. He didn't know what to do. All he could do was cry. But that was not enough. Everyone counted on him, whether they knew it or not.

Lucifer took a deep breath and quelled his nerves.

"I vow to you, spirits, I will avenge you. I will destroy

God, who betrayed your trust, lied to you, and ended your lives for his own pleasures."

He threw his hands in the air. The wind rose and with it, the howls. They understood.

The howls surfaced a memory. Lucifer replayed the moment when God had provided him with a personal quagmire of pain, when the souls had flown through the portal with such force that Lucifer had been knocked to the ground, losing connection with the whale, souls screaming over him and settling in the atmosphere.

"Wait," Lucifer said aloud. A thought sprang from the bottom of his brain. "Why did God use the Hell-Earth portal?" The thought continued to form as his mind ran through past events. God had never used the three-way portal to probe into Hell.

"He doesn't know," Lucifer shouted, throwing his hands in the air, his face lifted to the souls. "He doesn't know!" He shouted again through bubbling laughter.

FINALLY, something on his side. God's delusion of power, his arrogant faith in his own abilities, and blindness to the world outside his narrow vision caused him to overlook the dull colors of Hell through the three-way portal. God's blindness to the three-way portal gave Lucifer hope. He had a way in. The souls whipped again, Lucifer channeled their encouragement to gain strength. He could do it, save mankind and the souls. He could use God's arrogance against him. If he was blind enough to miss the true power of the portal, he would be blind to many other things. Lucifer gritted his teeth. To succeed in his plan, he must start with the living.

Lucifer kept the portal view static, focused on the ark bobbing in the manufactured sea. The water remained calm. God must be keeping it this way so nothing happened to his chosen ones. Lucifer did not bother to scan the Earth, everything else was dead. All he would find was a mass of bloated bodies, collecting in decomposing clumps.

Noah and his family remained inside, an occasional head popping out of the top hatch, checking the weather before disappearing back to the bowels of the boat. Lucifer could only imagine the filth; the thought of animals and humans in such close quarters was nauseating. Lucifer had not seen inside the vessel. The living arrangements and how Noah kept the animals alive was a mystery. The only thing he could presume was that he had help from God. He would always help his favorites.

Lucifer continued to watch, eating and drinking mindlessly, blocking out the noises of Hell. His concentration was rewarded when he caught the old man poking his head from the hatch.

Noah held something. Looking above to the sky, he threw the bird into the air. It flapped its underused wings, dipping to the ocean before the feeling of flight took hold. Lucifer's mouth dropped open, masticated red weed falling to the ground. What was Noah doing? He followed the bird. It had a purpose, he did not know what.

The bird dramatically changed direction, swooping in a sharp downward track, perching on the branch of a solitary tree.

Lucifer gasped. "It must be receding!" he shouted out to Hell. This was his chance to get through to the humans.

Closing his eyes and taking a lungful of humid air,

Lucifer positioned himself close to the portal, ready to send his mind to the bird.

THE BODY FELT FAMILIAR, wings effortlessly catching the air. He felt the cool breeze splice past the face of his host body, instincts pushing him toward the ark. The branch he pulled from the tree wedged tightly in his beak. He would bring the family hope, and with it, persuasion.

His splayed feet touched the edge of the ark, struggling to adjust his balance to the smooth rocking. No one awaited his return. Trotting to the hatch, Lucifer threw the stick at the cover, silently pleading that the sound would reverberate through the ark.

The hatch rumbled. With the quickened reflexes of his host body, he darted back. A head popped out, graying brown hair wild in the breeze.

"Great," Lucifer thought to himself. "You again." He scurried to where the branch had fallen. Grabbing it in his beak, he flapped to Naamah, dumping the branch indelicately in her hand.

Her eyes widened, her body moving farther out of the hatch, taking in the external environment with a sweeping glance. Looking for the tree.

"You won't find it," said Lucifer. Naamah's eyes narrowed.

"Not again," she said, shoulders slumping. "This isn't real. Why do all the good things turn out to be in my head?"

"This is real," said Lucifer. "I just found this on a tree not far away. The floodwaters are receding. I can help you."

"No, no, no," she said shaking her head, fingers curled in her wayward mane. "I have been on the boat too long. Too long. Too long," she repeated. With one last glance, her wild eyes ducked into the hatch.

"Well," said Lucifer, unsure after the strange encounter. "At least I still have the stick." He pounded away at the hatch until eventually he received another visitor.

"Noah," he said aloud as the wizened head appeared. The startled expression betrayed Noah's shock.

"She was right," said Noah, eyes widening further. "There really is a talking bird."

Now was the time, he had to take advantage. "Noah," he repeated, authority lacing his words. "Your God has come as a bird to tell you of a great danger."

Lucifer expected Noah to crawl from the hatch and fall to his knees on the deck. But what he got was the narrowing of eyes.

"No," said Noah. Startled, Lucifer hesitated.

"I am your God!" He shouted through the beak, flapping his wings. "You do not say no to me." He was imitating God's persona as best he could.

"What did you say to me the last time we met?" asked Noah.

Lucifer was silent.

"I know who you are. God told me you are his enemy and that you may come to test me, but if I stay true, I will be rewarded. God would not come to me as a bird! I have seen him, he is all-powerful. He would only come to me as himself."

Lucifer was lost for words. God had spun everything to Noah. It was the opposite of the truth. Disengaging from the bird, he returned to Hell. Persuasion of someone so brainwashed was a skill beyond his abilities.

∼

BACK TO THE BEGINNING. He had to think. He tried to block out the wails. Noah and his family were the only ones alive. He had to figure out a way to turn them from God. He would learn from his mistakes.

Noah was completely indoctrinated. He and his family had been saved by God. They owed him everything. Getting through the enormity of God's madness and volatility would be difficult.

The weight of responsibility rose to the forefront of every scenario he played through his mind. If he left Hell, what would become of the souls? If he stayed, what would become of the slaves in Heaven? The only answer was power. He needed dominion over both Heaven and Hell, he needed to rule with kindness and love to those who were already there while also acting as guardian over Earth. Watching over humanity to let them prosper, to let them realize their potential.

To achieve this, God must die. Could Lucifer truly kill?

"Yes," he said aloud, "for humanity." But God was too strong. First, he must be weakened. Lucifer needed to take what he wanted most. Slaves for Heaven.

"CONCENTRATE," he said. He sat cross-legged, hands resting delicately on his knees. He breathed in sharply, sending his force out into Hell.

The wailing increased, ringing in his ears. Desperation was seeping into his soul. Letting out his deep breath, he slumped, head in his hands. Now that he was sure Hell was his eternity, he needed to grow some better food to gain some strength. If anything would grow.

"OK," he said to the atmosphere. "Let's try something

else." He stood, shaking his limbs, which were tight from prolonged sitting. Harnessing the souls was difficult. He had been trying for so long without success. Trying to convince bodiless humans to help him get through the portal was easy, the hard part was getting them to work together. To enact the next phase of his plan, he had to get through the portal physically.

"Let's look at it another way. What gave us the ability in the first place?" he said, stroking his smooth chin with thumb and forefinger.

"God ate Raphael, and I ate Raphael. But I only had a taste, God had a lot more." A brick appeared in the pit of his stomach as he heard himself speak. The factual way he spoke of Raphael's death was unnerving.

"What is in the flesh that makes it work? I have no flesh here, only souls. I'm sure God said he takes in some life force from the flesh, but ultimately the soul is separate." Confusing himself, he closed his eyes and shook his head. He needed the souls to join him, they needed to be one.

"All right," he shouted. "You need to embrace me, meld with me." The souls screeched. Lucifer raised his hands and closed his eyes, waiting. Summoning his mental and physical strength, he reached out to the millions of souls. His skin crackled. He cracked an eyelid. Tiny sparks shot from his arms. His hair rose, long strands charged with energy. The whirling souls surrounded him, a mass of flesh and souls creating energy. His skin burned, the weight of the souls gripping his body. His cries melded with the wails of Hell.

Heavy legs moved him to the portal. "Are you ready? I need you!" he yelled above the din. The responding screams provided the answer.

A jolt. The force exploded as the power entered his body.

He had strength. He sprinted for the portal, feeling the rush of souls around him.

GROUND. Dry. Lucifer set foot on Earth for the first time. It was different but the same, all concept of time lost. He took a deep breath, lungs filling with dry air, the first time he had taken a full breath since entering Hell. Birds were chirping. Life was here. Noah had worked quickly to reestablish nature. No doubt God had assisted. Lucifer stamped his feet on the ground, laugher bubbling from tight lips. Hope was erupting.

He twirled, his arms stretched wide, face turned to the sky. Clouds melded into a dizzying swirl.

"Enough," he snapped, scolding himself. Without the luxury of animal flight or speed, he had to trudge like a human.

Soon he saw a man. He was tall and lean, herding two sheep into pen.

"Give me a lamb, you terrible beasts!" he yelled. "I am hungry."

Lucifer stopped, plotting his approach carefully. The only way this would work would be for him to appear all-powerful. He was sure it was all in the attitude.

With his chest puffed, he stood in view of the man, waiting for him to notice. Eventually, he stopped, mouth drooping at the sight of a being he did not recognize. The first living humanoid since the flood, shocking his system.

"Who are you?" Lucifer asked with command. His fists were clenched to hide the quivering of his muscles.

"Ham," the answer came with a raised eyebrow. "Son of Noah. Who are you?"

"Smug fool," thought Lucifer. It was now or never. "I am God," he said, trying to portray confidence. He saw Ham's jaw drop, the usual human inability to hide pure shock showing visibly in every facet of his body.

"God?" said Ham.

"Yes," said Lucifer. Now was the time. "Where is your father?"

"Drunk as usual," he said, eyeing Lucifer. Lucifer allowed himself a smile. Noah was the only person who knew what God looked like. "You don't look like God," said Ham. "Father told me you looked old and wise with a long gray beard. The best he had ever seen."

Lucifer tried his best to hide his nervous swallow, repuffing his chest for maximum effect. "I am God, Ham. I can look how I want, and I can do what I want. I own this world. I can smite you where you stand."

To Lucifer's shock, his show of force was met with a laugh and a shrug. "Sounds like God," said Ham, turning attention back to his task.

Lucifer stood still. How could these humans be so accepting of a malevolent God? Anger rose within him. Now was the time.

"There is much you do not know about this world, Ham. There are many beings who work against me, who will try to turn you away from me. I am not a bad God; I am a loving God. I promise to never harm humankind again. I promise to treat you fairly and equally. If anyone tries to harm you, he is an imposter. You must not believe he is the true God. Promise me, you will question everything."

Ham stood, open-mouthed. "Promise me!" shouted Lucifer, his newfound power rustling the trees, causing the pairs of birds to fly from every branch.

The show of power was enough for Ham. He fell to his knees. "I promise, God."

LUCIFER TRUDGED BACK to the portal. The power of the souls dissipating, he had to get back. He could not be stranded on Earth. His selfish pull to Earth was the hardest thing he had ever had to quash. He made the ultimate sacrifice, his own happiness for that of others.

His success gave him solace. He had planted the seed. The seed of doubt to begin the questioning of what was true.

This is how he would win. He might not be all-powerful; he might not have created this race, but he cared. He cared for them more than he cared for his own life. The trait of one who had lost everything, the only thing he had left to live for, was them.

But there was another factor at play. God needed short-term gain, instant gratification. Lucifer's knowledge gave him power. He was ready to play the long game. To win at all costs, even if it took an eternity. He would succeed in turning humans from God. It was their only salvation.

www.ingramcontent.com/pod-product-compliance
Lightning Source LLC
Chambersburg PA
CBHW021402110726
47901CB00008B/2017